The Hunt for the Crimson Queen

Duty Above Desire

Justin Shaughnessy

Justin Shaughnessy

Contents

Acknowledgements

To my beta readers, thank you for your invaluable insight, honesty, and encouragement throughout this process. Your feedback helped reshape this story into something far stronger than it would have been otherwise.

Special thanks to:

Shelly Ferry

Lauren Bussey

Aly Seaman

And to my editor, Roxana: thank you for your incredible feedback, guidance, and dedication. Your insight helped shape this story into what it was always meant to become.

Finally, thank you to every reader who picked up this book. Your support means more than words can express.

My wife Annie,

Thank you for supporting me every single day and encouraging me to keep going, even when inspiration felt out of reach. Thank you for listening to my endless ideas, helping me find direction when I'm lost in the storm, and reminding me why I started this journey in the first place. You are truly the lighthouse in the chaos of my mind, and I could not have done this without you.

Reader Discretion

This book contains mature themes and content intended for adult readers 18+. Reader discretion is advised.

1
Killian

Bad Habits is the beast that never sleeps.

I move through it all on autopilot. Wipe the counter, pull a pint, and slide it down the bar with practiced ease. I cash out a couple on a steady course toward morning regret and laugh as they stumble out the front door. I smile at the regulars' recycled jokes, knowing damn well they can't remember yesterday's punchline. Popping the top off another bottle, I pass it down and nod like I haven't done this a thousand times before.

Of course I look the part. Black T-shirt stretched across my shoulders, a faded OWNER tag stitched on one sleeve, and jeans worn soft at the knees. I'm just another man who pours whiskey and breaks up the occasional brawl. That's what I tell myself anyway.

But normal men don't carry scars like maps etched into their skin, marks from fights with things the average drunk at the counter couldn't imagine. Normal men don't keep a hidden compartment under the bar stocked with silver-tipped stakes and guns loaded for only one purpose. Normal men don't carry weapons everywhere they go like an extra layer of skin. They don't spend every night hunting the monsters that creep just outside of humanity's line of sight.

I've been a hunter my entire life. Raised by my uncle and his friends to protect humanity. I'm the best at what I do, and I take pride in leading my crew in our search for the Queen of Vampires. I opened this bar three years ago as a cover for us, but I've grown to love being its owner. It makes me wonder what life has to offer me outside of being a vampire hunter.

Even on weeknights, when the street outside falls still and the shops sit shuttered in darkness, Bad Habits pulses with life. The floors are sticky from decades of spilled drinks, and the walls wear their smoke stains like badges of honor. In the corner, the jukebox wheezes through the same late eighties tracks on an endless loop, fed by the same four regulars who swear it was "a better time back then."

Pool balls crack in the back like gunfire, sharp pops swallowed by thunderous rolls of laughter, slurred arguments, and the drunken mistakes that carry the sour tang of tomorrow's regret. The air is thick with the scent of stale beer mixing with fryer grease and sweat, the ghost of cheap perfume clinging to every booth cushion like a stain that won't wash out.

I glance across the thinning crowd and spot the hunters' table. My table. A semicircle of tired grins and raised glasses. Eli's arm is slung across the back of the booth, Helen props her boots up like she owns the place, and a couple of the newer recruits lean forward, hungry for scraps of praise. Tonight is a win. Two fewer vampires breathing, if you could even call it that. Another step closer to the prize we all want.

The queen herself.

"Hey!" David wobbles toward the counter, glassy eyes struggling to focus. His breath hits me in a hot wave of bourbon. "You promised me a free drink last night, remember?"

"I remember." I grab the disguised tap water bottle I keep for situations exactly like this and pour him three shots in quick succession. "On the house, Dave." Watching him take the shots, I wait for him to mention the lack of burn you would expect from alcohol.

"You're..." He downs the first, slamming the glass. "The..." Gasping and red-faced, he chokes down the second. "Best!" The third disappears.

I laugh, shaking my head as I realize he is too drunk to know the shots are only plain water. The look on his face almost makes me double-check the bottle.

I flip the switch behind the bar, and the lights overhead blink in a slow one-two-two-one pattern. A signal older than most of the patrons. "Alright, everyone!" I call out over the music. "Closing time! You don't have to go home, but you can't stay here!"

The room fills with groans and protests. One by one, bodies shuffle out with coats tugged on, cigarettes lit, and rides called. Albert and Monica, my bartenders, are already sweeping through tables, cleaning dishes, and swiping damp cloths across sticky surfaces.

"When are you going to let me get a piece of that hot ass, Killian?" Veronica slurs, throwing back the last of her beer before staggering toward the door.

I help her into her coat, laughing as I usher her outside. "Same joke every night. You never tire of it, do you?" The lock clicks behind her.

"I think the real question, "Helen drawls from behind me, "is why you haven't already let her get some of that 'hot ass'?" She teases.

"Never." I laugh. "I'd rather fuck a blood sucker than catch whatever she's carrying."

Helen barks out a laugh. "Fair point." Tipping her head toward the hunters' table, she looks at me expectantly. "So are you ready to drop the act and join us for the update? Or are you still playing bartender?"

I roll my eyes and slide into the booth. My shoulders loosen for the first time all night. The familiar faces, the edge of danger humming low in the air. This is the real heartbeat of Bad Habits.

"So," I say, scanning their faces. "Let's hear it."

Dakota leans back with a boyish grin still slapped across his face, excitement radiating off him after his first successful hunt. "They were fast." He shakes his head as if he still can't believe it. "Fuck, they were so fast. Strong too." His eyes find mine, still shining with adrenaline. "It's crazy how fast these things are, you know?"

"We know." Alice sighs. "Get on with the good stuff already."

Like Dakota, Alice is new to our crew. Unlike Dakota, she is military trained and isn't easily rattled. She keeps her hair braided back tight, her weapons clean, her hunting gear pristine. Dakota is all chaos with his shaggy hair perpetually unkempt; blades still covered in the sticky ash that killing a vampire leaves behind, clothes always wrinkled and stained.

Helen is my oldest friend, her black hair styled in a sharp pixie cut. I stare at her dirty boots crossed on the tabletop as she absentmindedly picks at her nails, the shine of her blade catching the low light above the booth. She acts as though she already knows how this all goes.

"Killian." Eli's voice cuts through my thoughts. "Did you hear any of what Dakota just said?"

I clear my throat and adjust myself in the booth. "Sorry, what?"

Dakota chuckles, though I can see the annoyance etched across his face. "I said you were right."

"I normally am." I smile, leaning back. "But how so this time?"

"The queen is coming to Colorado. To this very city, in fact."

Helen stops picking at her nails and drops her legs. Leaning forward, she raises a curious pierced eyebrow. "You got the bloodsuckers to talk?"

Dakota's grin widens, but it's Alice who speaks first. "They talked, alright. More than they should have."

Eli scoffs, arms still crossed. "Did they say where this queen of vampires was?"

Dakota's grin vanishes. "No. They didn't."

"It's more of a lead than we've ever had, Eli!" Alice growls.

I let them bicker back and forth about who is the bigger idiot, who asks the right questions, until Helen finally slams her fist down on the table. Everyone falls silent. She picks up a peanut from the glass bowl centered on every table in Bad Habits and begins picking at the shell.

"Killian." Her voice is steady, measured. "We're your hunters. You led us to this city with nothing but a feeling." Her eyes linger on mine for what feels like too long. "What are you feeling now?"

The weight of her stare gives me pause. Helen has always been like this—odd, intense—ever since I was a child and she and Eli trained me in the ways of killing vampires.

"Come on now," Eli barks. "We've been in this nowhere city for three years on nothing but this hunch of yours. New York is crawling with leeches. I vote we head out and keep doing what we've always done. Hunt and kill vampires."

"We've been stagnant here for too long." Bri agrees.

I can't help the quiet laugh that escapes me. Bri doesn't normally chime in on our meetings, but she would go anywhere and do anything for Eli. She's a skilled hunter, but Eli treasures her for more than the way she handles a knife.

"You don't get it." Alice leans forward, her voice sharp. "This isn't just a nest. It's a fucking convergence point. All four courts are meeting here."

My eyes snap to her. I lean closer. "All four?"

"The vampire said they were gathering for the first time in centuries for some kind of...hunt. That part was a little fuzzy." Dakota nods.

Alice continues, her words deliberate. "They said the queen's court is already here."

Helen huffs once, staring at me. "What's the plan, boss?"

I meet each of their eyes, one by one, landing finally on Helen. She's already smiling like she knows my answer before I speak it.

"You know I don't like being called that." I let the silence stretch. "The queen is here. I don't know how I know, but I know." I let the words settle over the table like dust. "We're in the right place."

Eli lets out a long sigh and runs his hand through his short hair, resigning himself to my choice. "Fine. Then let's kill the fucking queen of vampires."

My phone vibrates in my pocket. I pull it out and see the notification from Temptr—a message that makes me smile. "We will kill her." I say, distracted. "Just not tonight. Tonight, I have plans."

Everyone at the table smiles. They all know what I have planned. What I plan on most nights of the week. Another sad attempt to feel something that resembles a normal life. One without blood, guns, and monsters.

"Come on guys," Eli laughs, standing. "Let's go so Killian can get his dick sucked again."

"That's not—"

"Save it." Helen laughs, pointing to the front door. "Who's that?"

I turn to find a woman standing outside, her silhouette all curves and confidence.

"That is..." I struggle for words, then point to the door. "You know what? Shut up. Get out of my bar."

I stand, waiting for my friends to grab their things, then usher them out the door to stop them from making any stupid comments to the beautiful girl waiting.

"Did you get my message?" she asks with a smile.

I open the door wider, gesturing her inside before locking it behind her and closing the blinds. "Yes, Melissa. I got your message. We were just finishing up a meeting."

"I was worried you were standing me up." She pushes her lip out in a mock pout.

I let my gaze travel over her—the skin-tight black mini skirt that barely covers anything, the spaghetti strap tank top so thin it leaves nothing to the imagination. I lick my lips and take a step closer.

"I would never." I bring my eyes back to hers. "I've been waiting to meet you since we matched the other night."

"Oh, yeah?" Melissa crosses her arms, pushing her breasts together as she steps closer. "Now that I'm here...what are your plans?"

"I could cook you something if you're hungry?"

Melissa reaches out and grabs my arm gently, her hand running up and down my forearm as she bites her bottom lip and looks up at me with unmistakable hunger. Not the kind satisfied by food.

"Killian," she whispers. "Take me upstairs."

I glance over my shoulder at the stairs leading to my loft above the bar—to the bedroom where I'd told Melissa all the things I wanted to do to her over text the past few days. What I'd hoped was playful conversation, plans for something down the line, is happening now.

When I look back, Melissa has already slipped out of her tank top and stands topless in front of me, bouncing lightly on her toes.

I watch the overhead bar light reflect off the silver jewelry in her dark pink nipples, and the decision is made instantly.

I crush my mouth against hers, kissing her hard. My fingers trace up her sides until I find the hardened peaks of her nipples. I kiss down her neck, lower until I find her nipple and wrap my tongue around the piercing. The metallic taste gives me pause for only a moment before I suck her in and graze my teeth lightly against the skin.

Melissa lets out a moan as I kiss up her neck, my fingers working the button of my jeans. I pick her up and carry her toward the stairs, letting my pants fall as I walk. She wraps her legs around my waist and shoves her tongue into my mouth, biting my lower lip as I squeeze her ass. When we get upstairs, I toss her down on my bed and quickly shed my boxers, ripping off my shirt in a rush of need.

"Oh shit." Melissa gasps, staring at me standing at the edge of the bed naked.

I smile and step closer, grabbing the edge of her skirt and pulling it off her smooth legs. The scent of her arousal fills my senses as she parts her legs for me, already glistening. I crawl across the bed and settle between her warm thighs, tasting her, lashing my tongue across the sensitive spots that make her gasp.

Melissa runs her fingers through my hair and thrusts her hips against my face as I devour her. Her moans only make me want more. I pull back, kissing her thighs, kissing up her body until I reach her mouth and rest myself between her legs.

Her tongue slides into my mouth and the vibration of her moan fills me. With one thrust, I'm inside her and my groan rumbles deep in my throat.

"Oh, fuck," she moans as I pull back and thrust again.

"Is this okay?" I ask.

"More," she begs.

"Fuck, you feel so good," I moan.

Harder and harder I move, her breasts bouncing with each thrust. I cup one, squeeze, and watch her face contort with pleasure.

"Does this hurt?" I ask, slowing for a moment to check on her.

"I'm going to..." Melissa starts. "Don't stop, Killian. Please don't stop."

I thrust again, barely pulling back before I feel her tighten around my cock and throw her head back in a silent scream. I watch as she grasps the sheets and pulls to get leverage on her orgasm, and I keep a steady rhythm as she uses me to find her release.

It becomes too much, and I finish along with her, pulsing every drop into her as I moan, my legs shaking with every wave.

I collapse beside her, laughing as I try to catch my breath.

"That was..." Melissa trails off.

"Amazing," I finish for her, kissing her shoulder.

She sits up, already sliding back into her skirt with practiced ease, grabbing for her shirt. "Yes. And now I should be going."

I sit up beside her, kissing her shoulder again, running my fingers up her back before she stands suddenly.

"You don't have to go," I say. "You could stay. Maybe get some breakfast in the morning?"

"Tempting." She smiles, already heading for the stairs. "But it's four in the morning, and I have work in a few hours. I really should go."

I follow her downstairs, offering her a drink or a ride home so she won't have to walk. She rejects every offer politely. I've been through enough one-night stands to know I'll never see her again. By the time I lay my head on the pillow after a quick shower, she'll have blocked me on the app we met on.

Like all the others before her. The life of a hunter is a lonely one, but I'd be lying if I said I don't want more someday.

I watch as she leaves, listening to the click of her heels on the sidewalk as she disappears into the night. The door shuts with a hollow click. The bar is silent now, except for the hum of the refrigerator and the buzz of old neon lights still glowing.

I turn the downstairs lights off and climb the stairs with my phone in hand, already swiping through profiles in search of my next connection. Another pointless night. Another pointless hookup in a sad attempt to feel normal.

The same routine I've been stuck in for three years: swipe for dates, pour drinks, hunt vampires, sleep long enough to do it all again the next day.

The life of a vampire hunter.

2

Seraphine

The mirror lies beautifully to me.

Porcelain skin, soft mortal cheeks, and warm brown eyes that could belong to any twenty-something who still believes in happy endings. That's the glamour at work, and this is my favorite mask. It smooths away the centuries, tucks the truth out of sight. I twist a curl of hair into place, dab perfume at my throat, and there she is—the woman the world expects to see.

Pretty and harmless. Absolutely forgettable.

But the longer I stare, the more I feel the cracks pressing from underneath. Time doesn't forget me, even if the mirror does. This city hasn't changed.

Same cracked sidewalks, same crooked lampposts buzzing with moths. Even the still air smells like river water and dust. I've walked these streets before in past lives, when carriages rattled along dirt roads and the people who lived here did so in fear of what went bump in the night.

I smile at my reflection. I've danced this game in Paris salons and Venetian masquerades, in speakeasies where the jazz drowned out the hunger in my chest. Yet, standing here in the penthouse of some luxury hotel, about to charm some mortal man over dinner in a town that shouldn't matter...it feels strange.

Coming back here was supposed to be practical. Tactical. Safe. A nowhere place to disappear into. Instead, it feels like stepping into a dream I buried a millennium ago.

"My queen."

The voice is smooth as stone, carrying none of the warmth one might expect from a greeting. It slips into the steam-fogged bathroom like a blade sliding between ribs. I don't need to turn to know it's Marcella. No one else would dare interrupt me here. Still, I pivot slowly, letting the heels of my shoes click against the marble tile—a deliberate sound, sharp as a predator's warning.

"Yes, Marcella?"

She stands in the doorway, framed in the silver glow of the chandelier beyond. She wears her black hair in its usual severe twist, and she purses her lips as though the city's air tastes bitter. Marcella—my oldest friend, my fiercest advisor, and the one voice in all the centuries who dares tell me when I am wrong.

She's spoken more in the last few days than she has in years. Always about this town. Always about the mistake of coming back here.

"Rowena and Morgana will arrive soon," she says evenly, her gaze unflinching. "Amara will be here within the hour."

I can feel the unspoken words burning a hole in her chest. With a half smile, I gesture for her to step further into the room.

"Speak your mind." I order.

"Your sisters have agreed to a temporary truce in this war between our courts." Marcella's words are measured, deliberate. "They've agreed to meet you here, in this city where it all began." She pauses, and her eyes harden. "Do you truly believe now is the best time to be...messing with these humans?"

Her words drip with disdain, thick as venom. I let the silence stretch a moment longer before turning fully to face her, the glamour I'd worked so hard on shimmering faintly under the bathroom's gilded light.

"This war between courts has gone on long enough," I say, taking a dangerous step forward. "The hunters have grown stronger with each new generation. They've become more of a threat." I let my voice drop, cold and final. "It's time we put our differences aside and focus our efforts on eliminating the hunters once and for all."

Marcella bows her head and takes a nervous step backward as I approach. "Of course, my Queen."

A grin curls on my lips, sharp and amused. "Besides, if I'm going to be trapped back in this gods-forsaken city again, surrounded by enemies everywhere I look, I might as well have some fun."

This earns me a rare flicker of a smile from her—quick and humorless.

"I want the Crimson Court gathered by the time I return," I say, my tone snapping back to commanding. "How are the preparations going?"

"We've secured this hotel as you requested," Marcella replies. "The grand ballroom will make an excellent throne room for you to gather with your sisters. There are plenty of rooms for the generals to stay in while business is conducted."

"Good." I smile, satisfaction lacing my voice like silk drawn taut.

I reach for my phone on the counter, its screen glowing against the marble. Ryan has texted back—he's waiting in the lobby. The eagerness of men never fails to amuse me.

"They really forget themselves so easily." I say with a soft laugh.

Marcella's chuckle follows, lighter than her usual clipped tone. "Enjoy your dinner, then."

A wicked grin crosses my face. "Oh, I plan to."

The reflection in the mirror smiles back—a glamorous stranger, mortal-perfect. But for one fleeting moment, the mask slips and my true hunger presses through. My fangs gleam beneath my lips, a flash of ivory against the crimson lipstick. A glimpse of the monster beneath.

I let the sight linger just long enough to feel the hunger curl low in my chest. Then the glamour snaps back into place, flawless once more.

"Let's go have some fun." I murmur to the mirror, my wolfish grin glittering like a secret.

The restaurant smells of oak and pine varnish, roasted garlic and butter carrying on the air like perfume. The polished floors gleam under the low light, and servers in crisp black aprons move with the rhythm of practiced choreography, balancing plates, and wine glasses with solemn grace.

The walls are lined with framed photographs—black and white to color, snapshots of decades long past. My gaze catches on one in particular: opening night. A grainy black and white photo of the owner shaking hands with his first guests. And there, in the blurry background, sits a younger me, elegant in my formal dress, looking straight at the camera without realizing.

No one ever notices, of course. The faces of the long dead mean little to mortals rushing through their own fleeting days. I remember it vividly—the wallpaper was a suffocating damask red, heavy with dust and smoke. Gaslights hissed faintly with the tang of burning oil, and a quartet played a waltz, bows scraping with longing passion.

The laughter is the same now as it was then—bright and desperate. The laughter of mortals clinging to the illusion that forever is theirs.

"Nice, right?"

Ryan's voice brings me back to the table. I turn to find him beaming, gesturing broadly as though he built the place himself. He slides the leather-bound wine list toward me like an offering, saving face by letting me "decide" when it's obvious he hasn't the faintest idea what half the vintages mean. His boyish grin is eager, almost proud, as if bringing me here is an accomplishment.

"It's...lovely," I say, smoothing my tone into something polite. The smile I give him feels like slipping into another glamour.

He leans forward, elbows on the table, his cheap cologne sharp and synthetic. "So, tell me more about yourself. Your profile says you travel?"

Ah, so he has looked past the first two pictures. Most men lead with clumsy pickup lines and the graceless assumption I'd be in their bed before dessert. Ryan is at least trying.

"You could say that," I reply, letting the corner of my lips tilt up as though sharing a secret.

"Where to?" His eyes light, leaning closer as if the answer might give him a role in the story.

"Everywhere." I swirl the wine in my glass, watching the ruby liquid cling to the rim. "I'm looking for something."

"Oh?" His smile stretches, hungry for implication, as though he might be what I'm searching for.

"I haven't found it yet," I say softly, holding his gaze. My smile sharpens. "But it's out there."

The flicker of defeat across his face is delicious. His body slumps back in the chair as though I'd pressed a hand to his chest and pushed. For a moment, the silence between us is louder than the music.

Dinner drags the way it always does with men like him. He tells me about sales quotas and office politics, about his passion project for a podcast. I laugh where he wants laughter and nod where silence might embarrass him. My mind wanders as I count the cracks in the ceiling plaster.

I remember the taste of the man who once owned this build-ing—his ambition salted with fear. I'm bored enough to feel hollow by the time they clear the plates. I decide it's time to end my misery, calling the date to an abrupt end.

Back at his car, under the dim wash of the parking lot lights, I can see the question trembling on his lips. He wants to ask, wants to hope, but he doesn't dare. So, I place my hand on his chest, letting the heat of his heartbeat thrum against my palm—quick and eager.

"Your place or mine, handsome?" I whisper, watching the relief of victory light his face all at once.

"My place," he says quickly, grinning wide. "Just up the road."

We come crashing through his front door, his laughter caught in his throat as he fumbles with the keys, the hinge rattling when we finally shove inside. To Ryan, it must feel like a storm—clothes pulled loose in greedy hands, mouths flashing in the dark, a frenzy of what he believes is passion.

To me, it is choreography. A performance I've rehearsed for centuries. The house smells of leather and cedar polish. Beneath it, the faint musk of sweat and cologne soaks into the couch cushions. My eyes flicker across the walls as he paws at me—hunting trophies, framed photos of his kills, sharp steel blades mounted like art.

A hunter's den.

I smile at the irony, already imagining the look on his face when my glamour slips. He mistakes the curve of my lips for pleasure, growling low in his throat as if he's the predator here, and shoves harder, faster, eager to prove himself. He strips off his boxers, his cock jutting out as if it's the centerpiece of the evening.

"God, you're gorgeous," he mutters, collapsing onto the bed.

His eyes drink me in as I slide the dress from my body, his gaze ravenous, jaw slackening when I stand naked in the lamplight.

His hands reach for me the moment I straddle him, palms hot on my hips, pulling me down onto him. I let the practiced moan slip from my throat when he enters me—a sound pitched exactly right to stroke his ego. He groans, triumphant, burying himself deeper, convinced he has conquered me.

His hands roam freely, greedily worshipping the body I sculpted for him. I give him everything he wants to see: arching my back, lips parted, soft cries at the right rhythm.

The motions are mechanical. My hips rolling, nails dragging lightly across his chest, each movement designed to carry him faster toward the end he's so desperate for. His breaths become shorter, chest heaving, sweat beading across his skin.

His toes curl—the signal I've been waiting for. He thrusts hard, frantic, clinging to the illusion of control until he finally breaks and pours his release into me with a strangled cry of victory. I lean down, lips brushing his ear, my smile finally real. Sharp and cruel. As he shudders through the last of his relief, I let the glamour unravel like smoke. My skin pales, my eyes burn, and my fangs glint in the lamplight.

"Congratulations," I whisper, my voice velvet and venom. "You just fucked the monster hunters spend their entire lives trying to kill."

The terror that widens his eyes is sweeter than any climax. His hand shoots toward the nightstand, fingers scrabbling for the blade I can practically smell—silver-tipped, old, worn from use. Hunters always sleep with weapons within reach.

But he is far too slow.

I catch his wrist in a single fluid motion, bones splintering beneath my grip with a sound like dry twigs snapping. He screams—raw and panicked—the cry cut short as I crush the air from his lungs with the weight of my body. His curses never leave his tongue before my fangs split his throat.

The taste is exquisite.

Hot, metallic, spiced with the strange sharpness of his bloodline. The bitter tang of hunter's blood, rich with generations of obsession. It slides down my throat like a drug—burning and sweet, a flavor that thrums with memories of every ancestor who has stalked me and mine.

I drink and drink, deeper and deeper, until the pulse in his veins slows, then flutters, and finally stills. Even the wild heartbeat in his cock fades, leaving nothing but bitter silence inside him.

Pulling back, I lick my lips slowly, savoring every drop. A smear of crimson clings to the corner of my mouth. I wipe it away with a fingertip and paint the stain across my tongue, humming with satisfaction.

Rising, I slip back into my dress and smooth it against my body with deliberate elegance, as if I'm merely leaving a dinner party. The bed beneath him sags under his pale, cooling form, his eyes wide and still glassy with disbelief. A hunter undone by desire. What a fitting end.

At the door, I glance once more over my shoulder and let a smile curl across my lips, sharp and wolfish. "Sweet dreams, darling."

Then I slam the door behind me, the sound crackling through the empty apartment like a final heartbeat. The city blurs past me as I move, buildings and streetlights streaking by in a rush of neon and shadow, unable to keep pace. The night swallows me whole, its familiar darkness wrapping around me like a lover.

Home again. Already the city is bleeding for me. Two of my court guards pull open the heavy double doors as I approach. The ballroom reveals itself—what will now serve as my throne room while in the city. Whispers die in throats, laughter ceases, and spines stiffen as if strings are pulling them taut.

A hundred pairs of eyes turn in unison. The silence that follows is thick, oppressive, and trembling. Just how I like it. The echo of my heels carries across the marble like the beat of a war drum.

Each click rings sharp against the high arched ceiling, reverberating off the velvet banners that drip like streams of blood from the rafters. The floor gleams underfoot, polished so clean it reflects me back like a phantom.

A massive chandelier hangs overhead, light refracting menacingly across the walls. My chosen generals fall in line behind me—the rustle of silks and the whisper of bare feet mingling with the scrape of armor. All follow the rhythm of my heels as I approach my throne.

Three steps of marble lead to the gold-plated seat, its arms carved into snarling wolf heads and covered with red velvet cushions darkened over centuries of use. At the four corners of the dais stand my most trusted generals, silent sentinels, their eyes bright in the low light. Shadows cling to their armor and their blades. Loyalty and ambition paint their faces.

I ascend the steps slowly, each motion carved in grace and ritual. When I reach the summit, I turn and let my dress whisper around my ankles before sinking into the throne. Crossing one leg over the other, I let my gaze sweep the hall.

My generals meet my eyes without fear, but not without caution. They know power when they see it, and power now sits before them. Marcella's voice rings sharp and clear—the only one brave enough to cut through the silence.

"Her Eternal Majesty, Seraphine. Queen of the Crimson Court."

"Queen of the Crimson Court." The generals intone as one, their voices a low rumble as they sink to one knee with heads bowed. The sound fills the chamber like thunder in a storm.

My grin unfurls, slow and dangerous. Leaning forward, I lace my fingers together and let the silence stretch until it trembles like a bowstring.

"So," I purr, the word curling like smoke into every corner of the chamber. "What news do you bring of my sisters?"

3

Killian

The bar still smells faintly of stale beer and lemon cleaner as Monica polishes the countertop, her bracelets jingling with each swipe. The overhead lights hum to life, warming the dark wood with a golden glow. Chairs scrape as Albert lowers them one by one from the tabletops, his movements heavy and deliberate, like a man who would rather be anywhere else.

"Are you going to be working tonight?" Monica asks, glancing toward my office door. Her tone is bright, but there's a hint of hope underneath.

"Not tonight." I say, eyes still on the scattered reports in front of me. Numbers, addresses, leads—all blending together. I shuffle the papers absently, more for something to do with my hands than out of focus.

Albert's voice booms across the empty room. "It's not the same when you aren't on shift, boss!" He says it like a complaint but follows it with a grin that shows he means it.

"You two will do just fine." I call back, letting a chuckle slip as I lean in the doorway. "Besides, I'll probably be out more than I'm in. I trust you both to keep this place afloat."

Monica straightens, flipping her rag over her shoulder with a flourish. "We won't let you down," she says, smiling wide enough to flash the dimple in her cheek.

I give them a nod, but my mind is already elsewhere. Word of the queen's presence in the city has every hunter stretched thin. Helen and Eli are sweeping the abandoned hospital uptown, while Alice and Dakota are sniffing around the club on the west side—too loud, too flashy, the kind of place that always stinks of blood and smoke.

That leaves me and Bri with the foreclosed homes on the outskirts of town. Rotting wood, broken glass, and the quiet that can hide anything. I send a text to Bri, telling her to go to the club instead. I always hunt alone—partners are noisy, and noise gets you killed. I gather my phone and keys, pull on my riding jacket, its leather still carrying the sharp tang of motor oil. The back door groans open into the alley, where the chill of evening slaps against my skin.

My bike waits in the shadows, chrome dulled by dust, faithful as any weapon. The city blurs in my mind already, waiting to be cut open by speed. It's time to hunt.

The first two houses are nothing but hollow shells—empty windows gaping like blind eyes, doors hanging crooked on rusted hinges. No footprints in the dust, no fresh scent in the air, not even the scratches of rats in the walls. The yards have become overgrown, weeds tall enough to choke the chain-link fences that stand sentry in front of the abandoned buildings. Banks have given up on the houses, leaving the rotted structures to drag down the neighborhood like dead weight.

I sweep each property the same way I always do: slow, methodical, never trusting first glances. Every door jiggled twice, every window tapped, every step retraced. Hunters don't leave gaps. Gaps are where things wait.

By the time I reach the third house, I feel it before I see it. The air shifts—thicker, colder. My instincts prick like needles under my skin. I kill the engine and roll my bike into the shadows, the sudden silence making the night feel more alive.

Three men sprawl on the patchy lawn, holding bottles, their laughter bouncing off the hollow houses like breaking glass. At first glance, they look ordinary—beer guts, grease-stained work boots, the faces you'd pass at a hardware store and forget a minute later.

Then my blood stirs.

The hunter gene lights me up from the inside, an icy fire rushing down my spine. Muscles tighten, fingers flex against invisible tension, and the dark melts away until my vision is sharp as if it's noon. Every cricket chirp, every flutter of wings in the eaves strikes my ears with precision. The night unfolds for me, clear and merciless.

That's when their glamour slips. Their skin shimmers like heat haze before hardening into truth—flesh too tight, too dry, pulled cruelly over bones that have lived too long. Their smiles stretch wide, revealing fangs that glisten under the streetlight, nails lengthening into hooked claws.

I can't help but smile. My hand brushes the hilt of my favorite knife as I step off the curb, as casual as a man coming home.

"...told her if she doesn't agree to the terms, it'll mean war," one of them mutters, words slurring from beer and arrogance.

"Yeah? You think she's just going to hand over territory?" another man laughs.

"Not a chance," says the third. "That's why we're here. Pawns, sure—but someone's got to say enough is enough."

I clear my throat, loud enough to cut through their scheming. "Howdy boys. Lovely night for vandalism, huh?"

The nearest one sneers, flicking his bottle cap into the grass. "Fuck off, kid. You don't got any business here."

My grin sharpens. "See, that's where you're wrong. My business..." I draw both knives in one smooth motion, silver oil glistening faintly along their blades. "...is killing vampires."

They stiffen, eyes narrowing, laughter dying out. They rise to their feet in unison, predatory focus cutting through their sloppy disguise. This is the part of the hunt that gets my blood flowing, getting the chance to end the evil plaguing our world. I show no mercy when it comes to the creatures of the night.

"And business..." I say, teeth flashing as the night air holds its breath, "...is good."

The first one lunges before the others even process the words. Claws flash, catching the moonlight. I duck low and feel the swipe tear through the air above my head, close enough that it clips a strand of hair.

"Careful!" I spin on my heel and drive a knife into his ribs. "This jacket is vintage."

The vampire shrieks—a sound somewhere between a man choking and a bat screaming. He twists, claws raking my shoulder, and hot blood spreads down my sleeve. I wince but grin wider.

"Okay, okay," I say, staggering back a step. "You don't like my sense of fashion. Noted."

The second one comes in from the side, faster. His fist slams into my gut like a sledgehammer. My back hits the porch railing hard enough to splinter the wood. The air whooshes out of me, but I laugh through the pain.

"Damn." I wheeze. "Take it easy, I'm fragile."

The vampire snarls and comes at me fast. I roll under his follow-up swing, slashing my blade across his thigh. Black blood hisses against the silver oil, smoking where it spills. He roars and staggers back, giving me just enough space to catch my breath.

The third vampire circles behind me, voice a low hiss. "You'll bleed out here, hunter."

I spin the other knife in my hand and wink at him. "Maybe, but I bleed better than you boys sparkle."

He rushes me, claws raised. I pivot sideways and let the momentum carry him past, dragging my blade across his back as he stumbles. He whirls, face twisting in rage, and the first one catches me square in the jaw with a backhand that rattles my teeth. Stars burst across my vision.

"Son of a..." I spit blood onto the lawn. "That fucking hurt, you bastard."

They close in together now, no more games. Three sets of claws, three snarling mouths, circling like wolves. My heart thunders, my blood burns, and I can't stop grinning.

This is what I live for.

The first one lunges high, the second low. I kick the low one square in the chest, buying a heartbeat of space, while raising both blades to cross the strike from above. Claws scrape sparks off steel as I shove him back, twisting the knife deep into his forearm. He howls and I yank free, rolling clear just as the third tackles me from behind.

We hit the ground hard. His teeth snap inches from my throat, hot rancid breath washing over me. I jam a knee into his gut and shove my blade straight under his chin. His body convulses, then goes still.

"One down," I pant, shoving the corpse off me. "Two to go."

The other two are already approaching as I stand. The second one rakes claws down my ribs—hot pain flares, and I bite back a scream. The first tackles me, driving me into the dirt. I jam my remaining knife into his side, feeling it grind against bone. He screeches and thrashes. I roll with him as we lock in a bloody wrestle.

The second comes in again, but I yank the pinned vampire into the line of attack. Claws tear through his chest instead of mine. He shrieks and I shove him into the dirt. Pulling a third blade from my ankle, I drive it deep into the vampire's heart. Black smoke hisses from the wound as he crumbles to ash.

I stand, swaying, bloodied and bruised, with one knife left in my grip. "Man," I mutter, breathless. "You guys are terrible drinking buddies."

The last vampire snarls and charges, desperate and furious. I let him come. At the last second, I sidestep and catch his arm, spinning. I slam him face-first into the porch post. The wood cracks and his fangs snap shut on empty air. I pull my pistol from my waist and send three shots into his back.

He spasms, claws at the air, then sags into ash that spills through my fingers. Silence reclaims the lawn. Just my ragged breathing, the distant hum of cicadas, and the taste of copper in my mouth. I start back toward my bike when I realize my hunter gene hasn't faded.

The same gene that gives me strength and heightened senses, as well as quickens my healing, is only active in the presence of vampires—which means there are more bloodsuckers nearby.

A muffled groan comes from behind me. Turning, I find the first man I'd stabbed in the chin standing, rage blazing in his eyes.

"Oh yes." I laugh to myself. "How could I forget about you?"

The vampire bares his fangs at me, prepping to charge. I pull the gun from my holster and empty the clip rapidly into his chest. He gives a screech of pain before fading into ash with the rest of his kind. Wounding a vampire might slow it down, even incapacitate it long enough to deal with others. But only one thing can kill them for good—piercing their hearts with silver. All hunters carry weapons laced with silver oil, whether that be knives, stakes, or even a trusty bullet.

The hunter gene leaves my body with the threat removed. Sliding the gun back into its holster, I wipe my blade before sheathing it. I bend to pick up the other two blades, walking to my bike as I clean and sheath them.

My pulse is just beginning to settle when I thumb my phone awake. Notifications fill the screen, stacking one on top of the other like a series of warning flares.

Eli: *Nothing at the hospital, ran into a pack on our way back to the bar. Got an S.O.S. from Alice.*

Dakota: *S.O.S.*

Dakota: *Boss, answer me.*

Dakota: *Meet me back at the bar. Hurry!*

Alice is radio silent in the chat. I dial Dakota immediately and it goes straight to voicemail. No ring or delay, just dead air.

"Fuck." The word comes out in a whisper, swallowed by the night. "What the hell did you get into?"

I fire up the bike, the roar breaking the silence as I tear through the streets until the familiar alleyway swallows me whole. The bar's back door is cracked open, the metal frame streaked with blood. The sight tightens something in my chest as I slide my gun free of its holster. Pulling the magazine out, I count the rounds before pushing it back in and creeping forward.

Headlights sweep the alley as Helen and Eli pull up in his 1971 blue Mustang, their boots crunching the gravel as they hurry to my side, blades already in hand.

"You got the messages too?" Eli asks, voice low and taut.

"Yeah," I mutter. "I'd just finished three—"

I freeze mid-sentence. The shift hits me hard and sudden, like an electric surge through my veins. My muscles tighten, senses sharpen, and judging by the flicker in Helen and Eli's eyes, they feel the change too.

Our hunter gene activates. Vampires are near.

Words aren't needed. We exchange a look that feels like a silent vow and push through the door together. The stench hits first—copper-thick blood and the iron tang of death. Bodies litter the floor, slumped over tables, and sprawled across the sticky wooden planks.

Veronica, the bar's regular drunk, lies with her throat ripped open, eyes still glassy with shock. I step over her carefully, every nerve screaming.

"Alice?" I call quietly, spotting her hunched over a table.

At first, I think she's pressing a wound, trying to save someone. A spark of hope lights—only to die as we draw closer. She isn't saving anyone. She's feasting.

Dakota is pinned beneath her, or what's left of him. His arms are gone, ripped away at the shoulders. His chest cavity is split open like butchered meat. His head lolls at an unnatural angle, eyes staring past me into nothing. Alice tears another mouthful free, blood drenching her face.

"Fuck." Eli mutters.

"Alice!" I roar.

Her head snaps up, eyes blazing red, jaw unhinged. She screams—a sound that shatters glass, rattles bottles on the shelves, and makes the very air shake. She lunges, too fast, too savage.

Raising my gun, I fire. Two rounds find her, tearing flesh and slowing her just enough. Helen meets her head-on, blade flashing. With one brutal thrust, she drives the steel through Alice's face. Pulling the blade free, she repositions in the precious moment she earns and pushes the blade into Alice's heart.

Alice convulses and shrieks before dissolving into a heap of sticky ash at our feet. I stand there, chest heaving, when a dark laugh comes low from the shadows like smoke. A tall man in a crisp black suit steps into the light, his presence filling the room—casual, yet somehow suffocating.

"I wanted to return your hunter to you," he rasps.

His voice is low, gravelly, like old stone grinding against itself. I level the gun at him and pull the trigger.

Click click.

Empty.

"Fuck," I mutter, pulling my knife from its sheath and charging the man.

He catches my wrist like a child swatting a toy, twisting hard, and slams his elbow into my face. Pain explodes through my skull and stars flood my vision. I stumble, weightless, then crash across a row of tables.

Unfazed, he straightens his jacket. "I turned her," he says, almost bored. "It was only fair."

Helen hisses, blade ready. Eli shifts closer, fury blazing in his eyes. The vampire's smile widens, but his eyes darken to black pits.

"My Queen grows tired of your kind interfering," he growls. "She is here to end your disgusting bloodline. But I am generous." His voice drops to a growl that shakes the air. "You can join us...or die."

Silence fills the bar, broken only by the hum of the neon lights and the sound of blood dripping onto the floor.

Eli takes a step forward. "We would rather die."

The man grins. "So be it."

He lunges at Helen and Eli, speed blurring him into shadow. I'm already on my feet, blood pounding too loud to ignore. I intercept his movement, grabbing his collar as he passes and yanking him back. The momentum flips against him, and he slams hard into the ground.

I straddle him, blade raised, and drive it into his chest with every ounce of rage I have left. His eyes widen as the silver burns and his body convulses. Ash spreads from the wound like wildfire, and his voice cracks as he coughs out his last words.

"Long...live...the queen."

Then, he's gone. Nothing left but ash on my blade and the wreckage of everything we thought safe. For the second time tonight, my body heals itself from the wounds and aches left behind by the monsters in the night. The benefit of the hunter gene working its charms before it dies out with the threat now gone.

The bodies remain. Dakota, Veronica, and all the others I haven't even registered yet. And Alice—turned, fed, and then killed by our own hands.

I stand in the center of my bar, surrounded by ash and blood, and feel the weight of it settle like a stone in my chest. The queen has made her move, and this is only the beginning.

4
Seraphine

Large black banners drape around the ballroom, my court's symbol centering each one—a diagonal dagger with a single drop of blood dripping from the blade, highlighted by a red border. The marble floor catches every fragment of light from the crystal chandelier overhead, turning the room into a showcase of power.

Lounging on my throne, velvet cushion beneath me and one arm draped over the armrest, I watch as my generals below squabble like dogs over scraps. Power makes men hungry, and I keep four of the hungriest at each corner of my dais. They debate war strategy and how best to oversee the growing hunter problem. I listen closely, ears perked at the thrill of a good hunt.

"Hunters have been spotted trying to enter your lands, my Queen," General Kaelin announces. "They move in the shadows, working in packs."

I wave a lazy hand at him, urging him to move on. "We expected the hunters to make a move after we left."

"We killed most, but others..." His jaw ticks once. "...were more evasive, my Queen."

Across the ballroom, Jorah laughs—low and mocking. One of my sister's chosen generals, wearing his arrogance like the golden chain across his chest. The sound earns him more than a few glares.

"Evasive, Kaelin?" Jorah's weight shifts, the chain clinking. "Or perhaps your soldiers are simply...slow?"

Every muscle in Kaelin's jaw tightens. "Careful with your tongue, outsider. You are a welcome guest until your queen arrives. But you are just that." He pauses. "A guest."

Jorah smirks. "Yet the hunters still live."

Leaning forward, I click my tongue. "Now, now, Jorah. You may serve your Frost Court as ambassador until my sisters arrive, but continue with your mockery of my people and it will be the very last thing you do."

Jorah's eyes widen, his head bowing quickly as he takes a step back. "My apologies, your majesty. It was simply two warriors giving each other a hard time."

I stand and address the hall. "Onyx, Frost, and Ivory courts will join us soon enough. I expect you all to remember where you stand when they do."

A few heads lower, a few glares burn hotter.

Suddenly, the doors groan open and a figure stumbles in. One of my nightclub soldiers, reeking of cheap cologne and spilled blood. She falls to her knees before me, chest heaving, eyes wide.

"Your majesty," she gasps. "We were attacked by hunters."

Scoffs and whispers ripple through the chamber. Mutters of disapproval ring out, stopped only when I raise my hand to silence them. Leaning forward, interest piqued. "Go on."

"There were three, maybe four," she stutters. "They move like nothing I've ever seen. Quick. Coordinated. Cut through us before we could sound the alarm."

My fingers drum against the armrest as I gesture for her to continue.

She swallows hard. "We were establishing your feeding operation when they tracked us. One of your generals stayed behind and turned one of them." Her voice drops. "He said it was a gift for the hunters, from you. A message."

Hunters who could take on a club full of vampires and nearly escape. Hunters are strong—that pesky gene of theirs is remarkable, to be sure—but I've never heard of hunters who could stand against those numbers. My lips curve slowly. My tapping stops.

"Interesting." The word is barely a whisper. "Very interesting."

My court shifts, uncomfortable, waiting for my judgment. I sit back, one leg over the other. The weight of my gaze hangs in the air, and for the first time in decades, the hunters have my full attention.

"I'm done for tonight." My voice cuts through the chamber like a blade. "You may go."

Silence answers me first. Then the shuffling of feet, the rustle of cloaks as my vampires file out in clusters. They bow as they pass, their murmurs clinging to the walls even after the heavy doors groan shut.

The throne room is still. Only the five who matter remain—my most trusted generals, and Marcella. They stand at the foot of my dais like carved statues, but I know better than to mistake their stillness for calm. Their loyalty is sharp and their tempers are short.

"Vaelyn."

The general to my left bows instantly, dark hair falling across his brow—the picture of elegance and obedience. His beauty is the kind that makes mortals ache and rivals sneer. Sharp jaw, perfect smile, and a face designed to destroy.

"Yes, my Queen." Velvet wrapped around steel.

"Go to the club. I want the feeding operation secured and controlled before the others arrive. Take as many as you need, but keep it quiet." I meet his eyes. "No more interference from hunters. I will not have hungry mouths turning this city into a spectacle. We survive by being discreet, not reckless."

His lips curve faintly, though his eyes stay cold. "Of course, majesty. Discretion will be the mask of our hunger."

He bows deeper—theatrically—before rising. His boots echo across the marble as he strides toward the door and pushes it open.

My gaze slides to the others. "I want to know more about these hunters. What makes them different? Who trains them? Where do they live?"

On my right, Casen tilts his head in acknowledgment. Unlike Vaelyn, he carries no vanity. Only precision. His eyes are sharp as cut glass, his presence controlled and efficient.

"Allow me, my Queen." Calm and assured. "We will uncover their patterns."

I give him the smallest nod—all the permission he requires. In the next instant, the space where he stands is empty. His absence feels like a shift in air pressure. That leaves two more guards before me, waiting. They watch with a soldier's discipline as I lean back into the velvet embrace of my throne, letting silence stretch until it grows heavy.

"My sisters will be here before sunrise." I meet each of their eyes. "I want their rooms ready before they arrive."

They both bow and turn on their heels.

"It shall be done, my Queen." Andrew's voice echoes as they disappear through the doors.

My thoughts circle back to the hunters. For centuries, they'd been a nuisance, but always easy to deal with. Over the last few decades, they've become stronger. Wiser. More of a problem.

"My Queen." Marcella clears her throat, bringing me back. I raise an eyebrow, urging her to continue.

"What are your plans with the hunters in this city?"

I stand, taking slow and deliberate steps down the dais until we're eye level.

"I'm going to learn everything I can about them." I smile. "Then I'm going to destroy their cursed bloodline once and for all."

Marcella takes a nervous step forward, reaching out to touch my arm gently.

"Be careful, my Queen." Her voice softens. "This generation of hunters differs from centuries past. It's why we invited your sisters to meet in the first place."

I lay my hand over hers, showing my old friend the tenderness I rarely offer anymore. "I know."

Marcella bows her head and steps back. "My Queen."

Alone in the penthouse bathroom, I sink deeper into the porcelain tub. The water is hot enough to sting before melting into decadent warmth that eases every line of tension from my body. Scented oils—lavender and smoke—leave the air heavy. Steam curls upward in languid spirals, softening the glitter of the chandelier above until the entire room shimmers like a dream.

A red stained glass balances against the rim of the tub. Blood, bottled and repackaged into something delicate. I raise it to my lips and savor the way it lingers on my tongue.

In my other hand, my phone glows. Temptr—my new favorite pastime. The humans think it's for love, or at least lust. For me, it's a game. A way to play at being mortal, to dip my claws into their modern courtship rituals and laugh at how clumsy they are.

Swipe left. A pouty man with too much hair gel.

Swipe. A gym rat flexing in fluorescent light.

Swipe. A boy holding a fish.

"Absolutely not." I laugh, swiping again.

The motion becomes rhythmic. Profile after profile dissolving into nothing. Their opening lines fill my head like bad poetry.

> *Hey sxy, u up?*

> *Ever had a real man?*

> *That dress in your pictures would look great in a heap next to my bed.*

Tiresome. Predictable. And inevitably, no matter how clever the first few words, the same crude pattern emerges. Three or four desperate messages before a picture no one asks for. Why men think this is the way to interact with women, I'll never understand.

I swipe left so many times I lose count. The monotony lulls me to sleep. I tilt my head back and let the steam kiss my skin, nearly giving up.

Until him.

I pause, finger hovering over the profile of a man in his twenties. Broad shoulders that fill the frame, black hair cropped short, shirt stretched just enough across his arms to make me shift in the water. Heat rises for reasons beyond the bath.

His smile is arrogant—the kind that dares you to knock it from his face. It makes something stir deep inside me. He looks ordinary in every way. I swipe through his pictures—he leans against a motorcycle in one, a red-filtered bathroom selfie of him shirtless, and another with him holding a puppy and a bright smile slapped across his face.

"Killian Blake..." I whisper his name as I swipe right.

Instant match. Of course it is.

A slow smile curves across my lips as I swirl the wine in my glass. "Let's play."

The steam has gone hazy, softening the chandelier's light into a golden blur. My wine glass rests against the porcelain, half empty.

Killian: *Quick. Describe your ideal first date in three emojis.*

I arch an eyebrow. Emojis? That's new. Amusing, even. I send him a burger, wineglass, and eggplant just to test his reaction.

His reply comes fast. A steak, donut, and peach.

I snort into my wine, sitting up with a smile.

> **Me:** *Good to know you eat your fruits and vegetables with every meal too.*

> **Killian:** *Gotta keep this body in shape some- how. Right?*

The corners of my mouth curve before I can stop them. A laugh bubbles out—actual, genuine laughter. The sound startles me. I haven't heard it in centuries, not like this. I sit forward, ready to respond, when another message appears.

> **Killian:** *Sera is such a pretty name. Unique spelling too!*

> **Me:** *Thank you. It's short for Seraphine.*

> **Killian:** *That's so cool. Were your parents into old history stuff?*

I smile. If only he knew how old.

> **Me:** *You could say that.*

I add a laughing emoji to lighten it.

> **Killian:** *So what do you do for work?*

Of course. Men always ask this, as though your profession is shorthand for how you'd fuck. I let my fingers drift across the screen.

Me: *Acquisitions. High pressure. Lots of late nights. Clients can be a real pain in the neck.*

Killian: *That's pretty cool though. I own a bar. I would invite you out for a drink, but we're currently under renovation.*

A convenient excuse.

Me: *That's okay. Some other time maybe.*

The blood-wine and heat leave me restless. A flicker of mischief stirs as I slide the camera open and angle it at my legs stretched under the water, bubbles clinging to my skin. I hit send and wait.

His response is instant.

Killian: *Absolutely.*

With it comes another message—a set of eye emojis—letting me know he's replying to both. A beat later, a photo appears.

He's in what looks like a bar, jeans hitched up to show a hairy leg, mocking my pose. For the second time tonight, I laugh aloud. The sound is so foreign it startles me.

Me: *Let's see you copy this one.*

I snap a photo: peace sign, red-stained lips gleaming in a kiss. His response makes my eyebrows lift. He mirrors me perfectly—pose, pout, even tugs his shirt to show off his chest. More effort than I'd expected.

Me: *Well done.*

I take another photo. Bubbles sliding down my chest, skin flushed from heat. I let the cool air tease my nipples before hitting send with the caption: *If you're going to copy me, you'd better make it worth my time.*

Killian: *Oh fuck, it's like that?*

His reply nearly makes me choke on my wine. A shirtless photo appears—beer foaming down his chest, the empty glass on the counter behind him. I burst out laughing, shaking my head.

Marcella cracks the door at the sound, eyebrows arched. I wave her off, commanding her to prepare my nightgown. She lingers, eyes sharp with unspoken questions, but I give her nothing.

Me: *You are trouble.*

Killian: *Trouble is my middle name.*

Me: *Trouble can be…delicious.*

I smile at my innuendo, finish my wine, and stand from the tub. I reach for a towel when his next message appears. A picture of him in the bathroom, completely naked, though cropped just before it turns explicit. A deliberate tease.

Me: *Clever.*

In front of the mirror, I angle myself sideways enough to show the curve of my breasts and the swell of my ass. Unlike him, I make sure nothing is cropped, but also that he can't make anything important out. Leaving it all to his imagination.

I send the photo and set the phone down without waiting for his response, walking into the bedroom to find my silk ruby nightgown waiting. I slip into it just as I hear the vibration on the bathroom counter.

Smiling, I grab my phone and tuck into bed, reaching for the lamp. His message can wait until morning. Better to let him wonder, let him want. After all, this is half the fun.

As I set the phone on the nightstand, I catch myself thinking about him—about the way he makes me laugh. Actually laugh. When was the last time that happened?

I turn off the lamp and stare into the darkness. It's just a game, I remind myself. Just another mortal. But something about Killian Blake feels different.

And that makes him dangerous.

5

Killian

I stare at the photo she sent, the curves of her body framed like a weapon—the roundness of her ass, the soft line of her breasts, the way she knows exactly how much to show. My body reacts before my brain catches up.

Exhaling hard, I adjust myself before dragging my boxers back on and bending to pick up my jeans. She has me, at least this round. Not because she'd outplayed me, but because I'm not about to be the guy who sends an unsolicited dick pic. Instead, I thumb back my response.

> **Me:** *Oh, fuck. You're gorgeous. You win this round, but only because I don't want to be just another fuckboy.*

I add a winking emoji for good measure, pocket my phone, and make for the bathroom door. The smile I hadn't realized I was wearing falters the moment I swing it open and nearly collide with Helen. Her glare could cut glass.

"You ready to keep cleaning this shit up?"

"Yeah." I brush past her, grabbing the broom I'd left leaning against the counter. Right where I'd spilled beer foam on myself just to make Sera laugh. "Let's get back to it."

Worth it.

The hours that follow are nothing but the scrape of brooms, the chemical stench of bleach, and the steady ache in my shoulders. Tables reset, blood scrubbed from cracks in the wood floor. I sweep up broken glass until my knuckles are raw. The air grows heavy with lemon cleaner and old beer.

By the time we finish, the bar smells almost normal. Just in time for Donovan and Alex to show up for their shift. Thinking about Monica and Albert still makes my chest tighten, remembering how their bodies were shredded open.

"Something feels different about Bad Habits tonight," Alex says, glancing around.

I force a laugh. "We did a deep clean and rearranged a little. We open in thirty minutes, let's be ready."

They both nod and disappear toward the back. The illusion of normal is good enough for them. Helen leans against the counter, arms crossed, eyes piercing. "We have shit to talk about, Killian."

"I know."

The alley door groans open. Eli steps through, wiping his hands on a rag that smells of smoke and iron. He's back from taking what's left of Alice and Dakota, along with the other shredded bodies, to our dump site off Route 32.

"Upstairs." His voice is a growl. "We need privacy."

Before I can answer, the front door chimes and Bri stumbles inside. Her face is swollen, bruises blooming like ink stains across her skin. Her shirt is torn and her steps are unsteady.

"Shit!" I lunge forward, catching her just as her knees buckle. She sags against me, unconscious before I can call her name. I whip my head toward the back, making sure Alex and Donovan are still out of sight.

"Upstairs," I hiss. "Now, before customers start rolling in."

I carry Bri up the narrow staircase two steps at a time. The apartment above the bar isn't much, but it's convenient. It's home. The moment I lay her on the leather couch, she exhales a ragged breath and slips deeper into unconsciousness.

Helen and Eli collapse into their usual spots without ceremony, exhaustion heavy in every movement. I drop into my favorite chair, the worn leather creaking under my weight. For the first time since the bloodshed started, we all exhale. Even through the exhaustion, I pull out my phone to check for Sera's response.

Nothing.

I figure she'd gone to bed. She said she works nights. I should be asleep too, but first we have business—the business of what the fuck happened tonight and why I'd lost two of my hunters.

The apartment is heavy with silence. Only the faint hum of traffic below and Bri's ragged breathing fill the space. The room still smells faintly of bleach. My head rests against the back of the chair and my eyes half-close, until Helen's voice cuts through.

"What the hell happened tonight?"

I rub a hand across my jaw, stubble scratching against my palm. Leaning forward, I shrug. "I started with the foreclosed homes. The first two were empty, but the third had three vamps camped out on the lawn like they owned it."

Helen raises an eyebrow. "What happened to them?"

I smile grimly. "They didn't last long. But one of them was talking about terms, some kind of deal. How war was brewing. I didn't stay long enough to get the details. As soon as I finished them, I checked my phone." My smile fades. "That's when I saw Dakota's messages."

Helen and Eli share a look before telling their story. "The hospital uptown was abandoned." Helen says, fingers drumming against the armrest. "Rotten gurneys, broken glass. Hell, we didn't even find corpses. Just dust and silence. But on the way back..."

"We were jumped." Eli finishes gruffly. His eyes narrow as if he can still see it happening. "Five of them. Two Frost Court, three Onyx Court. I can still see the icy blue shine in their eyes."

My gut tightens. We haven't seen any court outside of Crimson in years. Ever since discovering the queen leads Crimson Court, we've stayed in her territory, hoping to draw her out and end her.

"I guess Dakota and Alice were right," Helen mutters. "The four courts are meeting here."

The words hang in the air like smoke. My jaw clenches. "That means more deaths than we can clean up. We need to find the queen and put her down before this city drowns."

Eli leans forward. "I still want to know what the hell happened to Dakota and Alice. How did it flip like that?"

"Agreed," Helen growls. "That was a Crimson Court general. The smug bastard turns Alice right under our noses. But why?"

I think for a minute. "Not just turn her—he parades her back into our bar. Which means he gets her to talk before she loses herself. Names, places, secrets." I shake my head slowly. "He might have already compromised us if he carried that information back to the queen."

"Maybe," Helen says. "But I don't think so. He came here alone. That tells me he had his own agenda."

Eli grunts. "Or he didn't need more. We don't know who else he spoke to before showing up here. If word reaches the queen, she'll send her armies. We'll be dead before we see her face."

My gaze flicks to Bri, her face pale against the leather. "Then we wait. When she wakes up, we'll know what she saw, what she heard. Until then, speculation won't save us."

None of us speak after that. The weight of it presses down heavier than exhaustion. I lean my head back against the chair and let my eyes close. The leather is warm against my skin.

The next thing I feel is Eli's rough hand shaking me awake. "Bri's up."

Just like that, rest is over.

I glance at the clock above the TV. I'd only been out for an hour. Sitting up, I watch Bri drink from a mug of what looks like tea—Helen's doing, no doubt.

The bass from the bar below throbs through the floorboards, muffled but insistent, like a second heartbeat none of us can ignore. Even up here, the insulation can't drown it out. Still, it's quiet enough that we don't have to raise our voices.

"The second we got to the club," Bri begins, voice hoarse. She coughs, swallows, then continues. "We knew we were out of our league. All four courts were there. The place was crawling with them. More vampires than humans."

The weight of her words presses the room into silence. I meet Helen's worried gaze. She reaches over, squeezing Bri's shoulder, urging her to continue.

"Dakota?" Bri's voice cracks. "Alice?"

I shake my head slowly. No words, no comfort, just the truth. Her face crumples and tears slip free, tracking down her dirt-smeared cheeks.

"I told them we had to wait for you. They didn't want to. They went in together."

Her voice breaks, but she forces herself on. "I found a way in through a rooftop vent. I thought...I thought I could at least keep my eyes on them." Her hands twist the blanket in her lap, knuckles white. "But by the time I got inside, I saw them. One of their generals was turning Alice. He held his fingertips against hers and let the blood transfer happen while she answered his questions."

My jaw tightens and I wait.

"It was like she was in a trance," Bri continues. "She told him about our crew, our safe house, and how we operate. She told him everything. You can't blame Alice; she didn't know what she was doing."

Helen flexes her fingers. Eli leans back, running a hand through his hair, and exhales hard. Rage burns in my chest as I lean forward, resting a gentle hand on Bri's knee.

"It's okay. We don't blame her and he's dead too."

Something in her shoulder's eases, though her smile is weak and trembling, tears still collecting in her eyes. "Good. He deserves what he got. Probably worse."

Bri takes another sip, shakily inhaling.

"The vent I was hiding in gave out. I fell straight onto the dance floor and they swarmed me. The one who turned Alice stopped them. He wanted me alive, wanted me to carry the story back to other hunters. To scare them." Her eyes drop to her bruised wrists. "He tied me up, knocked me out, but not before letting two of his soldiers beat me. When I woke up, I was in the alley. They'd let me go."

The silence that follows is colder than any grave. Helen is the first to speak. "Sounds like they're setting up a base of operations."

Eli shakes his head. "That's not their style, though. Every vampire we've ever hunted keeps to ruins, abandoned places. Never something so...public."

"Maybe the queen's the reason for the change?" I ask.

Bri's voice is barely audible, but it cuts through the room like glass. "She is. I heard them talking before I fell. They sent one of their own back to report to her. They mentioned a luxury hotel on the west side of the city."

The words sink in, heavy and final. I lean back, hands curling into fists. "This changes everything we know."

Eli crosses his arms, frowning. "The club's their anchor. We stake it out and see who comes and goes. That's where the answers are."

"We'll need backup," Helen adds. "If all four courts are here, this isn't something we can handle alone."

I grab the notepad off the coffee table, pen scratching furiously. "Then it's settled. Helen, you call our allies. Spread the news. Get them here now. Eli, dig into the records of every high-end property in this city. Hotels, penthouses, luxury homes. Anything recently bought out or leased. Get blueprints so we can plan."

"What about you, boss?" Eli asks.

"I'll go to the club and see what's really happening."

"You can't go alone," Helen says, shooting me a glare. "We can't lose anyone else."

"I'm the only one who can go. My blood is different. They can't scent me like they do you. I can blend in, see who's human and who's not." I meet her eyes. "It's the only way."

Helen's jaw tightens, but she doesn't argue. She knows I'm right. Bri's lips press tight. She takes another sip of tea. "We regroup here in the morning. Keep in constant contact."

We all nod.

"You stay here and heal," I say to Bri. "Rest and run point for us."

I hand each of them the sticky notes I'd written, outlining the plan. We stand, sharing a worried look before the meeting dissolves. Helen and Eli slip away to begin their tasks. I move into my bedroom, the familiar weight of my gear pulling me back into focus.

I strip off my stained clothes and step into the shower, letting scalding water wash away the grime and blood. My muscles ache, my shoulder throbs where the vampire had clawed me earlier. The hunter gene had done most of the healing already—knitting tissue, fading bruises. By morning, I'd be whole again.

I dress in clean jeans and a black T-shirt, nothing that will stand out. Strap a knife to my ankle, tuck another at the small of my back. My gun stays holstered under my jacket. I look like any other guy heading out for the night.

Before I leave, I check my phone one more time. Still nothing from Sera. A strange hollow feeling settles in my chest. I tell myself she's just a distraction, a game to pass the time. The truth is, I'd been looking forward to hearing from her.

After the night I'd had, after losing Dakota and Alice, after scrubbing their blood off my floors—I want something good, something normal.

I pocket my phone and head downstairs. Saying my goodbyes to Alex and Donovan, minutes later I'm astride my bike. The night's cool air rushes against my face as I rev the engine.

My texts with Sera run through my mind as I pull down the road, closer to the club. She said she works long nights, so at first I thought she was asleep. But now that night has come and still no text, part of me worries I might have already scared her off.

Focus. I tell myself. *You've got a job to do.*

The bass of the club thumps down the street as I approach. Driving past, I can see the humans standing in line, waiting to enter. The bouncer, doormen, and a few security guards are all vampires. Their glamour shimmers across their faces as my hunter gene comes alive with the threat of their presence.

I circle the block, park my bike two alleys over, and walk the shadows of the sidewalk. Finally, I join the line that stretches down the block. My hunter blood keeps me warm while everyone else's teeth chatter against the autumn chill, desperate to get inside.

They don't know they aren't waiting for a party. They're waiting for a slaughter. I stand here, hands shoved in my pockets, watching the crowd. Young people, laughing, drunk already. A girl in a short dress shivers next to her friends. A guy checks his phone, grinning at something. All of them oblivious.

All of them prey.

My jaw tightens. This isn't just reconnaissance anymore. This is personal. The queen wants a war? Then she'll get one.

6

Seraphine

Smiling at the bright glow of my phone, I read the text Killian sent in reply to my photo. Sitting up, I toss my phone to the edge of the bed and stand. Walking over to my closet, I run my fingers across the silk gowns and velvet cloaks that whisper against one another. Finally, I pull free a crimson dress that catches the light like fresh blood. The fabric slides over my skin—cool at first—before clinging to the curve of my waist.

I trace ruby-red lipstick over my lips and lean close until my reflection stares back at me with a predator's smile. My bedroom door opens, and Marcella steps in, ever silent until the moment requires her voice.

"Your sisters are waiting for you in the throne room downstairs, my Queen." Marcella bows.

"Good." I smile, bending to slip into my matching red heels. "Time to prevent more needless bloodshed."

Marcella clears her throat, clearly wanting to speak more but holding her tongue.

"Speak your mind, old friend," I say.

"Your sisters have been plotting to overthrow the Crimson Court for centuries." Marcella huffs. "Do you truly believe they will end the war for territory and join us in this fight against the hunters?"

I think about her question for a moment. A question I've wondered for many sleepless days. The fact of the matter is my sisters and I need one another if we're going to defeat the ever-growing threat of this new breed of hunters.

"We can only hope they see the urgency like we do, Marcella." I sigh. "But I must admit, I don't trust them. Which is why the Crimson Court has orders to kill without mercy while I am gone."

"Of course." Marcella bows. "When you're ready."

The ballroom doors groan open as I push them wide, the sound echoing down the chamber like a warning. The throne room has been remade in my absence. No longer one throne at the head of the room, but four—arranged in a semicircle. Each a symbol of sovereignty, three of them already occupied.

My heels click against the marble floor as I cross the chamber. The air hangs heavy, charged, as though the city remembers our last gathering centuries ago. Three pairs of eyes follow me: the first daughters of the dark. My sisters. My rivals.

Rowena, ever draped in midnight, sits stiff-backed in a gown of black silk, her crown of onyx burning against her pale brow. Shadows curl faintly at her feet, restless, like hounds on a leash.

Morgana shimmers in ice-blue, her crown a frostwork of sapphire. The air around her is colder than the rest of the chamber, her throne rimed faintly with frost.

Amara, in stark white, lounges with feline grace. Her bare feet tuck beneath her gown and her laughter hovers, ever present at the edge of her lips. Warmth and cruelty mix in her like perfume with poison.

As I ascend the dais step by step, my crimson gown spills over the marble. The weight of my crown is cold against my palm before I set it upon my brow. When I lower myself into my seat, the silence thickens as each of us waits for the other to flinch first.

No guards, no generals. Only four queens. Four predators with one ancient feud hanging over us all. Finally, I break the silence.

"Sisters. It has been too long."

Amara tilts her head, smiling faintly, almost indulgent. Rowena's eyes burn with quiet disdain. Morgana's expression is a mask of ice.

"You have called us here." Amara says softly, her words floating like music. "Why?"

I tap my finger against my throne's armrest, rhythm steady as I let my gaze move across them. "This war between our courts must end, sisters."

Rowena scoffs, the sound like claws on glass. "A war you started." Her crown glimmers like oil-slick stone as she leans forward.

Amara rolls her eyes, sighing through her smile. "Oh, must we start with grievances older than our fangs?"

"Do not defend her, sister." Morgana growls. "It is her love for humans that broke us apart. Her desire for more power drove the wedge deeper. Seraphine's lust for dominion drove the final nail in the coffin."

A sly smile slips across Amara's lips. "Pun intended, I'm sure."

I hold Rowena's gaze for a beat longer before letting out a long breath. "Whatever might have happened in the past, sisters, the hunters have grown bolder. Stronger, even. They multiply unchecked, and I propose we set aside our strife and work together to end that cursed gene once and for all."

I reach to my side and grab the map I had Marcella prepare earlier, unrolling it on the ground before them. The parchment crackles as it opens and reveals our lands sectioned off and colored distinctly to represent our four courts.

"What is this?" Rowena huffs.

Morgana gasps as realization hits her first. Amara stands, examining the details of what I propose.

"You mean to—" Amara starts.

"Yes," I interrupt. "I am tired of fighting, sisters. I wish to make amends, and to show how serious I am, I would like to redraw the boundaries of our territories."

I bend down, pointing to a spot on the map. The land divided cleanly and equally, all radiating outward from this very city—the very place it all began a thousand years ago. I look to Rowena first and soften my voice just enough to suggest concession.

"Onyx should expand into the northwest. You will gain more of the mountains. A greater reach leading to greater strength."

Her eyes narrow, suspicion warring with satisfaction, but she leans back in her chair. "A correction...long overdue."

My gaze slides to Morgana next. "The Frost Court will remain in the southwest, but your domain will stretch further into the waters, reaching Hawaii. Let your ships sail again, sister. Your people have starved for water too long."

The ice building on her throne thickens, cracks echoing like distant thunder. She doesn't speak, but gives a slow and shallow nod.

Finally, I look at Amara, who is running a finger across her new lands. "The Ivory Court will expand northeast past the Great Lakes. You will have the biggest territory, but your people are wanderers by nature. Let them wander farther."

Her smile blooms, her eyes shining with a pleasure too sharp to be kindness. "You are too generous, Seraphine. It almost feels like bribery."

I ignore the bait. "Crimson will take the southeast. I have ceded much of my land so the balance tips in each of your favors. Do not mistake this for weakness, sisters. I only wish to make amends for my past...wrongdoings."

Rowena's glare softens slightly. She leans forward, raising an eyebrow. "This is very unexpected of you, Seraphine. I must admit, I'm surprised by all of this."

"There is one last thing," I say. "I think we should open our borders and allow our people to cross without fear of harm."

Morgana's lips peel back in a snarl, frost crawling over her armrest. "We have never allowed boundary crossings."

"No," I agree simply. "We haven't. But we've also never faced hunters like these. Their numbers grow, and their weapons evolve. They are a nuisance—"

"A threat." Amara interrupts.

"One we cannot ignore," I finish.

For a moment, silence hangs in the air again. The weight of the decision presses down on all of us. At last, Rowena laughs.

"Well, sisters, for once, Seraphine might be right. This may be the only way to keep the hunters from thinning our numbers."

Morgana gives a curt nod, suspicion still in her eyes. Amara follows, the gesture stiff. I let my shoulders ease fractionally, though inside my thoughts roil. They have agreed, but I know better than to trust it.

Rowena and Morgana have been plotting against me in secret for decades. This truce is nothing more than a pause in their plans. Still, I smile. "Then it's settled. We call our people and announce the new order of things. Let this city be the center of our power once more."

For the first time since this war began, the four of us have agreed. I pray it will last long enough that I won't have to kill my own blood.

The chamber fills with the shuffle of footsteps, cloaks brushing across marble. Whispering vampires file into place. My sisters preen on their thrones—Rowena taps her lacquered nails like claws against obsidian, Morgana whispers ice-laced commands to her guards, and Amara smiles lazily at her reflection in a polished goblet.

My crimson gown pools elegantly over my throne as I let my gaze wander to the small glow in my hand. Hiding my smile in the curve of my knuckles, I swipe open the message thread with Killian and type out my first message to him since sending that photo.

Me: *Did you get any sleep last night, or did you spend all night thinking about me?*

His reply comes quick, desperate, like he'd been waiting for me.

Killian: *I slept like a dream.*

I can almost hear his laugh through the screen.

Me: *Is the bar busy tonight?*

Killian: *It is a busy night, but I am out with some friends tonight. You should come over later, have a drink.*

Bold. I have to give him that. He's putting in the effort most men don't. I clear my throat to hide the laugh I'd just let out, checking to make sure no one is paying attention as the rest of our four courts file in.

Me: *I am finishing up meetings tonight, big decisions are happening.*

Killian: *Gross. Sounds like you need a drink.*

Me: *You just want an excuse to see me.*

His reply brings another smile to my face. This human has a way with words.

Killian: *Can you blame me for wanting to see such a beautiful girl?*

Me: *We will just have to see how lucky you are, I suppose.*

Killian: *I'm feeling pretty lucky.*

Before I can type my message, Marcella clears her throat beside me. As I look up, I see my sisters staring at me, waiting for me to address our now-gathered court.

I let the screen dim in my palm, slipping the phone back into the folds of my gown as the herald's voice rises to announce the beginning of the session. My sisters stare outward, regal and cold. I straighten on my throne, the weight of my crown firm against my brow, and smooth my face into something unreadable.

Deep inside, under velvet and steel, I carry the warmth of his words like a secret ember. A towering brute in a black suit emerges from the sea of vampires. His voice rolls through the chamber, deep and commanding, as he sweeps his hand from left to right.

"The Four Courts are gathered. Hear now what your Queen's decree is."

He bows low, retreating into the shadows as all eyes turn to me. Slowly, deliberately, I rise. The velvet of my gown whispers against the throne, the weight of my crown catches the chandelier's light. The air is thick with anticipation, the silence broken only by the faint hiss of braziers.

"Welcome, all," I say, my voice carrying easily across the vast hall. It echoes off the marble, filling every corner until even the boldest murmur dies. "As many of you know, our courts have been at war for centuries."

A ripple of whispers spreads through the hall—some excited, some wary. I let it run its course, savoring the tension before continuing.

"It is the decision of your Queens," I announce, each word sharp as glass. "That the war between us be halted. And the boundaries of our courts be redrawn."

The chamber erupts at once. Cheers and sighs of relief clash against growls of discontent. Some press hands to their hearts in reverence while others cross their arms, flashing their fangs in open defiance. The roar swells like a storm until Rowena rises from her throne.

Her black gown shimmers like oil, her voice cuts clean through the hall. "The borders will remain open. Anyone who wishes to move may do so without fear of punishment. We will need each other if we are to defeat the true threat to us all."

Morgana stands next, her presence brings with it a breath of frost. Her words spill like shards of ice. "The hunters." She pauses. "They have been allowed to prosper for far too long. We will call upon our allies among the mortals, and they will make good on the reason we allow them to live."

The crowd shifts uneasily. A few smirk, a few pale. Finally, Amara stands, her white gown trailing like spilled milk across the dais. Her smile is sweet, her tone deceptively gentle.

"We all remain in this city until these matters are completed. There will be no massacres and no reckless displays. You will remain discreet and feed only at the nightclub that Seraphine has so generously set up for us all. Keep it orderly, or face the consequences."

A hush falls and the tension clings to the air like smoke. I step forward, letting my shadow stretch long across the marble. My grin sharpens as my eyes burn darker.

"Kneel before your queens," I command. "Four Courts united at last."

The response comes all at once—the scrape of armor and the rustle of cloaks, heavy as hundreds lower as one. Every vampire, from ancient generals to fledglings, drops to their knees. A difference of how to rule, bickering between four power hungry immortals, and an imbalance of land division separated my sisters and I for centuries. Now, for the first time, the four of us stand united.

If only in appearance.

7

Killian

Inside the club, the bass pounds through my bones, and the floor trembles beneath every step. Lights strobe in red and violet, washing the crowd in waves of shadow and glow. Heat presses in from all sides, the smell of perfume mixing with the coppery tang of fresh blood and sweat from the patrons dancing.

I weave through the crowd of humans and vampires mixed seamlessly—at least to the untrained eye. But not to mine. My hunter blood reveals the truth of what this club is. I can see through the glamour to skin stretched too tight and eyes that glimmer a fraction too long under the strobe. Teeth hidden but itching to be bared as they dance close and whisper promises that lead their prey toward the darker corners of the room.

Behind thick curtains are private rooms, cleverly disguised feeding stations. VIP lounges with fogged glass doors that no one bothers to look through. Passing by one booth, I glimpse a woman leaning back, eyes rolled white, neck bared.

Anyone just passing by would assume she's enjoying a private, intimate moment with a man whose lap she's sitting on. One extra glance would reveal the truth: the vampire is feeding on her, draining her dry.

I force my expression flat, casual, as though I'm just another guy out on a Friday night. But inside, the rage coils tight. From the corner of my eye, I catch movement—a vampire stepping down from the balcony. Broad shoulders, sharp suit, his gaze sweeps the crowd like a predator looking for a loose calf in the herd.

When his eyes pass over me, my grip tightens around the bar top. Turning back toward the dance floor, I force my body to sway with the beat. A woman approaches and runs her finger across my chest. She's beautiful—curvy in all the right places. Except for the fangs that threaten to show, her true age shimmering, peeking through her glamour. My hunter blood boils, urging me to act.

"Care for a private room, handsome?" she asks sweetly.

I stare at the way her pale skin stretches around her skull. She must be centuries old to appear so...refined.

"I should probably get going." I yell back, making my voice carry over the heavy beat.

The vampire leans in close to my ear. "On the house." She yells back, the smell of blood thick in her words.

I give her a curt nod, following her to the private rooms in the back of the club. She sweeps back the curtains and opens a fogged glass door, urging me to go in. I hesitate for only a moment before stepping past her and taking a seat in the leather chair.

The music is lower here, like the room must be soundproofed to prevent passersby from hearing the screams of the victims. The woman reaches for a dial on the wall and the lights dim. Soft music begins playing as she moves her body to the rhythm and teases at the hem of her shirt.

I lean back in the chair and watch as she peels off her shirt, her breasts bouncing free. On the surface, she runs her hands up her slim, beautiful body, dancing seductively as she makes her way closer to me. The hunter blood coursing in my veins reveals the aged, pale skin of the truth beneath.

"My name is Emma." She smiles. "Are you new to this kind of thing?"

I watch as she peels her mini skirt down until the fabric pools at her feet. She turns around and bends over as she peels the lacy thong off. I stare at her ass, both holes parting slightly as she shakes it in my face.

I adjust myself slightly, shifting in the seat as she stands back up and begins grinding in my lap. This is truly one of the most confusing lap dances I've ever had. The beautiful woman luring me into her trap is ruined by the monstrous creature beneath.

Her gentle fingers running up my thighs are rough with calluses, claws that scrape lightly across my jeans. Emma turns and straddles me, wrapping her arms around my neck. She leans over and brushes her chest against mine, kissing my neck. I can feel her fangs grinding against my skin, and I know it's only a matter of time before she strikes.

"I am new to this," I say, producing a mock shy tone. "I've never had a lap dance like this before."

"It's about to get so much better, sweetie." She teases, pulling my zipper down and running her hand across my hard cock.

She pushes me back against the chair, holding me in place as she lets out a laugh that disappears into the soundproofed walls. Finally, she drops her glamour and reveals the truth I'd already seen. Any normal man would have been terrified by this moment—panicking, pulse racing, scrambling to find a way out.

I simply smile and stare up at her, and wink. "Now this." I laugh. "I am not new at."

Emma gives a confused glance at my smile. "You aren't afraid?"

"Of a vampire?" I laugh harder.

Moving quickly, I pull the pocketknife I keep behind my belt and flick it open, plunging the blade deep into her heart. She gasps in pain and shock.

"I've been killing you bloodsuckers since I was a kid," I say, twisting the blade as her pale skin turns to ash.

With a last effort, she lunges forward, attempting to dig her teeth into me. I don't flinch. The vampire is ash before she gets halfway.

Standing, I brush the sticky remnants from my clothes before zipping my pants back up and tucking the knife away.

"The crew will never believe this." I whisper to the scattered ashes still smoldering on the ground.

Pulling back the thick curtains of the private room, I make my way back to the main club. Across the room, I catch sight of two men—generals by the cut of their suits and the way the crowd bends to give them space. Their voices carry over the music, sharp with anger. They're arguing about a kill. One snarls about restraint, about keeping the feeding clean and taking just enough to taste before releasing.

The other scoffs, dripping arrogance, saying the body was weak and useless. The truth is clear: killing isn't part of the plan. Not here, not now. It's too risky, too loud, bringing too much unwanted attention.

Too late, assholes. We already figured you out.

The front door opens. A burst of light spills in briefly across the floor as four more humans stumble inside, oblivious to the wolves circling them. The rising sun is my cue to leave.

I turn away, moving with the crowd until I slip through the exit, then cut into the alley where my bike awaits in the shadows. The air outside is cooler, quieter, but the thrum of the bass still rattles the brick walls behind me.

A buzz in my pocket.

I pull my phone out—a message from Sera. My lips twitch into a smile despite the weight in my chest. After the blood, the screams, and the predators playing house in that club, her words are a strange lifeline—normal, even sweet. Just a conversation with a beautiful girl.

I thumb a reply, slide my phone back into my pocket, and swing a leg over the bike. The engine roars to life beneath me, echoing in the alley. By the time I hit the street, the bar will already be closed and silent. Just how I need it.

I sit in my office, feet propped up on the desk after finishing paperwork from closing, smiling like an idiot at my phone as I watch three jumping dots appear in our chat thread.

Sera: *How was your night, handsome?*

Me: *It was a busy one. Ready for bed.*

My eyes are growing heavy, but I'm enjoying talking to Sera. It's refreshing to have someone to talk to who makes it feel so easy, so natural. Just a normal girl who makes me feel like I'm more than a hunter.

Sera: *Oh, headed to bed?*

The message is simple, but I can't help but read into it. Is she upset that I'm heading to sleep?

Me: *I don't have to if you have something in mind?*

I stare at my phone and anxiously wait for her response.

Sera: *I wanted to meet you, and I thought we could break the ice with a little friendly competition.*

Smiling, I thumb back a response.

Me: *I would love to meet up. If you can handle losing well?*

Sera: *Bold man. Are you saying you won't let me win?*

Me: *I would never.*

I add an emoji of an angel to make the message more playful, hoping it doesn't ruin the mood. She texts me back a picture—she's laying in bed with covers pulled up to her nose. I stare into her hazel eyes longer than I would like to admit before replying.

Me: *Let me shower, I'll meet you there. Where do you have in mind?*

When she sends me a pinned location, I let out a laugh. It's an old building that was recently renovated into a laser tag arena. This girl has no idea who she's up against, but I decide to play it cool and send her a simple thumbs up emoji.

I realize as I'm walking toward the shower that I just agreed to meet this girl. Not a hookup, not a quick dinner—an actual date in the daytime that could lead to doing something after. I don't think I've ever felt this nervous in my life.

8

Seraphine

I do want to meet Killian Blake. The couple of days we've been texting back and forth have been a welcome distraction from the constant plotting and planning with my sisters and generals. Waiting for Casen to return with intel is beginning to get to me. I could use more of his distraction.

"You ready to have your ass beat?" I ask, walking up to Killian as he leans against his parked motorcycle.

The afternoon sun hangs low and golden, casting long shadows across the cracked pavement. I can only hope the gentle smile I've given him hides the blush I can feel warming my cheeks. He's not at all what I expected from the app. His shoulders are broader somehow, filling out his frame in a way the photos didn't capture. The way the sunlight reflects off his sharp jawline causes me to pause when I see him.

He's wearing a pair of blue jeans that form around his ass perfectly, and a dark blue long-sleeve shirt with the sleeves rolled to the elbows. The fabric squeezes tightly against his muscles, and I can see the faint outline of scars beneath the thin material—old wounds that tell stories I suddenly want to know. I have to clear my throat before extending my hand to offer it to him.

Killian eyes my hand before smiling at me and extending his own. Gods, even his smile is better than his photos—crooked at one corner, confident, with just a hint of mischief. He takes my hand and squeezes firmly. His palm is warm, calloused in places that suggest demanding work, and his grip is strong enough to make my pulse quicken.

"Only if you can agree to lose gracefully." Killian laughs, the sound low and genuine.

"Seraphine," I say.

"Killian."

We end up being part of a group of eight others. The building smells of industrial paint and new carpet, the air conditioning fighting a losing battle against the packed playroom. The woman helping everyone check in asks if we want to be on a team or not, and Killian and I both quickly say no. We both are here to silently prove to the other who's better, and we can't accomplish that on the same team.

I stare at the red flashing light on his chest as we wait for them to open the doors, watching it pulse like a mechanical heartbeat. I'm hardly listening to the training video that plays—something about avoiding headshots and staying in bounds—and Killian isn't listening either. He's staring at me with intense green eyes, a smirk on his face that I can't wait to wipe off.

The doors open with a pneumatic hiss, and both teams rush inside, footsteps echoing off concrete floors as we quickly find our starting spots. I listen, tracking his heartbeat as he settles on his side of the dark arena. The sound is steady, strong, pumping beneath muscle and bone. I lean against a wall that's been painted black, except for some glow-in-the-dark markings that pulse faintly under the UV lights. Neon lights hang from the ceiling like electric vines, casting everyone in a weird blue glow that makes teeth and white clothing shine like beacons.

A woman's white shirt is practically a lighthouse, and I know she's going to be a quick target for the other team. My sights are set on one person and one person only. As I listen for his heartbeat, I find it easily. Unlike everyone else whose hearts are pounding with excitement and nerves, a frantic drumbeat of adrenaline, Killian's heart is steady, calm, unnaturally so.

Maybe he's used to the dark rooms and loud environments since he owns a bar. Either way, the moment the start alarm sounds—a sharp electronic blare that cuts through the bass-heavy music—I move with one goal in mind.

In a matter of seconds, I'm lost in the maze of strobe lights and dark walls. The air smells like plastic and fake smoke from the fog machine, thick enough to taste. I take nervous shots at anyone who turns a corner, the gun vibrating in my hands with each pull of the trigger, blue laser cutting through the manufactured darkness. I manage to get our team seven points before finding Killian, and as I stare at the scoreboard—glowing numbers suspended above the arena like a neon constellation—I see his team has nine points. I curse silently to myself when my chest piece lights up blue and vibrates against my ribs, the sensation both startling and annoying.

"Oops," I hear Killian mock from behind me, his voice cutting through the pounding techno beat.

He's gone by the time I turn around, swallowed by shadows and synthetic fog.

Two minutes left in the game and I'm determined to get the upper hand on him. I climb stairs that lead to a second-floor crosswalk area, metal grating rattling under my feet, and spot Killian below. He's leaned against a wall, perfectly still, trying to peer around each corner before making a move. He's good, and if I hadn't known any better I'd say he has a background in the military with how he's clearing rooms—methodical, efficient, always checking his six.

I aim my gun at him and smile to myself. As if he senses his doom, he looks up at me just as I pull the trigger. The laser finds its mark, painting his chest piece with red light. I jump with glee as I watch it blink frantically, a strobing admission of defeat. I hold my gun up and pretend to blow smoke off the barrel.

"Oops." I tease back.

It's too loud for him to have heard me over the music—something with heavy bass that makes my bones vibrate—but I know he knows what I said by reading my lips. He glares at me before giving me a slight head nod, acknowledgment and challenge rolled into one gesture. When his chest piece stops blinking, I aim at him again but he ducks behind a wall before I can shoot, quick as a shadow.

The lights in the arena come back on, fluorescent and harsh after the darkness, and the music dies out as the game ends. His team won by one point and there's a fire in my stomach that I have to put effort into not letting show. I start to take off my chest piece when I feel Killian's presence behind me—the heat of him, the scent of his skin mixed with sweat and something clean, like cedar.

"Want to go again?" he asks, close enough that I can feel his breath on my neck.

I turn to face him, all smiles. "No one else is in line." I point out, gesturing to the family gathering their things by the exit. "This family is leaving too."

"I paid them extra to let us go again." Killian says, grinning like a man who's used to getting what he wants.

I give him a smile. "We are technically tied 1-1." I shrug.

We enter the room again, and find our starting points on opposite ends of the arena. I close my eyes and listen for his calm heartbeat, finding him in the right corner of the arena. When the lights go out and the blacklight comes on—turning every surface into a strange otherworld of glowing paint and shadow—the starting alarm sounds and I move.

I clear each corner efficiently, not wanting him to get the first shot off in our five-minute match. I catch his scent just seconds before he turns the next corner—masculine, earthy, with a hint of leather and gunpowder that clings to him like a second skin. I drop to my knees just in time for him to turn the corner and fire at where I would have been. I drink in his confused look as I aim at him from the ground, and he barely manages to look down before I'm firing at him and causing his chest piece to light up frantically.

"That's too bad," I say with a smile. "2-1."

Killian glares at me, already aiming his gun at me and waiting for his chest piece to stop vibrating. I get to my feet and run, my footsteps echoing off the walls. I hear him pursuing me, his breathing steady and controlled even as he moves fast, and I'm hit with an urge to let him catch me.

Shaking my head, I get rid of the thoughts of him pinning me against the neon-lit wall and focus on making sure he loses. I turn a corner and collide right into a waiting Killian, the impact solid and breathtaking.

He grabs my gun and pins it against the wall, the barrel trapped beneath his strong hand. I can't help the noise that leaves me—half gasp, half something else entirely. He leans in close and I can feel his breath hot on my cheek, smell the mint of his toothpaste mixed with coffee, as he whispers, "2-2."

I push him back, looking at him confused. "What? You didn't—"

My chest piece lights up in a blinking blue light and vibrates against my chest. I look down and see his gun aimed up at his side, the barrel still pointing at me even as he'd distracted me with his proximity.

"You distracted me. Doesn't count," I say.

"Distracting isn't against the rules." He winks. "What are you going to do about it?" He asks and disappears down the next hall, laughter trailing behind him.

Two minutes left in the match and neither of us have gotten off another shot since Killian pinned me against the wall. It's exactly what I wanted him to do, and it had the exact effect on me that I knew it would. This human is bringing out a side of me I haven't felt in so very long—something warm and reckless, something that makes me forget what I am.

I watch him round another corner from the second-floor crosswalk, and lift my gun to fire at him. I hesitate, with only one and a half minutes left—if I fire now he can get his revenge before time runs out. I drop down onto the main level, landing silently on the balls of my feet—probably not something any normal human would do, and I have to just hope no one was watching at that moment. I weave around corners until I find Killian checking the next hallway, his broad back to me, muscles shifting beneath his shirt.

I run at him, and just as he turns to block me I pin him against the wall, making sure to pin his gun down so he can't surprise me. His body is warm and solid against mine, his chest rising and falling beneath my palms.

"Now who's distracting who?" Killian breathes, his voice rough.

I stare at the sweat building on his forehead, tiny droplets catching the blacklight like liquid stars. The flush of his cheeks, the way his pupils dilate in the darkness. I watch his chest rise and fall rapidly, each breath making the space between us feel smaller.

"Sorry." I say quietly, my voice barely audible over the music. "Am I distracting you?"

He leans in slightly and I'm tempted to meet him halfway, to taste whatever truth his mouth might hold. I pull back, aim my gun at his chest, and wait. Thirty seconds left in the match. I half expect Killian to try and make his move, to fight back or twist free, but he just waits patiently, his eyes never leaving mine as he grins back at me.

"You have me," he says, the words heavy with double meaning. "Take your shot."

"You don't tell me what to do," I say, trying to be seductive and not authoritative. However it comes off, it seems to work on him. His breath catches, just slightly.

"Yes ma'am," Killian drawls, the southern edge to his words making something low in my stomach tighten.

I press the trigger and get my one up on him, winning the match. But the way Killian makes my heart race, makes me want to crush his lips with mine, makes me feel alive in ways I'd forgotten were possible...he's the true winner today.

"That was fun," I say as we walk to Killian's bike, the late afternoon sun painting everything gold and amber.

The parking lot is nearly empty. Birds chatter in the trees nearby, and somewhere in the distance a car alarm bleats once before falling silent.

"More fun than I've had in so long," Killian agrees, running a hand through his sweat-dampened hair. "Thank you for suggest-ing this."

"I'm glad I did," I say. "Thanks for not being a sore loser."

Killian raises his hand and brushes his knuckles across my cheek, the touch feather-light and electric. His skin is warm, slightly rough, and the tenderness of the gesture catches me off guard. I lean into his touch before I realize I am, my eyes fluttering closed for just a moment.

"I'll lose anytime against you," he whispers, his voice low and sincere.

I look up at him, realizing now just how much bigger he is than me. He's a giant standing next to me, broad-shouldered and solid, and all I can think about at this moment is climbing him right here in this parking lot. Gods, what is wrong with me?

Instead of acting on impulse, I pull back and offer him my hand in return. He takes it politely and shakes it, much gentler than our first handshake, his thumb brushing over my knuckles before he releases me.

"Would you want to go get some lunch?" He asks suddenly, hope and uncertainty warring in his expression.

"Right now?" I ask. A stupid question, I know.

"Yes." He smiles. "If you want?"

Killian's phone goes off before I'm able to answer him, buzzing loud in the quiet parking lot. He apologizes and reads the message on his phone. I see his eyes go wide, the color draining slightly from his face before he pockets the phone with hands that move just a fraction too fast.

"I am so sorry." He says, and I can hear the truth in it. "I have to go. I had so much fun, and I will text you. Rain check on food?"

His sudden shift in demeanor gives me pause—the way his entire body has tensed, the way his jaw has set, the way his eyes have gone hard and distant. But I reluctantly nod my head, not wanting him to see my sadness in him leaving so suddenly.

"Of course. Rain check," I say, keeping my voice light.

He sits on his bike and starts it, the engine roaring to life with a throaty growl that vibrates through the ground. He backs it up before revving and taking off, tires squealing slightly as he accelerates. He pulls out of the parking lot and speeds down the road before disappearing behind some buildings, the sound of his engine fading like a promise broken.

My phone rings and I answer with a hint of annoyance in my tone. "What." I demand, watching the empty street where Killian disappeared.

It's Marcella. I can hear a sense of urgency in her voice—tight, clipped, the way she only sounds when something has gone very wrong—and I'm running down the street before she finishes her sentence. The city blurs past me as I run with supernatural speed back to the hotel, buildings and cars becoming streaks of color, the wind whipping my hair back and stealing my breath.

"We have a problem."

9

Killian

No matter how fast I ride, or how hard the wind whips against my skin through the open visor of my helmet, I can't get the smell of her out of my nose. Not that I want it to leave. Sweet vanilla mixed with something floral—jasmine—clings to my senses like a memory I'm desperate to keep. Images of her smile dance across my vision as I turn down the last street leading to the bar, and my chest tightens when I remember the feeling of her pressed against me, warm, solid, and real.

I roll into the alley behind the bar and turn off the bike, the engine's rumble dying to silence. As I set my helmet on the handles, I smile at the memory of our game. She wasn't shy like other women I've talked to—hell, she asked me out before I could. This woman is different, and I need to know more.

Fuck Eli and his interrupting text.

I rush upstairs to find Helen, Bri, Eli, and two others I don't recognize sitting in my living room. The air is thick with tension, cigarette smoke curling toward the ceiling from the ashtray on the coffee table. I glare at the two men as I slow my run, approaching cautiously and trying to read the room. Both are broad-shouldered, dirt still clinging to their boots, the smell of road dust and gunpowder following them like a shadow.

"What is it?" I ask. "Who are you?"

"They are the reason we're here," Eli says, gesturing to the strangers. "After Helen sent out the message, Cole and Michael were finishing up a hunt in Kansas. On their way into town, they passed the abandoned hospital and noticed a group of vampires taking it over and using it as their den."

I cock my head and raise an eyebrow. "I thought they were using the club as their den? Isn't that why we're watching it so closely?"

Bri laughs, the sound bitter and sharp. "Who's to say they aren't using both? All four courts are gathered in this city, Killian. It's going to be a bloodbath."

I don't give her a response. She's been too ready to kill since Dakota and Alice, a fire in her eyes that burns too hot, too reckless. Instead I turn to Helen. She's looking at me with a smile on her lips, picking at her nails again as if she hasn't a care in the world for the threat in this city.

"Care to give your input?" I ask.

She lets out an annoyed sigh, examining her thumbnail. "We're hunters. The club isn't killing innocents, they're just feeding. The hospital group is killing. Seems simple to me."

I consider her words carefully, weighing lives against strategy.

"Listen." The man introduced as Cole stands, his chair scraping against the hardwood. "My brother and I are going to that hospital tonight to end the killings. We just thought we'd give y'all a heads up since this is your operation."

"I agree that we should end the killing," I say. "But is no one worried about retaliation from the four queens occupying the city? Or their hundreds if not thousands of generals with them?"

Eli shrugs, Bri copying the motion with mechanical precision. "We're here for war anyways, Kil. Retaliation is expected no matter what move we make," Eli says.

"The four queens need to die, no matter the cost. Duty above desire," Bri agrees, using our hunter motto as emphasis of her stance to fight.

"How many are we talking about?" I ask with a frustrated sigh, rubbing my temples as I wait.

"I've seen fifteen." Michael chimes in, his voice rougher than his brother's, gravel, and whiskey. "But that was just watching the day we rolled in, could be more I 'spose."

The silence hangs thick in the air as I contemplate the best option that allows us to all survive this. Guns, obviously, are the best route and the hospital sits on the end of a long road, part of the reason it was closed and moved to the center of the city. This means sneaking in won't work—they'll see us coming. Finally, I nod.

"Let's come up with the plan."

I follow Eli's mustang as we barrel down the road leading to the hospital, gravel crunching beneath my tires, dust billowing in the headlights. Helen is riding with him, much to Bri's dismay. They're following Michael and Cole's Hummer that's been tricked out with all kinds of weapons—reinforced plating, mounted guns, the works. It's also armored which is why they're leading the way. I spot Bri in the back of the Hummer, shifting in her seat and ready to swing her door open the moment we stop.

I barely scrape through the gates after Michael rams through them, metal screaming as it bends and tears. They rebound instead of staying open and I have to go faster to clear it, then immediately slam on the brakes so I don't run into Eli's Mustang. I kill the engine and get off the bike, quickly slipping into my armored mask that not only protects my skin from teeth and nails, but gives me a heads-up display that allows me to see in the dark. The HUD flickers to life, painting the world in shades of green and digital overlays.

"Ready?" I ask over comms, my voice crackling through the speakers.

Once everyone confirms, we advance to the hospital. It's quick, precise, and uniform. We move as a unit, staying close to one another and constantly watching all around us for surprises. Our boots crunch over broken glass and scattered debris—old medical equipment rusting in the moonlight, wheelchairs tipped on their sides like metal skeletons. Cole and Michael place charges on the doors and we duck as the doors explode open with a deafening boom that echoes across the empty landscape.

I throw three smoke grenades into the lobby of the hospital and we advance forward, the acrid smell of burning chemicals mixing with dust and decay. Each of us carries rifles, holstering pistols in multiple places and an array of knives. I haven't hunted in a group in so long and the sense of pride and brotherhood I feel right now is otherworldly. It's a high I constantly chase, this feeling of being part of something bigger.

My muscles tighten and my senses heighten the moment we stop in the middle of the empty lobby. The hunter gene flares to life in the presence of vampires, my blood singing with recognition. Though there aren't any here now, they're close. Waiting. Watching. I turn off the night vision of my display, but keep the helmet on for protection. My hunter blood allows me to see as clear as daylight in this dark abandoned hospital—every crack in the tile, every spiderweb in the corners, every shadow that moves wrong.

We hold our position in silence, listening for any sign of foreign movement. The building creaks around us, settling like old bones. Water drips somewhere in the distance, a rhythmic plop that counts the seconds. We don't have to wait long. Bri and Eli begin shooting down the wings they're watching, the rapid crack of gunfire splitting the air. Helen and Cole fire down theirs, muzzle flashes lighting up the darkness. Michael and I watch the overhead space, not giving the vampires the chance to drop in on us from above.

I can't help but feel like I'm in the worst zombie movie ever as hordes of vampires fill the halls and rush us, their feet slapping against tile, their snarls echoing off the walls. So much for roughly fifteen.

"It's a trap!" I yell just as movement in the shadows above draws my attention.

Michael is firing into the ceiling, plaster and dust raining down in chunks. I watch the walkways of the second and third floor, tracking movement in my peripheral. Fuck the exposed architecture of the building—it's too much to cover for just the six of us.

The horde of vampires is on us before we can get a reload in, so it becomes a close quarters fight too quickly for my liking. This is supposed to be an in and out hunt, and it's gone fucked quickly. Bodies slam against me, claws raking across my armor with sounds like nails on chalkboard. The air reeks of death and ash and something sweet like rotting fruit.

"We need to go. There's too many." I say, driving my knife up under a vampire's jaw.

"Absolutely not!" Bri growls. "These fuckers die tonight."

My clip is empty, ash is smothering the already damp, musky air. Another reason for the mask—to filter out the suffocating air that tastes like copper and decay.

"Don't be ridiculous," Helen says, her blade flashing silver in the darkness. "Killian is right, there are way too many."

"They knew we were coming!" Cole growls into his mic, his voice breaking with static.

"No shit." Eli says.

We move toward the doors before we can be surrounded. I bring my knife up, plunging it into the throat of an incoming vampire with piercing blue eyes—Frost Court. I watch Helen throw a blade at another with soulless black eyes—Onyx.

"All four courts are here," I say, breathing hard. "The queens must be close."

As if being summoned by my words, four women step out of the oncoming horde of vampires in armor that matches the color of their respective courts. I have to admit, they're breathtakingly terrifying.

Beautiful, in a dangerous way. They'll draw you into their orbit just to rip your heart out. Cole lunges for the blue queen and I gasp at how quickly she rips him apart.

In the blink of an eye, one second he's beside us fighting, and the next he's being torn in half and tossed aside like discarded trash, his scream cut short with a wet crunch. Michael roars in rage and Eli has to pin him to the ground to stop his assault. It's then when I notice the vampires aren't pushing anymore.

They've formed a circle around us, except for the small opening we managed to get to the front doors. They close in, but no longer attack. Eli gets Michael to calm down, and they stand back up, Michael's chest heaving with fury and grief.

The queens step forward, a smile on each of their faces—predatory and pleased.

"Look what we have here," the white queen says, her voice like honey over razors—Ivory Court.

"Hunters, trying to disrupt our operations." The black-court queen laughs, the noise high-pitched and forced, grating against my ears.

"We aren't going to let you feed in this city." Eli growls.

They go back and forth, insulting each other while I quickly assess the best option out of here alive. It's the middle of the night, so they can follow us if we run. We don't have the ammunition or the numbers to fight this many. The only real option I see is an all-out assault on the queens, targeting the red queen—Crimson Court. If we're right about our theory, killing her will kill the rest.

Helen glares at me as I come to an insane conclusion in my head. She's always been good at reading me and she takes a step closer as Bri joins in on the taunting.

"Don't do anything stupid," she hisses.

I laugh. "Stupid is all I do."

I move to step in front of my hunters when I freeze. Michael has charged toward the Ivory Queen and is pumping his fist in the air at her, scolding her as if he has any right to speak to her this way.

"You promised my brother and I would be left unharmed!" He yells, voice cracking. "You lied!"

Eli stops talking. All of us stand frozen at Michael's words. Did he just say—

"I have served you faithfully for six years! I told you where the hunters would be tonight! Why did you kill my brother, Morgana!"

I'm struggling to process everything Michael is saying. Because it sounds like he sold us out to the vampires, and not only that, but that he's been working with them for...six years? I see the confused looks on everyone's face as we all come to the same conclusion.

"You serve the vampires?" Bri asks before anyone else can, her voice hollow with betrayal.

Michael doesn't even acknowledge her. He drops to his knees and cries out at the feet of the queens, tears streaming down his face. Crying for his brother and begging the queens to answer him.

They don't.

They don't get the chance. Eli pulls his gun out and shoots Michael in the back three times. It is quick, brutal, but efficient. The body slumps forward, blood pooling on the tile like spilled ink. The horde of vampires stirs but doesn't press forward.

"That was rude." The Crimson Queen sneers, her voice smooth as silk over steel.

"He was our pet to play with." The Frost Queen—Morgana apparently—hisses, frost forming on the ground around her feet.

I take a step forward. "How many humans are working with you?"

The red queen laughs at me, and it takes everything in me not to pounce on her and kill her. "More than you could ever imagine, boy."

There is something so familiar about her voice, and the longer I stare at her the more I feel like I know her. The ancient wear of being an immortal creature is making it hard for me to figure it out. Her hair is long and as black as night, flowing over her crimson armor like liquid shadow. She's toned perfectly and although her fangs gleam brightly in the moonlight streaming through the broken windows, I can't help but think she has a certain...beauty about her. Something that makes my chest tighten.

I push those thoughts out and focus. "What is the end goal here?"

I take another step forward and I watch her eyes dart to my arms, to the scars that litter my body. She takes a step closer until we're only two feet apart. I can't help but take a deep breath, the smell of her filling my senses and distracting me from the real danger at hand. Vanilla and jasmine mixed with something darker—blood and smoke and ancient earth. My fingers twitch with the need to reach out to her, to touch her—

What the fuck? No. The woman is an ancient immortal creature of the night. She's the enemy. Fuck her and her supernatural aroma that distracts me.

"Well, we're going to rip the four of you apart," she says plainly, her lips curving into a smile that's all teeth. "Then finish our business here and continue ending the disease that is the hunter's bloodline."

"How about we end this right now," I suggest, grasping at straws. "You and me. One fight to decide the rest."

She cocks an eyebrow and Eli steps forward.

"No," he yells.

"Killian, she'll kill you," Bri says.

I wait for Helen to put in her two cents, but she just stays silent. I glance over my shoulder to find her picking at her nails and smiling to herself. What a time to check out.

"Interesting." The red queen smiles, looking back at her sisters. "A hunter who thinks he can match a queen."

The sisters laugh, and even the surrounding vampires begin to laugh—a chorus of cruel amusement that echoes through the hollow building—until the red queen snaps her head back to me.

"Deal." She grins. "You win; you walk away—all of you. I win, I slaughter your entire group slowly, painfully."

I don't wait for an invitation. I use the knife I had already pulled from my waist and I thrust it upward. Her hand catches my wrist and twists sharply, bones grinding together. I drop the knife with a hiss of pain. I drop to my knees to duck from her swing, her claws barely missing the top of my head as she swipes, the wind of it ruffling my hair.

The red queen grabs my throat and lifts me off the ground like I weigh nothing. My boots dangle in the air, kicking uselessly. I struggle against her grip, but she isn't making an end of me like I would expect her to. I use the minute of hesitation to kick off her stomach, throwing myself backward and forcing myself out of her grip.

I roll back to my feet, pull a pistol from my thigh and fire off four shots. I watch, stunned and amazed, as she dodges each one with lightning reflexes—a blur of crimson and shadow. I drop the gun as she runs toward me, bracing for impact.

"Come on, you immortal bitch," I growl.

When she drives her shoulder into my stomach, I bring my elbow down sharply into her spine. The impact reverberates up my arm but it does nothing but piss her off more. The red queen lifts me off the ground and drops me on my back behind her. The air leaves my lungs as I hit the tile floor hard enough to crack it, and she's on top of me seconds later.

Vampires cheer around us, their voices rising in bloodthirsty anticipation. My hunters take an uneasy step, unsure if they should help or not. I hope they don't—no one else needs to die. Just the red queen.

She smiles down at me, grabbing my throat again and squeezing harder this time. She leans over me, I feel her lips brush against my cheek as she whispers into my ear, her breath hot and smelling of wine and copper.

"Is this the fight you wanted, little hunter?"

I gasp at her words, and the heat of her breath as it warms my chest. I realize my hands are on her hips and I'm not fighting her, I'm...caressing her? The fuck?

"What are you doing to me?" I ask through choked breaths.

"I'm not doing anything." She smiles wickedly at me, her face inches from mine. "Except ending your life, of course."

Her claws extend into my neck, nails piercing my flesh. I feel the warm blood trailing down my neck and the wounds trying to heal around her nails as she digs deeper. I grunt out, refusing to show her my pain.

"I'm going to enjoy peeling the skin off your friends." the queen growls into my ear. The scent of her sending blood flow to a part of my body that has no place being aroused right now. "We're going to drain them, nice and slow. Too bad you won't be there to witness their deaths, little hunter."

"Stop...calling...me...that," I demand.

Thrusting up with my hips, I get the leverage I need and manage to flip her onto her back. I'm pinning her down before she can react and though she fights me—writhing beneath me with inhuman strength—I manage to hold her down. The vampires growl and take a threatening step forward, but the other three queens stop them with raised hands.

"We agreed!" the white queen hisses.

I look over to Eli, Bri, and Helen. "You guys go. Now!"

"Not without you," Eli says.

"Go!" I yell.

They hesitantly back up, boots scraping on tile, before Helen all but pushes Eli and Bri out and they take off. I wait to hear the car start and peel out, gravel spraying, before I put my focus back on the red queen under me.

"You," I growl, leaning down until our faces are inches apart. "The queen of vampires. You die tonight."

"Don't tease me with a good time." She whispers back, her eyes dancing with something that looks like amusement.

I pull my knife from my hip and hold it to her neck. I take a long pull and smile as she grunts in pain, the thin line of blood pooling in her neck before trailing down and dripping on the floor. Her wound heals the second I stop pulling the knife, flesh knitting back together.

I trail the knife down her chest, over her breasts—feeling her breath hitch—before turning the tip to point at her heart. My eyes are watching her parted lips, her fangs inside her mouth gleaming white. I look up at her eyes and can't help but get mesmerized by the light brown flakes that float in them like amber in honey.

I find myself leaning in closer, so close my lips are almost touching hers.

"What are you doing to me?" I whisper against her skin, breathing in that maddening scent.

Before she answers, I sit up and start to thrust the knife through her heart.

"Wait!" The white queen steps forward, her voice sharp. "Go. Get out of here."

I shoot her a look. "The deal was her or me."

"Another day," the black queen says, shadows curling around her feet. "The hunters will be left alone as long as they leave us alone."

I watch the blue queen roll her eyes, obviously not agreeing to this deal being made, ice crackling along her armor. "We will keep our generals in check. No more killing, we promise. We're almost done with this city, anyways."

I turn to face the red queen. My hand wrapping around her throat for other reasons than to pin her down—to feel her pulse, to understand why she makes me feel this way.

"Live to fight another day...little hunter." She grins.

I watch her for a second, memorizing the curve of her smile, the way her eyes catch the moonlight. Then I stand, backing up slowly and memorizing the faces of the queens. I'll take the win. We need to wait for our backup before we face this horde again. I'm no fool.

I point my knife at the vampires, sweeping across the vampires glaring at me. "This isn't over."

My threat sounds better in my head. And though I mean it for each vampire in the hospital, it's aimed at the red queen laying on the floor and glaring at me. Whatever magic she's using against me to make me feel that way when near her—I need to know what it is and how to end it. She needs to learn to fight fair, not to cheat with supernatural magic, distracting my brain during the most crucial fight of my life.

I start my bike and peel out down the long dirt road, the engine roaring into the night. Trying, and failing to get the red queen out of my head. There is something so familiar about her, and no matter how hard I rack my brain, the connection isn't clicking. And one thing I don't like more than vampires, is mystery.

I need answers.

10

Seraphine

Back in my penthouse suite, I unclip my armor and let it fall to the ground in a heavy thud that echoes off the marble floor. I peel off my sweat-soaked undershirt that clings to my filthy skin like a second layer. The fabric reeks of battle—ash and blood and the acrid smoke that lingers after vampires turn to dust. Making my way to the bathroom, my thoughts keep going back to the fight with that hunter.

I should have killed him. I had my chance and I hesitated. Why? Was it the look in his eyes when he stared back at me through his mask—green and fierce and somehow familiar? The way he made my body feel when I was pressed against him, heat coiling low in my stomach despite the violence between us?

I stare at myself in the mirror while the tub fills with water, steam beginning to fog the glass. Watching the glamour I prefer wash back over my form—softening edges, warming skin that's gone pale and cold in my true form. My phone buzzes on the counter and my chest immediately tightens, an anticipation I haven't felt in centuries.

Killian: *Wanted to check in. I'm so sorry I had to leave so suddenly.*

I can't help the smile on my face. My date with Killian had been such a welcome distraction from every day duties as queen. I was hurt when he had to leave suddenly, but I had my people to think about and hunters to kill. Even that I failed at, because of him—the masked hunter.

Me: *No need to apologize. Turns out I had to go just seconds after you.*

Killian: *Well, I still feel bad and want to make it up to you as soon as possible!*

Turning the water off, I step into the steaming water and lower myself into the tub. Heat envelops me, soaking into muscles that are still tense from the fight. I pour some scented oils into the water—lavender and floral—and take a deep breath in, feeling my muscles relax as the fragrance rises with the steam.

Me: *What did you have in mind?*

I can't help the smile on my face, hoping he's catching on to my playful mood. My breath catches in my throat when his reply comes—a photo of him fully naked, fresh out of the shower with water still dripping off his chiseled chest. Droplets cling to the ridges of his abdomen, trailing down in paths I want to trace with my tongue. My eyes dart to the bottom of the screen, but his photo cuts off at the worst spot and I can't see anything. It doesn't stop my imagination from running wild.

Me: Sir.

It's the only thing I can manage. I keep opening the photo and staring at his body—at the scars that pattern his skin like a map of violence, at the breadth of his shoulders, at the V of muscle disappearing beneath the frame.

Killian: *I need to see you again. You are so fucking beautiful Sera.*

Me: I would love to see you again.

Killian: *I have some paperwork to finish up from the bar. I'll text you tomorrow, I hope you get some good sleep.*

I can't help myself. I open the camera on my phone and lift it high above my head, making sure my entire body is in the photo. I'm covered by bubble-filled water so I have no fear of revealing anything that might be too much too soon. The bubbles catch the light like tiny pearls floating on the surface.

Killian: *Or better yet… you should come to the bar for a drink.*

I let out a genuine laugh, sinking lower into the tub until the water reaches my nose, warmth surrounding me completely.

Me: Oh man. If only I knew where the bar was and it wasn't sooo late, or early I guess, depending how you view it.

I watch his chat bubble appear and disappear a few times as he contemplates what to say. I add a winking emoji to let him know I intended the message to be sarcastic flirting, which I hope is how it comes off.

Killian: *Oh come on beautiful, don't pretend you haven't already searched me. You know the name of my bar and exactly where it is.*

Arrogant. But he's right. I looked him up right after we messaged for the first time, and found everything I would need to know about the owner of Bad Habits. Purchasing the business from some old man three years ago when he moved into the city.

Three years ago.

The thought niggles at me. But as badly as I want to see him again, to feel him pressed against me like he was in that laser tag room, I decide to let the tease continue just a little longer. I'm the queen of Crimson Court, not some horny woman who needs a man's attention.

Me: *Good night, handsome.*

I set my phone on the floor with a soft click. Sinking into the water, I let it wash over me and dull my senses while washing out the dirt and debris from the fight we had tonight. The water turns cloudy with ash and blood, swirling around me like diluted ink.

So those filthy hunters killed many vampires. They would pay for the lives they took as soon as Casen could find their identities for me. I hear my phone vibrate from through the tub—a muffled buzz against tile—but I stay submerged under the water and mourn my fallen generals. Imagining all the horrible things I'm going to do to the masked hunter who dared to challenge me in front of my people.

ONE WEEK LATER

My nights are filled with meetings with my sisters, councils with my generals, and quick texts with Killian when I'm able to spare a minute of time. We haven't been able to text much, and it upsets me more than I want to admit it does. He's getting to me, and I find myself craving his attention more and more every day—checking my phone between meetings, smiling at notifications like some lovesick mortal girl.

My sisters and I finalized the new boundaries and terms of inter-border travel amongst the courts yesterday. Most of our time is now spent discussing the hunters and our plans to destroy them. Morgana and Rowena are content with causing a scene until they show their face so we can wipe them out. Amara and I have disagreed with that plan, not wanting to cause needless bloodshed when we know a face-off is inevitable.

The club is running smoothly. Offering free dance nights and discounted drinks is bringing in more people than we're able to feed off of. Rowena clears her throat and brings me out of my thoughts. I'm slouched in my throne, resting my chin on my fist and trying, and failing, to pay attention. The throne room feels stifling today—too many bodies, too much hot breath and cologne mixing with incense. Gods I need out of this hotel.

"Are we boring you, sister?" Morgana says, her voice sharp as cracking ice.

I meet her glare with one of my own. "Not at all, sister." I say. "I was just thinking of all the ways I could thank you for what you did during our fight with the hunters."

Rowena laughs, the sound like wind through dead leaves. "If anyone is going to kill us, it's going to be at one of our hands. No filthy-blooded hunter is going to get the best of a queen."

I offer her a rare smile, feeding into her delusion that they saved me for anything other than to save thousands of vampires from dying too. They care only about numbers and bolstering their own armies.

"I'm going to bed." I say, standing. The velvet of my gown whispers against the throne as I rise.

Killian: *When do I get to see you again?*

Me: *Are pictures not working for you anymore?*

Killian: *I love seeing your face, but I have this urge to smash my lips into yours.*

I laugh at his message, the sound echoing softly in my empty bedroom. We've been taunting each other with cuddling and kisses for three days now. Teasing one another with photos that are getting closer and closer to being explicit. The tension being built between the two of us is like the static build-up in the air before lightning strikes—electric, inevitable, dangerous.

Me: Dinner. Soon. I promise.

I set my phone down and slip into my silk nightgown, the fabric cool and smooth against my skin. Three soft taps echo off my door—measured, respectful.

"Come in!" I answer.

Marcella slips in with her usual silent grace, her footsteps barely audible on the marble. She gives a crisp bow, but her tone is clipped, urgent. "General Casen is here with news, my Queen."

He enters, filling the frame of the doorway as he crosses the threshold. His ruby-red cloak flows dramatically behind him, the fabric catching the lamplight and shining like fresh blood. His boots click against the floor with military precision.

"What is it?" I growl, annoyance sharpening my words. "You better have a good reason for disturbing me just before bed."

"The hunters." Casen says, getting to the point. His voice is steady, controlled. "The ones who disrupted our feedings. The ones who attacked the hospital. I found them."

The words light a spark in me. I step forward, my robe brushing the marble floor with a whisper of silk. "Go on."

"They're organized. A small group—not more than five or six. They've been following the false trails we left of your whereabouts." He pauses, swallowing. "Until three years ago. Then everything changed suddenly when their leader shifted course. He brought his crew here to this city."

I tilt my head, eyeing him and urging him to continue with the weight of my gaze. "And why did they change course?"

He hesitates, then shrugs, the movement uncomfortable. "No one knows. Not even the hunters themselves. Their leader simply...decided. The rest followed."

Something coils low in my stomach—unease mixed with curiosity. I let the silence drag long enough for him to squirm before sipping from my glass of wine I poured seconds before I was interrupted. The liquid is rich and dark, sliding down my throat like velvet. I watch my phone light up with my nightly call from Killian, the screen glowing against the dark wood of my nightstand. We've been Face Timing each other when we can and I find myself getting irritated missing his call.

"Interesting," I say as his call turns into a missed notification. "Where are they now? Why do you stand in front of me alone, after over a week of searching for information?"

That's when his lips curve, not the smile of a soldier, but of a man savoring the game. "The hunter who follows your sister—he's in town and gave me their base of operations. I thought you might want to end this yourself. A demonstration of your strength. While your sisters are here."

The idea is intoxicating. Blood spilled across my city, my sisters watching, my power undeniable. My smile stretches sharp. "An excellent idea, Casen. Tell me, where is this nest I'll burn to ash?"

He meets my gaze squarely, unflinching. "A bar. They run their operations out of a bar."

The words land like a blade between my ribs. My eyes cut to my phone, thinking back to the man who has my attention so pulled from my duties as queen. To the masked hunter who wears scars so similar to the same man I had a blast with in a laser tag arena. Surely, Casen has to be mistaken. I would have smelled him, I would have sensed that disgusting hunter blood.

"Did you just say...a bar? You're certain?"

"Yes, my Queen." He says carefully, brow furrowing at my sudden tone shift. "Their leader owns it, but they run the operations—"

"Out." My voice cracks like a whip. "Now."

He freezes, then bows low and retreats, his cloak swirling behind him. Marcella follows him after giving me a silent look that I ignore—concern mixed with curiosity. The heavy doors close with a thud that echoes through my suite.

Alone again, I set my wineglass down, hand trembling faintly though I force it steady. The wine sloshes slightly, catching the light like liquid ruby. My phone lights up again, screen glowing with another call.

Killian.

A rush of something unfamiliar—heat, dread, intrigue—tightens in my chest. I think back to every word, every laugh, every photo. My sisters and I are of the original magic that made vampires, allowing us to sense the hunter gene. I should smell him. I should sense the hunter's blood in him.

Unless...

11

Seraphine

My internal struggle with my feelings for Killian and the revelation that he may be my enemy causes me to push him into the background. I put more focus on my sisters and the rebuilding of our relationship. Now, three days of short texts and avoiding his phone calls later, I find myself craving his attention again. It's time to get answers once and for all.

Me: *How was your night, handsome?*

Killian: *It was a busy one. I'm so glad I have tomorrow off.*

I raise a curious eyebrow. He's never mentioned his days off before, so why make it a point now? Is he just as tired of being apart as I am? Something about that thought tightens something in my chest and warms me as I reply.

Me: *The bar is closing tomorrow?*

I suppose he could have a regular day off while someone else covers for him...so I don't know why my first thought is the bar closing. Hope.

Killian: *Monday's we close so I can deep clean and take inventory. It's a tedious all day and night thing.*

Me: *Sounds…fun.*

I add a laughing emoji to let him know I'm being playful with him. I imagine him shaking his head and rolling those piercing green eyes at his phone. My phone vibrates.

It's a picture of him sitting in his office, doing the paperwork after closing. He undid the top three buttons of his shirt and I feel my cheeks heat when I see the strands of hair poking through his chest. His lips are pursed so that he looks pouty. The caption he adds is "I'd much rather be asleep."

I take a moment to look at his photo, tracing a thumb over his lips on the screen before taking my own photo. I'm still in my crimson dress from meetings but I make sure to show my unmade bed in the background—silk sheets rumpled and inviting.

Me: *Mine is pretty comfortable.*

Killian: *It sure looks big enough for two.*

I smile at his text. Without responding right away, I set my phone down and strip out of my dress, letting it fall to my feet in a whisper of fabric and stepping out of it, making my way to the shower. I don't want to come off too eager and reply too quickly, but I find myself rushing through the shower to text him back.

I text him while drying off, water still beading on my skin.

Me: *What are you up to?*

Killian: *I'm going to take a quick nap and then head into town to get some things done before starting inventory. Lunch date?*

Me: *I would love to see you again. Soon. I can't tomorrow though.*

It isn't an outright lie. I am busy tomorrow, and he doesn't need to know that he is my plan. I let my screen dim before going black and see my reflection staring back at me. Shops don't open for another three hours, so I set my alarm and turn off my nightlamp next to my bed.

I walk to the closet and pick out a pair of blue jeans with a spaghetti strap top, pulling on a light green button-up shirt that I leave open as I step in front of the mirror. I shift quickly through the many glamours I've built over the centuries, and smile, settling into one of a woman with black shoulder-length hair, thin eyebrows, and pale lips. She's ordinary looking—perfect for blending in with the people of this city.

A floral tattoo wraps up my wrist and ends in the middle of my forearm. A few finger tattoos appear on my other hand as I finalize the details of the glamour. With a satisfied grin, I slip into some tennis shoes and make my way to the door.

The warmth of the sun feels good on my skin after so many days and nights spent in the hotel—meeting after meeting. The heat soaks into me, chasing away the perpetual chill of my true form. As a queen made from the original magic, I have the luxury of enjoying daylight without fear of my generals following me. The curse of the sun is nature's balance to my sisters and I creating more vampires. The witch warned us not to do so, but we four sisters were stubborn humans and even more stubborn immortals.

The hotel isn't too far from the part of town I figure Killian would have gone to. I grab my phone and open the messages between us, rereading every line to get clues of where to look first. Sighing with frustration at the realization he never mentioned what he's actually doing today.

I stop in an alley, shifting my glamour into the woman he'd matched with before I snap a picture. I send it with the caption: *Needing a bite to eat, but where to go?*

I laugh at my joke, laced with double meaning. To him, it would be a request for his location, a hint I want to meet him. And though that's true, we have vastly different intentions for our meeting today.

His reply takes a minute. By the time my phone buzzes I've already shifted back to the ordinary girl with tattoos and walked another three blocks, the morning air crisp and carrying the smell of coffee from nearby cafés.

Killian: *Can't go wrong with Al's chicken.*

Me: *Are you asking me to meet you there?*

I roll my eyes. Why are men so dense?

Killian: *Oh, yeah! We can meet there! I'm getting my hair cut right now, but give me twenty minutes.*

Pocketing my phone, I make my way to the nearest barber. The scent of aftershave and hair products hits me before I see the striped pole. My heart skips when I see him in the barber's chair, a black drape around his neck. He's so much more handsome in person than his photos—the line of his jaw sharper, the breadth of his shoulders wider, the way sunlight catches in his dark hair making something in my chest ache. I have to remind myself that he's potentially my enemy, and this is a stakeout. Not a date.

I walk past a news cart seller, and snatch a pair of sunglasses from the end display. Ripping off the sales tag, I sit on a bench across from the barbershop. I cross my leg over the other and scroll on my phone casually as I watch Killian get his hair cut, the barber's scissors flashing in the light streaming through the window.

I don't want him to think I'm standing him up, but there's no way I'm confronting him in public during the day. Not with my sisters in town, and not while we're in the middle of such high-tension negotiations.

I pull up the Temptr chat thread and quickly type.

Me: *Last minute meeting. Let's facetime tonight.*

I hit send, waiting for him to read my message. Sure enough, seconds later he's pulling out his phone and letting out a sad sigh that I can hear even from across the street. He lifts the phone to show his barber and I find myself focusing my hearing on them, drowning out the surrounding noise—the cars passing, the chatter of pedestrians, the hum of the city.

"Do you think this is just an excuse to dodge me?" Killian asks his barber, his voice carrying a hint of vulnerability I've never heard before.

"No, man," the big-bellied man replies, his clippers buzzing as he works. "Women get scared easily. She doesn't know if you're a creep or a serial killer. Or worse...ugly."

I can't help but laugh. The barber is right—I don't know if he's a killer. But we've met before so he should know I don't find him ugly, quite the opposite according to the ache in my chest and the tight ball my stomach is in seeing him tick his jaw. Either way, it doesn't matter. I'm here to find out how much pain I need to cause him before I kill him.

Killian laughs, the sound warm and genuine. "She's seen my pictures. What should I say back?"

"Just play it cool. Don't let her know how heartbroken you are about it." The man laughs, his belly bouncing.

Killian rolls his eyes. "Shut up. I'm not heartbroken."

They share a laugh, and a moment later my phone vibrates in my hand.

Killian: *Not a problem. I would love to talk tonight.*

I thumb up his message and pocket my phone, listening back in.

"See!" The barber laughs. "She liked it."

"I've hooked up with plenty of girls, David." Killian smirks and for some reason, I want to knock that smirk off his face for saying what he did. "But she just...I don't know man, she just gets me."

The barber finishes trimming his neck and grabs a brush, cleaning him off with swift strokes. "Alright. I'm intrigued. Show me her pictures."

Killian's face lights up as he opens my profile and swipes through my photos. I lean in on the bench, ready to rip his throat out if he shows some of the other photos we've exchanged.

"Damn, man." The barber laughs, his belly bouncing harder. "She's hot. If things don't work out, send her my way."

Killian closes his phone and I lean back on the bench, relaxing slightly. I wonder if he would still think I'm desirable if he ever saw my true face, the one behind the glamour. The one he will see seconds before I kill him.

"You're all finished up!" The barber announces, whipping off the drape with a flourish. "That's going to be forty bucks."

Killian hands the man a single bill and slaps his shoulder. "Keep the change, Dave. You're the best."

I watch as Killian waves goodbye to the barber and makes his way down the sidewalk, his boots clicking against the concrete. I follow on the other side of the street, keeping behind him just slightly to stay out of his peripheral vision.

He stops at the chicken place he mentioned and dips inside. The smell of fried food and spices wafts out as the door swings closed. I follow and stand behind him in line. Killian takes out his phone and lifts it to the menu. A second later, my phone vibrates and I see the image of the menu board with the question: *What should I get?*

I decide to tease him a bit, wanting to lighten the mood after I made him feel like I didn't want to see him.

Me: *I don't see 'Seraphine' on that list.*

After I hit send, I hear Killian gasp to himself. "Oh, shit."

Before he can reply, it's his turn to order. I can't help but step closer to him. Partly because I want to scent the hunter's blood in him, the other part is just enjoying his scent. It's earthy but sweet-smelling too—like cedar and something darker, like gunpowder masked by cologne.

I jump back, startled, as he turns around quickly. With a toothy grin, he points at me. "And whatever she's having."

"You...you don't have to do that," I stutter, caught off guard.

"Nonsense." He smiles, gesturing me forward. The genuine warmth in his expression makes my chest tighten. "I insist."

I glance at the menu, having no actual intention of ordering anything. I scan it before blurting out a random number.

"I'll take the number seven."

Killian smiles, handing the woman his card. "You like spice?"

I most certainly do not.

"Uh, yeah. Who doesn't?" I say with a smile.

Fuck.

"That's pretty cool. Not many girls do. Well, enjoy your lunch, ma'am," Killian says with a smile as he makes his way over to the pickup counter.

I follow him, keeping my phone in hand and aimlessly scrolling so as not to draw too much attention to myself. It seems to work—Killian doesn't so much as glance in my direction. He grabs his food and goes to sit down. I watch him pull out his phone, and seconds later mine vibrates.

Killian: *So, beautiful. Any big plans for the day?*

I grab my food and sit at a table on the opposite side of the restaurant. The chicken even smells spicy, the heat of the peppers making my nose tingle, and there's no way I'm going to eat this. I grab a few fries and eat them as I reply.

Me: *Following a lead on a new potential client.*

I add a smiling emoji to lighten the chat. I watch as Killian bites into his chicken sandwich, a glob of sauce on the corner of his mouth as he chews. He wipes it off with his thumb, and licks the sauce off.

I clear my throat, looking around to make sure no one sees me watching him.

> **Killian:** *Sounds fun. I'm about to head back to Bad Habits and call in a couple of bartenders.*

> **Me:** *Oh? I thought you were closing tonight?*

Killian leans back in his chair, grabbing a handful of fries and stuffing them into his mouth. A typical man, I see. He wipes his fingers on his jeans and types back his reply.

> **Killian:** *We were going to be. But I just got a message about my uncle being back in town and we always celebrate his return. I might as well make some money too.*

I raise a curious eyebrow at Killian after reading his text. Watching him finish his food and clean his plate, I suddenly become aware of how little I'd eaten and don't want him to see the meal he paid for go to waste.

I pick up a piece of chicken and bite into it, quickly taking another bite and then another.

The heat hits me all at once, halfway through my second piece of chicken. My eyes water and I down the water I'd gotten. It does nothing to soothe the heat that now spreads across my tongue, coating the roof of my mouth like liquid fire. My eyes are watering, and I eat the ice in the cup to give any kind of relief.

I am the fucking queen of vampires, an original creature of magic, and a piece of meat is bringing me to my knees.

I need more water.

Standing, I grab my cup and turn to head to the fountain when I run into the firm chest of Killian fucking Blake.

"I'm so sorry!" I say, my glamoured voice is mousy and higher than normal.

He laughs, wiping water that splashed on his shirt. "Don't worry about it. They don't call the number seven Diablo Fire for nothing."

He grabs some napkins and helps me wipe off the spilled water, then offers me the rest of the wipes to clear the tears streaming down my cheeks.

"To be honest, I hate spicy things," I admit, my voice is still rough from the heat. "I was just distracted and said the first number I saw."

He raises an infuriatingly charming eyebrow. "Distracted?"

I glare at him, wanting to use his blood to soothe the burn in my mouth. Before I can respond, he laughs again, reaching into his pocket and pulling out a business card. "I own a bar. You should come get a drink...on me." Killian takes my cup and refills it, handing it back to me with a gentleness that makes my heart skip. "As an apology for distracting you."

He leaves me standing there, gulping down the ice water, and watching him through the glass window as he gets on his motorcycle and slips the helmet over his head. He looks over at me, winking before pulling down the visor and starting the bike.

Oh, how I wish that bike would have stalled, embarrassing him the way I feel now. But no, the gods are on his side and it starts right up, the engine roaring to life. I watch as he takes off down the road, exhaust shimmering in the afternoon heat.

I look down at the business card, the embossed letters catching the light.

"Killian Blake, owner of Bad Habits." I read aloud.

I throw my food away and step onto the sidewalk. The sun is high in the sky now, and not a cloud is in sight. I know the guards Marcella would have insisted follow me would be trapped in the buildings they're hiding in until the shade returns to the alleys.

So I take off running.

I watch Killian for hours setting the bar up, cleaning, talking with his staff that showed up. The sun dips lower, painting the sky in shades of orange and purple. None of the bartenders smell like hunters, and that gives me hope. Maybe Casen is referring to a different bar.

However, as evening falls and night begins, the evidence confirms Casen's information.

Three hunters get out of a Mustang in the alley and enter the same back door Killian had hours before. Two men, who look and smell like hunters—that distinctive bitter-copper scent mixed with adrenaline—get out of the car. The woman with them is small, with a pixie haircut. Although she smells like a hunter too, something else radiates off her as well. Something old. Something familiar that makes the hair on my neck stand up.

As the two men enter the bar from the alley, she stops and peers over her shoulder, her eyes scanning the rooftops with unnatural precision.

I drop below the half-wall and check my glamour to make sure it's still in place. When I look up again, she's no longer in the alley.

I leap from the roof and land gracefully on the sidewalk, joining the growing line of patrons as the bartender unlocks the door and greets the first couple of guests. Music thrums from inside, bass vibrating through the brick walls. My heart beats a little faster. Tonight, I will know the truth. As I step closer to those doors, I realize something that makes my chest tighten in a way I don't recognize: I'm not sure what I want the answer to be anymore.

12

Killian

Hours into the night, the smell of fried food, spilled beer, and cheap perfume mixes in the air like a cocktail you wouldn't want to drink. Music plays from the old jukebox in the corner, just loud enough to weave into conversation and laughter. Glasses clink, coins rattle into tip jars, and my staff calls out orders as they come from the kitchen.

I slip behind the sticky bar top and begin mixing drinks, popping bottle tops, and sliding them to customers with practiced ease. Beside me, Alex balances trays of food and weaves in and out of the crowd with precision, their movements a choreographed dance through the packed bodies. Donovan is breaking up a fight before it can escalate, his bulk enough to make drunk idiots reconsider, then clearing tables and wiping them off before jumping back behind the bar to help me make drinks.

By the time the rush dies down, my shirt is wet with sweat and my voice is hoarse from calling out orders. I'm wiping off the counter when Helen saddles onto an empty bar stool, her expression all business.

"Tommy's waiting for you." She says.

"I know." I pop another bottle cap and slide it down the bar. "I've had his drink ready. Just waiting for him to show his face."

"He's upstairs, Killian. Debriefing the team about his journey west." Helen sighs, clearly annoyed with me. "You coming?"

I stop wiping, meeting her annoyed glare with one of my own. "After we close. I'm not leaving Donovan and Alex to fend for themselves."

Helen huffs, twisting and hopping off the barstool. "Sometimes I wonder where your loyalty truly lies. Us or this bar."

She begins walking toward the stairs that lead up to my home when I laugh back at her. "Sometimes I wonder the same thing."

She stops and looks over her shoulder, a thin smile on her lips. "Who's the girl?"

"Who?" I ask, though I know who she's talking about. "Oh, just a girl I ran into at lunch."

Helen raises her eyebrows suggestively before turning and walking upstairs, her boots heavy on each step. I flip the light switch that signals the patrons the heads up that we're closing. The rhythm of the lights overhead gives way to groans and moans of disappointment.

"Last call for the kitchen. We close in twenty minutes!" I call out.

Alex and I put in the last orders, Donovan begins making the last round of drinks. As I type in my last order of food, in the mirror behind the bar I see the woman from lunch sitting alone at a four-top table, brushing off a few guys with ease.

I've seen her throughout the night. She's been here since we opened, but every time I call her over, she acts like she can't see me. I'd catch her multiple times watching me, her eyes tracking my movements like I'm something to be studied. But finally, as the bar thins out, she stands and walks over.

She's still in her blue jeans and tank top—the shirt she'd been wearing was taken off when a drunk woman tripped and spilled her beer on her. She sits atop the stool and interlaces her fingers on the bar top as she watches me type in my last order.

That's when I realize I haven't been typing anything for a few minutes. Hitting send, I close the monitor and turn slowly, forcing a cool smile as I glide over to her and lean across the bar, our fingers only inches apart.

I've been looking at her all night. There's something familiar about this girl. Now that she's closer, the feeling is stronger, but I still can't place where or how I know her.

"What'll you have?" I ask, keeping my voice smooth.

Her lips curve up and she squints her eyes just lightly as she says, "Bad Habits. That's a unique name. I'll have whatever your favorite drink is."

Her smile is warm and infectious, but wicked and dangerous all at once. The shy girl from the restaurant is no longer in front of me. This girl is trouble.

I'm in the mood for some trouble.

I turn and grab a tall glass, pouring in two shots and adding some mixes. I slice a strawberry in half, the juice sticky on my fingers as I slide it over the rim of the glass. Cutting open a pineapple, I place it on the other side and slide the drink across the counter.

It catches the low bar lights—red and orange swirling around the ice like trapped embers. She picks it up and licks the salt rim before taking a sip. I can't help but watch her tongue glide across the glass and the way her lips are now wet from the drink. Realizing I'm staring, I clear my throat and step back, raising a curious eyebrow.

"What do you call this?" she asks with a smile.

"I call it the Killian Special," I laugh, leaning on the bar again.

"Clever," she teases, her voice carrying an edge I can't quite name. "It's good."

Her fingers brush against mine for a moment. Goosebumps crawl up my arm, electric and sudden, and her eyes widen like she feels it too.

"Sorry." I blurt. "Hands are cold from the ice."

For a moment, her eyes stay fixed on mine. There's a weight in them, something more than playful curiosity.

"I never got your name," I say.

"That's because I never gave it." She smiles.

The silence holds for a moment. I'm internally hitting myself for how stupid I am for not asking the girl her name at the restaurant.

"It's Alison," she finally answers.

I smile, trying to deflect my own internal embarrassment. "That's a beautiful name. I'm Killian."

She slides my card across the bar. "I assumed as much. Let me guess—you're the owner too?"

She points playfully at the badge on my shirt, and again I force a smile, though I feel anything but confident in this moment. She's sharp, keeping me on my toes. My normal flirting isn't working on her. Her voice rolls off her tongue like silk dipped in honey and for a second, I swear I've heard it before. Something in the cadence, something in the way she looks at me.

"You seem familiar," I admit, squinting like I could put it together. "Have we met before?"

Her smile sharpens. "I think I'd remember your face."

That lands like a spark. My chest tightens, but I force a smirk. "Fair enough."

She taps her finger in a steady rhythm on the counter, never breaking eye contact. She drinks slowly, listening intently as she guides the conversation. Questions roll off her tongue like casual small talk, but the way she asks them makes it feel like something else entirely.

"How long have you been here?" she asks, tilting her head, black hair catching the neon glow.

"Three years," I say it easily. "I'd dreamed of owning a bar, and when the opportunity came, I took it."

Her eyebrows lift with genuine—or perfectly performed—interest. "And you plan to stay?"

I shrug, grabbing a rag and pretending to wipe the counter even though I never look away from her. "Depends. Got other... business in the city. Once that's sorted, maybe I'll move on."

Something flickers in her eyes then, quick as lightning. Intrigue? Satisfaction? It vanishes before I can name it.

I don't care that it feels like an interview—she has me hooked. Her laugh, her gaze, the way she leans in like every word matters.

Eli's sudden shadow looms at my side, breaking the trance. He bends close, voice low and urgent. "We need you upstairs. Now."

I catch the edge in his eyes and know this isn't optional. When I glance back at Alison, her focus isn't on me anymore. Her gaze has shifted to Eli—sharp, assessing, almost hostile beneath the softness of her expression. Her tapping has stopped.

For a heartbeat, I swear she's glaring at him. I straighten and reach for the light switch. The overhead lights flicker, signaling the end of the night. "Closing time, everyone!" I call.

Turning back to her, I try to salvage the moment. "You can stay if you'd like. I'll just be a minute, then maybe we can hang out?"

Her smile is quick and enigmatic, flashing like a blade. She rises with the grace of someone who'd already decided her course. "Thank you," she says. "But I only wanted to see this place for myself. I've heard...so much. I got what I needed."

No payment, no hesitation. She just turns and moves through the bar with purpose. The sway of her hips, the gleam of her hair—every detail pulls me in, but I force myself to look away only after she vanishes around the corner.

Something about the farewell feels final. It's like a door closing that I didn't know was open.

"Killian." Eli's voice snaps me back, sharp as a growl.

I sigh and rub the back of my neck. "Coming." But I can't shake this feeling that I'd just let something important slip through my fingers.

Upstairs, the air feels heavier than in the bar. The apartment smells like sweat, old leather, and the faint metallic tang of weapons that have been sharpened too many times in one room. Helen and Eli are sunk into the couch, Tommy is sprawled like he owns the place, his maps and journals spread across the coffee table like artifacts from a war. Bri appears from the bathroom, toweling her hands, dark circles bruising her eyes.

I collapse into my chair, groaning. "Alright. Someone tell me what's so important you had to stop me from getting laid...again."

Helen arches an eyebrow, her lips twitching with a knowing smile. "Poor Killian. Think of all the women you'll never get to disappoint."

"Cute."

Tommy rumbles in his gravel voice, "If you ladies are finished, I was just getting to the good part."

Tommy raised me after my parents died. He taught me how to fight before Eli and Helen joined. When we discovered my hunter gene was different from theirs, they trained me to be a leader. Although they're older and much more experienced than me, they trust my intuition and instincts to guide us to the queen.

I narrow my eyes at him, though my grin tugs anyway. "You can fuck off too. How do you show up after five damn years and not even say hello first?"

"You're right." He says, the corner of his mouth lifting like he knows he'd won the point. "I should have said hi, but I was excited to share the news."

"Well..." I lean back in the chair, stretching until the leather creaks. "Spill it."

That's when I focus on the mess on the table. Maps inked with notes, journals scarred with years of travel—all of it screams one thing: trouble.

Tommy's voice drops low, steady. "Hunters have been tracking the queens for centuries. I went west and watched the Onyx and Frost Courts. They're moving."

I lean forward, the weight of it already prickling in my gut. "Moving how?"

"They're making a play against Crimson." he says.

My chest tightens. "So what you're saying is, there's about to be a war between four of the most powerful evils this world's ever known?"

He nods once. "They've gathered here in the city. On the surface they talk of treaties. Peace. But peace isn't what they came for."

Helen straightens, fire sparkling behind her eyes. "Then we stop it before it starts."

Eli snorts, shaking his head. "How the hell do we stop something like that?"

Tommy's gaze shifts, his voice lowers until we all lean closer. "That's not even the worst of it."

Bri's tone is sharp, brittle. "Then quit dragging your feet. Some of us still have vampires to kill."

Tommy's next words chill the room. "They're working with humans...hunters."

The words hit me like a knife, and my thoughts go back to Cole and Michael. "Actually, we know."

His eyes hold mine. "How?"

I spend the next few minutes discussing the fight in the abandoned hospital, the betrayal of Michael and how he lost his brother to the Frost queen.

"It makes sense. They use humans to break past our hunter gene. We can sense a vampire coming, but not our own people." Eli says.

"Exactly." Tommy nods.

The room falls silent, the weight of it presses in like a storm brewing against the windows. Someone shifts on the couch and the leather groans.

"So, what do we do?" Bri asks finally, her voice clipped, her jaw trembling with barely contained rage.

"Reinforcements are days out." Eli mutters. "Three hundred hunters, maybe more, are gathering as fast as they can."

"Three hundred against thousands of vampires." I add. "And that's before we add in the vampire-on-vampire pissing match. This city won't survive it. Hell, this entire state might not."

Helen lowers her gaze, voice softer. "The hills and countryside give us some advantage, but you're right...it won't be enough."

"The queen." I say suddenly, the word punching through the air. "The other vampires don't matter if we can get to the crimson queen and kill her. If she goes down, they all go down.

"The one who turned the rest. The mother of them all. We know she's one of the sisters, and we already assume she's the crimson queen. We find her, we kill her, and everyone else burns."

Tommy's face is grim, his eyes hollow. "That's always been the mission, Killian. We're no closer now than the hunters were a century ago."

I run a hand through my hair, forcing a smirk. "Then we do our homework, don't we?" I look around at their faces—tired, furious, and determined. "So let's get to work."

Even as I say it, my mind drifts back downstairs to the black hair catching neon lights, to the smile that felt like a weapon. To the woman who said she got what she needed, and I can't shake the feeling that I'd just been played.

13

Seraphine

The alley is damp, reeking of oil and rain-soaked garbage. The kind of place humans pretend not to see when they hurry past. I press my back against the brick wall, cold and slick against my skin, and let the night settle around me. My chest rises and falls with a slow, controlled rhythm as I replay what I'd just walked into.

A bar full of hunters. Their base of operations, hidden beneath neon lights and beer-stained wood. But Killian didn't smell like them. Hunters carry a scent unique to their gene, like the taste of a blade held too long in the mouth—metallic, bitter, sharp. I haven't sensed it in him. Not once. Which means either he's very, very good at hiding it...or I'd let myself be blind.

Then I remember the way one of them had looked at him, how they'd said they needed him. Hunters don't "need" ordinary men. My lips curl into a dangerous smile and though he may not have smelled like my enemy, every instinct tells me he's the masked hunter that I want so desperately to find.

I cross the street in a blur, the night air rushing cold against my skin. Fingers hooking into the cracks in the bricks, I scale the wall with effortless grace, crouching just below a narrow window where voices drift into the night like smoke.

"...They're making a play against Crimson..."

I still, lashes lowering. I know this already of course—my sisters whisper treason like it's their native tongue. But hearing it from a human's lips is curious. Hunters shouldn't have known such things, which means my sisters' secrets leak more than I'd realized. Someone in the inner circle could be betraying us.

Still, my attention isn't on the old one speaking. It's on Killian. He leans forward, voice firm and jaw hard. "...we find her, we kill her, and every one of them burns with her."

For a moment, I simply watch him through the window, the light throwing shadows across his face. The muscle in his jaw ticks with every word, veins flexing along his forearms where his hands curl into fists. The conviction in his voice is ...beautiful.

He wants me dead. And the certainty of it lights him like a flame. I smile, slow and sharp, lips parting into something halfway between amusement and hunger. The idea of him putting a blade to my heart, a bullet to my skull, stirs something dangerous inside me.

He wants to hunt me. Very well, I'll let him try.

My fingers loosen and I drop from the wall, landing soundlessly in the shadowed alley. I crouch like a predator before straightening, the glamour of the black bob already peeling away from me in strips, like a snake shedding its skin. My hair lengthens and bleeds back into the auburn-brown, lower-back length it normally is. My features sharpen, my true face settling like a crown.

The city blurs around me as I move faster than night could follow, buildings streaking past in ribbons of light and shadow. The penthouse waits for me—my wine and velvet nightgown. If Killian Blake wants to kill the Queen, I'll give him the fight of his life. But first, I'll have my fun.

Steam curls around me in languid ribbons as I slide into the bath, the water licking my skin until the heat settles into my bones. The porcelain edge is cool against the back of my neck as I lean my head back, eyes closing for just a second.

Then, my phone vibrates against the marble tray. I don't even need to look to know it's Killian. My lips curve as I reach for it, anticipation already sparkling in my chest.

Killian: *The bar was swamped tonight. Sorry for being a little MIA.*

I trace a finger through the bubbles, leaving faint trails like constellations in foam, before typing back.

Me: *Not a problem. My lead panned out, and I'm glad to be home now.*

Killian: *Glad you got home safe.*

Me: *I'm more than safe.*

His three dots appear instantly. I bite my lip, already picturing his face. That cocky half-smile like he just won something.

Killian: *Oh? What's more than safe?*

I angle the phone, raising it above my head until the camera catches just enough—my breasts hidden beneath the froth, bubbles sliding over my pale skin, hair fanned out like ink in the water. I close my eyes, turn my cheek, making the image suggestive without giving away too much. Just enough to drive him mad.

The reply is instant.

Killian: *Oh, fuck. Definitely safer for me, too.*

I laugh low in my throat, shifting in the water, warmth spreading through my limbs.

Me: *I wish you were here with me.*

Killian: *Say the word and I'll head that way right now.*

The thought of him marching through the lobby of a hotel crawling with vampires makes me smirk. Brave, foolish, and delicious.

Me: *If only I didn't have all this work to do…*

Killian: *Then when are you finally going to let me take you out?*

I let the anticipation stretch a beat before replying.

Me: *Tomorrow night.*

Killian: *Absolutely. I'll pick you up around seven?*

Me: *What a gentleman. I'll meet you there just in case I need to make a run for it.*

Killian: *Perfect. Can't wait!*

The warmth that spreads through my chest genuinely startles me. I tell myself it's just the water.

Me: *What about tonight? What are you up to?*

Killian: *My uncle is in town. Been gone for years. We are catching up. I've always been close to him.*

I file that away, my mind already turning. Old men carry old secrets. If I want leverage over Killian, I've just received a string to pull.

A notification pops up and my breath catches. A photo. His muscles gleam in the dim bathroom light, water beading on his shoulders, and his shirtless body looks like it's been sculpted for battle. But my eyes don't stay there. Something in the background makes me smile to myself.

Me: *You're hot. But hey… is that a mask behind you?*

Killian: *Give me a second.*

My heart kicks faster as I wait, steam beading on my collarbone, the anticipation coiling low in my belly.

Then the next photo arrives and my jaw actually drops. The light is filtered crimson, casting him in shadow and fire. He's naked, but positioned perfectly to hide the one thing I most desire, which taunts me. His hand grips the top of the doorframe, biceps taut, his body a silhouette of power and control. And on his face…a black fabric, a mask that hides his mouth but not his eyes.

Those eyes—dark and burning—hold me captive. Heat floods me, sudden and sharp. A darkness in him mirrors the hunger in me and gods, I want his hand at my throat.

I have to clear my throat before typing back.

Me: *Wow…*

Killian: *What's the matter? Cat got your tongue? Did that satisfy your book girly dreams?*

Cocky bastard. But he earned it.

Me: *That was not nice.*

Killian: *I never said I was nice. Or that I play fair.*

My lips curve into a predatory grin. Oh, two can play this game.

I get out of the water, droplets trailing down my skin, and grab a towel—soft against my damp body. I set my phone on its stand, checking the angle, and then I hit record. My gaze smolders into the lens as I step back, bouncing lightly on my toes, letting my chest rise and fall with the motion.

I unwrap the towel slowly, revealing my naked body to him, give a wink, a sultry smile, then I turn and bend over slowly and deliberately, knowing the camera catches the perfect angle of my ass, water still glistening on my skin.

I trim the edges of the video, leaving only what I want him to see and hit send.

The silence afterward gnaws at me. A flicker of doubt stirs—had I gone too far, perhaps? Shown too much?

Then his reply comes. A video.

At first, it seems like nothing but his bathroom countertop, until my eyes adjust to the reflection on its glossy surface. A shadow moving. My pulse jumps as I realize what I'm seeing.

His hand. His cock. The slow, deliberate rhythm of him stroking himself, the angle catching just enough to show me, to torture me. I watch the shadow of his cock being pulled when I realize the sound is on. He left the fucking sound on!

His low groans fill the bathroom around me, guttural and raw, until my breath hitches. I hear him moan my name softly, "Serrrra," as he draws out my name like a prayer or a curse. He comes, spilling across the counter in heavy pulses and I gasp aloud, hand gripping the porcelain edge of the tub.

Me: Not. Fucking. Nice.

A beat later, his reply: a simple devil-smiling emoji.

I stare at it, my heart pounding, heat curling like fire through my veins. This isn't a game anymore. This is war.

I towel myself dry and slip into a simple dress, braiding my hair and pinning it into a tight bun. I reread the quick exchange of messages Killian and I share. His words are reckless in their simplicity—talk of dinner tomorrow, even a walk along the river before. Innocent things. Mortal things.

I indulge him, savoring the novelty of a man who wants nothing from me but my company. I've just begun typing my reply when a knock sounds sharp against the doorframe. Marcella slips in, silent as always, dipping into a bow before announcing, "General Vaelyn requests an audience, my Queen."

I stifle a sigh and wave her aside. "Send him in."

The door shuts softly behind him. Vaelyn enters with his usual poise, every line of him carved in discipline—broad shoulders, dark hair pulled back, the same handsome face I've trusted for centuries. Yet, there's something strained in the way he holds himself, like a taut bowstring waiting to snap.

"Yes, general?" I ask, letting indifference lace my tone.

"The feeding operation is proceeding smoothly," he reports, his words clipped, professional, as though this were an ordinary update.

"I'm aware." I roll my eyes. "Get to the point, Vaelyn. Why are you really here?"

Silence stretches between us, heavy and suffocating. Then he draws a breath, his voice even though the faintest tremor betrays him.

"I have served you faithfully for five hundred years, your majesty. But when the borders open...I wish to follow Amara. To Ivory."

His words strike like iron across my chest, though I keep my expression perfectly still.

"You...wish to leave me?" My voice comes softer than intended, a dangerous whisper.

His eyes don't falter. "I wish to serve Amara."

The room suddenly feels colder. Centuries of loyalty, battle, and blood unraveled in the space between us. I remember the first night he knelt, the cities we've burned together, the enemies who fear him because of his association with me.

Vaelyn has been more than a general—he's had a piece of my reign, a thread in the tapestry of Crimson itself. And now that thread is severing.

Rage coils hot in my veins, demanding to be released. I want to lash out, to remind him what eternity means under me. I force the fury down, locking it behind the cage of my ribs. Queens do not beg. We do not break.

I draw in a slow breath, letting indifference mask the wound. I give a careless wave of my hand. "As you wish. When the borders open, you will be free to go where you please. As will all vampires."

He bows low, the movement respectful yet final. "My Queen."

Then he's gone. The silence that follows presses heavy, suffocating. I let myself sink back against the bed, phone forgotten in my lap. Centuries of loyalty reduced to ashes in a single conversation.

How many others will follow when the borders open? How many threads of the Crimson Court would unravel before I'm left holding scraps of what had once been my empire?

I stare at the ceiling, my jaw tight, my hands clenched in the sheets.

Let them go. Let them scatter.

They'll see soon enough that no Ivory throne, no wintered Frost, no Onyx shadow could shield them when the time comes. When the tide turns, when the war truly begins, the only court left standing will be mine.

I recline against the pillows, phone in hand, words from Killian glowing softly across the screen. Of all the chaos unraveling around me—whispers of war, the treachery of bloodlines—it's here in this fragile thread of conversation that I feel something I haven't in centuries.

Happiness. Peace.

How strange, how dangerously ironic, that it comes from a human...a hunter. The one man who wants me dead is the only man who makes me feel alive. I place my ruby crown on my head, fix my face, and force my emotions down. I have a meeting with my sisters tonight, and I refuse to let them see a crack in my armor.

The betrayal of my generals, even these dangerous feelings for a man could all wait. But even as I stand and smooth out my dress,

I catch my reflection in the mirror. For just a moment, I don't see a queen. I see a woman who's tired of being alone.

14

Killian

Early mornings in the bar are some of the most peaceful times. No laughter, no music, just the silent hum of the fridge and the occasional creaking of the old pipes behind the walls. I lie in bed, arm resting behind my head as I swipe through profile after profile on Temptr. None of them interest me.

Finally, her message pops up, and I happily click it.

> **Sera:** *So, do you just own the bar as a great pickup line?*

Smiling, I thumb a quick reply.

> **Me:** *If it is a pickup line, it seems to have worked.*

> **Sera:** *Mhm, answer the question, bartender.*

> **Me:** *No. I own it because it makes me happy. You'd have known that if you had come last night.*

I know I'm playing a little loose, risking upsetting her by being too pushy. But a little teasing can't hurt. It seems to be her style too, so it's a risk worth taking.

Sera: *It's like that, huh?*

She follows it with a smirking emoji, and I feel relieved, knowing she has a good sense of humor about it all.

Sera: *And do you sweep the floor yourself too? Or do you make the "new girls" do it for you?*

I roll in bed, smiling at the realization that she's come by the bar, just not come in.

Me: *So you have been stalking my staff, huh? Kind of a red flag don't you think?*

Sera: *Red is my color.*

I laugh, shaking my head at the photo she follows up with: she's in a red dress, a deep V that reveals her cleavage. I can tell she's pulling the dress down to reveal more than it normally would. The edge of her nipple shows and it makes me adjust myself.

Me: *You are dangerous, you know that?*

Sera: *Dangerous? I'm in bed eating chocolate and messaging you. Hardly lethal.*

Me: *Depends, dark chocolate or milk?*

Her response is quick.

Sera: *Dark. Obviously.*

Me: *See, that's serial killer energy. Milk chocolate is the way to go.*

Her response is instant and sharper this time, almost cutting.

Sera: *Maybe I just like a challenge.*

My thumb hovers over the keys, instincts tugging at me like a warning. Still I type,

Me: *Good. So do I.*

The dots return, slower this time.

Sera: *Don't forget. Tonight at seven. Don't keep me waiting.*

I smirk, tapping the mattress with one hand while I type with the other. Bossy. Gods, I like it.

Me: *What if I show up five after? Do I get scolded…or punished?*

The dots flare up again, immediate. She's right there with me.

Sera: *Depends. Do you deserve punishment already?*

I laugh aloud, the sound echoing too sharply in the room's stillness.

> **Me:** *Probably. I have that kind of face.*

> **Sera:** *You have one of those mouths.*

I freeze, staring at the words until a slow grin spreads across my face. She knows exactly how to twist the knife and make it hurt, but still feel good.

> **Me:** *Careful. Keep talking like that, and I'll start thinking you like me.*

There's a pause. Then her answer hits, sly as a blade across the throat.

> **Sera:** *Maybe I do. Maybe I don't. Guess you'll have to show up on time to find out.*

I drop the phone on the bed, dragging a hand down my face. Every part of me knows this is a bad idea. I can't remember the last time I'd felt this reckless. A date. An actual date. Not a one-night distraction, not a meaningless warm body to forget by morning. Sera feels different. Talking to her these last few weeks has been too easy, like we'd known each other longer than we should have.

It feels dangerous to admit how much I want tonight. But before desire...duty.

I grab my keys and slip out the back door, the smell of stale beer and bleach from the bar clinging to me as I swing my leg over the bike.

The engine rumbles low and steady, vibrating through me like an extra heartbeat. The morning air is heavy, charged. The clouds above are already thickening, a storm rolling in. Perfect cover for the monsters I hunt.

I park two streets over from the club, killing the engine in the shadows. The building looms ahead, its neon sign a pulsing red heartbeat against the darkening sky. I scale the fire escape quickly, muscle memory guiding me until I reach the rooftop. From there, I have the perfect vantage point of the club.

For hours, I sit crouched in the rain. The grit of tar paper rough under my palms, the smell of ozone sharp in the air as lightning teases the horizon. I scribble notes, cataloging movements, memorizing faces. Vampires move in and out like clockwork, their patterns as telling as their colors. Subtle signs mark each court.

One court stands out. Crimson.

Over and over again, they come and go in greater numbers than the rest. They don't just move—they command. The others defer, even when they think no one is watching. That tells me enough: Crimson has the lead here and their queen is pulling the strings.

Leaning back, I pull out my phone, thumb brushing over the screen. A notification lights up—a photo from Sera earlier, slipping into a new dress, the image that makes my chest tighten and my brain stop working for a few dangerous beats.

Smiling despite myself, I send her a saved photo from this morning that I debated sending, but didn't want to come off as too much. I hit send and then exit the Temptr app.

I hesitate before calling Tommy. When his gravelly voice answers, it's the same anchor it's always been.

"Hey, got a second?"

"Heading to stake out the club myself. Thought I'd get some intel." His tone is clipped.

I chuckle. "Too slow, old man. I've been here for hours."

Silence. Then a growl of irritation. "Why the hell didn't you tell me before you left?"

"Got distracted. I just decided to come. Anyways...want to hear what I found?"

A pause and then gruffly, "Go on."

I lean forward, the rain splattering against the roof. "I think the queen is Crimson. I'm sure of it. The vamps dominate the club, and the others listen to their orders."

"If that's true, then we go for the queen and end her."

"That's why I'm here." I smile into the speaker. "If we wait long enough, they'll show. Queens need to feed, same as the rest. I'll call you guys when I see her and we'll take her down."

Tommy exhales. "As good a plan as any. Want backup?"

"No." I say firmly. "This is my ground. I've got all the angles covered."

Before he can argue, I end the call and slip the phone back into my pocket. The air shifts suddenly—my hunter gene surges like static under my skin and I freeze. Tires roll slowly over wet asphalt, the hiss of rubber on the rain-slick street. My veins pulse as my senses stretch, every nerve alert.

Below, tinted cars ease to a stop outside the club. The guards stiffen, their postures snapping like soldiers waiting inspection. Even in the storm's dark belly, I feel the weight of power pressing down from those cars.

I sink back into the shadows, body low against the rooftop edge, heart hammering steadily. Whoever has just arrived isn't ordinary, and this is what I've been waiting for.

A blur of motion cuts through the rain-slick street. A figure cloaked in black sweeps to the tinted car and pulls open the door. From within steps a woman—tall, striking, her hair jet black and sleek as ink spilled over her shoulders. Her dress clings like a shadow, a slit daring up her thigh and black heels clicking like gunshots on the wet concrete. The Onyx queen, though she now wears a glamour so she appears human, beautiful even.

The man guiding her holds a clear umbrella over her. I scribble notes, forcing myself to memorize every detail, though my pulse hammers harder with each second.

Another blur, another door. This time, ivory and gold. A woman with blond curls, shoulder length and perfect, dressed in white that shimmers even in the storm. Pearls wrap her throat and wrists like chains of moonlight. Her guard also covers her with an umbrella as they walk into the club.

The air seems to thicken. My phone buzzes in my hand, cutting through the sound of thunder.

> **Sera:** *Three more hours. Are you excited to see me?*

Despite myself, I smile. My chest eases for just a second. My thumb flies across the screen.

> **Me:** *Of course. I'm pacing my room, trying to figure out what to wear.*

Dots dance across the screen, then her reply comes sharp and teasing.

> **Sera:** *Oh my. I'm going on a date with a diva.*

> **Me:** *A handsome diva.*

I laugh under my breath, covering my mouth so it won't echo off the roof.

> **Sera:** *I've got a quick meeting, then I'm all yours. Make my time worth it.*

> **Me:** *I plan to.*

I slip the phone back into my pocket, heartbeat steadying again—until movement below drags me back.

The Frost queen steps out of the car and her guard is instantly covering her with the umbrella as they walk into the club. I can't help but note the similarities in the queens' glamours, their bone structure, their perfectly smooth skin, and elegant curves. It makes me wonder if their glamours are what they looked like before they became monsters.

My pen scratches furiously against the page. Three queens, three courts. Then the last car door opens and a hulking man in a crimson suit steps forward. He looks like a wall of muscle, holding an umbrella for his queen.

She steps into the rain and it's as if the rain bends itself away from her. The Crimson Queen steps out wearing a gorgeous red dress that hugs her curves perfectly. Her heels click in a rhythm that matches my own heartbeat as she hurries into the club. A blood-red jeweled necklace wraps around her neck. A neck I've become familiar with over the last few weeks.

I stare at her long brown hair tumbling in perfect curls that frame a face I know all too well. My pen falls from my hand and my jaw clenches so hard it hurts. The rain cover I'd fashioned slides from my shoulders as I stagger upright, blinking against the downpour. I wipe my eyes, desperate for the rain to blur her into someone else. Anyone else.

It doesn't because it can't. It's her.

She moves with elegance, each step claiming the world beneath her. At the threshold of the club, she pauses and tilts her head ever so slightly. Then she glances over her shoulder—a glance so casual, so unbothered, it's lethal.

My chest squeezes until I can hardly breathe. My hand aches, fingers locked tightly around the hilt of my knife before I even realize I'd drawn it.

Every word, every photo, every text we'd shared tumbles through my head like shards of glass. The woman I text in my bed at night, the laughter I haven't heard from myself in years. Her smile in those photos, her bone structure, the same face, refined into something impossibly ancient.

Sera. My Sera. The Crimson Queen.

The truth slams into me so hard I gasp, sucking in the cold wet air as though it could steady me. Stumbling forward, I fall to my knees and grab onto the building ledge. The rain falls heavily on me, soaking through my clothes. I wasn't preparing for a date with a fascinating stranger. I have a date with the Queen of all vampires.

I don't tell the others the truth when I get back to the bar. I give them the rundown on the queens I'd seen but tell them the rain had gotten too heavy for me to stay. The Crimson queen never showed.

Tommy's eyes narrow as if he can see straight through me. Helen is furious I hadn't just waited it out. I brush them both off, but the lie sits heavy in my chest.

Later, as I dress, my thoughts circle like vultures. One part of me—the part carved into me since childhood, the hunter's blood—screams that I have the answer. That tonight could be the end if I play it right. Take her out, lure her back to the bar and let my team finish the job. Clean. Efficient.

But another part of me, a quieter, more stubborn part, wants something else.

I want to walk into this night as just a man, not a hunter. To see what it feels like to sit across from her without blood and war between us. To let the moment play out.

I hate myself for admitting it, but I'm also excited.

At the club, every vampire has revealed itself to me through my hunter gene. Their glamour falters in my sight, their actual faces bleeding through. But not her. Not any of the queens.

Sera has stayed untouched, human, and flawless. Maybe that's what makes her so dangerous. It lets me keep lying to myself, telling myself she's just a girl who likes my stupid jokes and wants to see me smile.

Not the oldest, most lethal monster ever to walk the earth.

The night air bites cold against my face as I ride, the storm's breath still clinging to the city. The rain has eased, but the clouds hang low, heavy with promise for more. My mind buzzes louder than the bike's engine.

I park outside the restaurant five minutes early, heart thrumming faster than I want to admit. My palms are damp on the helmet when I set it down.

Inside, warmth washes over me in soft golden lights, the hum of voices, the faint perfume of food and wine. A hostess looks up from her podium, her smile polite.

"Are you Killian?" she asks.

"Uh...yeah," I say curiously.

"Your date is waiting for you." She gestures with a smile. "This way."

I follow her through the dining room, my pulse in my ears louder than the clinking of silverware or the indistinct murmur of conversations around us.

And then...

There she is.

Back of the room. Alone at a table draped in white linen, she looks like she belongs entirely to another world. A red dress hugs her curves, the fabric alive in the light. Her hair curls into brown waves that spill over her shoulders.

For a heartbeat, I could have sworn the whole place dims, like every candle bends toward her.

My knees go weak.

The hunter in me—the one who has memorized her face on the rooftop, weapons in hand—should have surged to the surface, should have screamed at me to run, to fight, to end her here.

But that part of me falls utterly silent as I approach her. Because when her eyes lift and find mine, when she smiles, it hollows me out.

There's no queen. No centuries-old predator.

It's just Sera. My Sera.

The girl who makes me laugh in the dead of night. The girl who knows how to get under my skin with a single line of text. My throat tightens and my hand twitches against the hilt of the knife hidden beneath my jacket. I loosen my grip and relax, as if the thought of raising it against her is the most impossible thing in the world.

I clear my throat and force my legs to carry me forward, every step betraying me. She looks me over slowly, her light brown eyes catching every detail, and there's a sparkle there like she already knows exactly how undone I am.

I sit, the chair creaking beneath me, and feel heat crawl up my neck. What I hate is her ability to make me nervous. I hate it more that I like it.

"You look stunning, Seraphine." I manage, my voice rougher than I intend.

The server appears, but I barely glance at him when asked for my drink order. My focus never leaves her. And as she smiles I realize with terrible clarity that I've already lost. Hunter or not, this woman has me. I have no idea how this night is going to end, and that thrills me.

15

Seraphine

"Thank you." I smile, letting my gaze drag over him a little longer than necessary. "You clean up nice yourself."

It isn't just a polite compliment. I'm genuinely stunned. In the bar, he'd been all sharp edges and unflinching calm, a predator in his own right. Across the table now, in the soft golden light of the restaurant, he looks...different. His hands betray him, fidgeting against his coat pocket. A faint sheen of sweat clings to his forehead. The hunter who slips beneath even my senses is nervous...about a date. With me.

Interesting.

"Have you been here before?" Killian asks, his voice cutting through the silence I'd been savoring.

I tilt my head, studying him. The way his eyes dart from my hands to my face and back down to the tablecloth, as if unsure where it's safe to land. The faint tremor in his voice. "No." I lie smoothly, letting the smile reach my eyes. "It's a nice place. What made you pick it?"

"I heard good reviews." His laugh is quick, self-effacing, like he's trying to soften the fact that he actually thought about it. "I don't get out of the bar much. My nights are mostly spent eating burgers or fried chicken."

I lean in, the scent of roasted garlic and wine curling around us. "We need to get you out more."

"Are you offering to show me?" His grin is crooked, half shy and half daring.

The server brings the first course, steam rising from bowls of bisque, and conversation spills more freely than either of us expects. He tells me about working behind the bar—brief stories about eccentric customers and the regulars who treat it like a second home. I counter with feigned tales of university days, slipping just enough truth into the lies to make them shimmer with credibility.

We trade stories like cards, teasing each other when one detail sounds a little too outrageous. Through it all, I laugh—sharply and unexpectedly—the sound warming my chest.

The food is exquisite, even by immortal standards. Tender steak, seared perfectly. Buttery potatoes, crisp greens with a hint of citrus. He cuts into his portion a little too fast, as though afraid he'd reveal how much he's enjoying this if he slowed down. I let my fork linger, savoring each bite, savoring the way he steals glances at me when he thinks I'm not looking.

At one point, he leans forward, his voice quieter, thoughtful. "I used to think...the job is all that mattered. Lately, I keep wondering if I missed something. The normal things—sitting across from someone and having dinner, talking about nothing important."

For a moment, I forget the crown that weighs heavily on my head, the bloodthirsty hum in my veins. His honesty pierces me sharper than any blade could.

"You didn't miss it," I say. "You just...postponed it."

His smile is small, vulnerable, like he wants to believe me. By the time the server places the check on the table, hours have slipped by unnoticed. Killian reaches for it without hesitation, sliding his card across with an ease that doesn't quite hide his nerves. Then he leans back, shoulders loosening as if he's passed some invisible test.

"I'm sorry the weather ruined our chance to walk earlier..." His voice carries the same softness again, a thread of regret woven through it. "...if it's not too late, we could still take that walk?"

I let the silence stretch for a beat, savoring the flicker of antici-pation in his eyes. Then I smile, slow and deliberate, the kind of smile that promises more than words.

"Let's walk to your bar for a drink," I suggest, tilting my head just enough to let him think it's his idea. "It's pretty close, right?"

"Close enough." He laughs, but his eyes linger on me a moment longer than they should, as though the world outside this table can wait.

The night air is cool and damp, carrying with it the faint scent of rain on brick and the musk of the city winding down. The earlier storm has broken, leaving the streets slick and shining. Lamplight reflects in fractured pools at our feet. I draw in a breath, letting the freshness of it coat my lungs, letting the quiet of the hour settle between us like something intimate.

Killian walks beside me, his arm brushing mine every so often—the accidental touch feeling anything but accidental. Each time, a spark chases through me. He's more at ease now, laughter loosening his posture, his eyes catching mine boldly before darting away again.

"So," he says, bumping my shoulder. "All these meetings you've been having...are they going well?"

His tone is casual, but the question lingers, layered. A hunter testing the waters? Or a man trying to get to know me? I study his profile for a moment, the way the streetlight catches in his hair, the cut of his jaw softened by shadow. Suspicion tugs at me, but I let it go. Tonight isn't for suspicion.

"They're going as well as expected." I admit. "Honestly, I'm over them. I'm ready to get back to my normal routine again."

He glances at me sidelong, lips curling. "I'm glad you finally let me take you out."

The sincerity in his voice makes me pause. "I'm glad you finally asked me out." I tease. "I was running out of angles to show you."

That earns a genuine laugh, warm and unguarded. Up ahead, the neon glow of his bar's sign cuts through the night, a beacon calling us closer.

We reach the door. He slides the key into the lock, hesitating just enough for me to catch it. I arch an eyebrow. "You aren't open tonight?"

"I gave everyone the night off." He says, sheepishly, flashing that grin that doesn't quite match the careful thought behind it. "I was hoping you'd want to join me for a drink. I wanted us to have some time alone..."

"Smooth." I laugh. "But thank you."

Inside, the bar is quieter than I'd ever seen it. No clinking glasses, no chatter, only the faint hum of the old jukebox in the corner. Shadows stretch across the polished wood, and for once the place feels like it belongs entirely to him. To us.

"What do you want to drink?" He asks, slipping behind the bar with easy familiarity.

"Surprise me." I say, leaning an elbow on the counter, letting my smile linger.

He works with practiced hands, flipping bottles, shaking tins. The faint scent of citrus and rum blooms into the air—a show just for me. When he slides the glass across, sugar crusting the rim, fruit perched at a careful angle, I already know what this drink is.

I take a sip, letting the sweet familiar burn dance on my tongue. "It's good," I say.

"Thanks." He beams. "I call it the Killian Special. I just perfected it...you're actually the first person I've made it for."

I raise an eyebrow, hiding my amusement. I remember this drink, remember sipping it under another face, another name. He doesn't know that, though. "Oh...really?" I smile.

"Yup. So I'm glad you like it." His grin is boyish, almost disarming.

He runs over to the jukebox and selects something to play—a country song, evenly paced and clearly setting the tone of the night. When he comes back to the bar, he leans across the counter.

I let my gaze drop to his mouth, then back to his eyes. "Are you planning to get me drunk and take advantage of me, Killian Blake?"

He leans forward, forearms resting on the bar, until only inches separate us. His voice drops low, daring. "I would never dream of doing such a thing. But I wouldn't say no if you offered."

The tension coils so tightly between us it's almost unbearable. I tip the glass back and drain it in one long swallow, never breaking eye contact. The sugar clings to my lips like a promise.

"I'm offering." I say, my voice velvet and fire, sliding my hand across the bar until my fingers brush his. The touch is electric, sending sparks up my arm. "Take me upstairs. Now."

In an instant, he's out from behind the bar, his arms scooping me up as if I weigh nothing. Our lips collide, all the heat and want we'd been stoking, pouring out in a furious rush. The kiss is rough, desperate, like the night itself has been building toward this single, inevitable moment.

He kicks the door shut and tosses me onto the bed. The sheets are cool against my heated skin. Before I can sit up, his fingers hook into my dress and yank it over my head, flinging it across the room. My body hums with anticipation.

Killian grabs my ankle and pulls my leg straight as he kneels at the bed's edge. His mouth moves up my calf, kissing, biting lightly at my knee, then devouring my inner thigh with desperate hunger.

Each press of his lips is demanding, leaving marks that burn with delicious intensity.

Then his mouth is on me, tongue exploring with raw need. I gasp as his fingers slide deep, curling inside to hit that spot that makes me arch against his mouth.

He pulls back, eyes locked on mine, dark with desire. He flips me over, my body pliant under his hands, and I feel the weight shift as he strips off his clothes. Without a word, he lines up and thrusts in, filling me completely, stretching me in the most exquisite way.

He kisses a gentle trail down my spine as he pushes deeper inside me. I can't help the noises escaping my throat—they only get louder when he reaches around me and buries his hand between my legs, rubbing slow circles across my clit.

"Killian," I gasp.

His breath is hot against my skin as he moans. "Does it hurt?" he asks.

"No. More. Please," I manage.

He stops and I whine when he pulls out of me. I'm desperate to have him back so I roll over and meet his gaze. He's staring at me with a hunger in his eyes and it takes only a smile before he grabs me behind my knees and lifts my legs up. He rests my ankles on his shoulders and buries himself again.

"Fuck." I moan. "Just like that. Don't stop."

He leans down and takes my mouth desperately. When I part my lips, I feel his tongue push greedily against mine. It's too much for me—this man is going to be my undoing. I feel it edging closer and closer.

"I'm..." I breathe against his lips. "Killian... I'm..."

I can't finish what I'm trying to say because I'm screaming out my orgasm into his neck. I feel his cock pulsing inside me as he chases my finish with his own and I feel a satisfaction I've never felt wash over me as he collapses on top of me. His sweaty body glides off mine as he slips out and lays next to me.

Both of us breathing raggedly as we stare at each other. I watch his green eyes, refusing to look away. I know what has to happen next, and I'm drawing it out as long as I can.

"Fuck." I smile.

"That was..." Killian gasps.

"Amazing." I finish for him, lips curling as I stare at the cracked ceiling above.

When I roll onto my side, his eyes are already on me. Unblinking.

"What?" I ask, my voice softer than I ever intended it to be. Vulnerable.

"Just admiring you." His smile is small, disarming, more human than hunter.

I crawl onto his lap, his arousal already pressing against my thigh, eager. His hips roll in a slow tease as I bend to kiss his lips, trailing down the curve of his neck, tasting the salt of his skin and then lower to the plane of his chest. I brush my lips over each scar that I find, his body's story now making more sense.

His hands find my hips, rough palms sliding upward, grip tightening as a growl rumbles from his throat. I can't resist anymore. I let my mask slip and my voice drops low, edged with hunger. "It's such a shame you've spent your life hunting down my kind. We could have been so good together."

The shift in him is immediate. His hunter gene snaps awake, pupils flaring, muscles straining with sudden, unnatural strength. His body coils beneath me, instincts rising.

I expect panic, horror, revulsion at what I am. Instead, his gaze is steady. Darkened yes, but steady. He's still hard under me, his body betraying no fear—only desire. I feel the head of his cock press gently against my entrance and I have to force myself not to grind against him.

"You knew?" I whisper, surprised by the calm in his eyes.

"I knew," he breathes, the confession slipping from his lips like it had been waiting.

"Then you know I have to kill you now." My voice is a growl.

"And you know I have to kill you first." He smiles at me.

I don't wait. With a snarl, I sink my fangs deep into his neck. He gasps but doesn't fight me. He lets me drink from him, and gods, his blood.

It's hot, thick, coursing down my throat like molten fire. The taste is wrong and right all at once—rich and wild, laced with something I haven't tasted in centuries. Something ancient. Older than the hunter gene. As old as I am.

It's intoxicating.

My body trembles as realization coils like ice down my spine. "You're the—" I gasp, pulling back, lips smeared with his blood.

The cold press of steel meets my throat before I can finish. He pulls the knife from beneath the pillow in one swift motion and shoves me off, pinning me against the wall. His blade is steady against my skin, his grip iron.

My eyes flick to the blood trickling from his neck, the wound I'd left—despite that, he stares at me with aching tenderness.

"You are so beautiful," he whispers. "Even with the glamour down...I can't deny it."

His knife lowers slightly. His voice cracks with something like awe. "You're the Queen, aren't you? The original?"

A slow smile curves my lips as I nod, wicked delight lacing my words. "The one and only."

My fingers graze his cheek, smearing blood across his skin. He inhales sharply, torn between reverence and duty. "We could have been so good for each other." He murmurs, echoing my own words.

He leans in and kisses me. I can't help but kiss him back, deeper. My eyes go wide with the sudden pain that flares in my belly. I pull back to see his blade buried in me, the apology in his eyes giving me pause. The burn is sharp, molten, shocking enough to draw a gasp from me. He twists, hating himself but pushing through.

"I'm so sorry," he whispers, tears in his eyes. "I'll make it quick."

The knife plunges again, heat exploding through me as I snarl, eyes blazing red. My hand shoots out, shoving him across the room with supernatural force. His body slams against the wall, cracking plaster, his knife clattering to the floor. In a blur, I'm on him, my fingers wrapping around his throat, pressing hard enough to feel the panic twitch beneath his skin.

"You just fucking stabbed me," I snarl.

He claws at my wrist, gasping. "Duty...above...desire."

I squeeze tighter, then let him go. His body slumps to the floor, gasping for air. My wounds close before his eyes, knitting together as if he'd never touched me. I lean in close, lips brushing his.

"We aren't done," I whisper. "Not even close."

I turn to gather my dress, but the hunter in him isn't finished. He lunges, blade flashing. This time I catch his wrist mid-swing. With a twist, bone cracks beneath my grip. His scream splits the air.

I shove him back onto the bed and straddle him with a predator's smile. My gaze rakes down his body, hungry and taunting all at once.

"As much as I'd love to take you for another ride... I have a meeting to attend."

I let the words linger, my smile cruel, before slipping into my dress. At the door, I pause and look back at him—broken, bleeding, his wrist shattered, neck still leaking blood. Even through the pain, I see the heat in his eyes. The desire that neither of us can deny.

"Next time," I whisper, "don't hesitate. It might be the death of you."

Then I fade into the night, leaving him burning with something far more dangerous than hatred.

Want.

16

Killian

I sit on the edge of my bed, elbows braced on my knees and hands clawing through my hair as if I could scrub her out of my mind the way I tried to scrub her blood off my skin. But she still lingers. The ghost of her lips at my throat, still wet with the taste of me, whispering the truth I've chased my entire life like a fool chasing shadows.

Seraphine. The Queen of Vampires.

My wrist aches, the bones having knitted back together minutes ago thanks to the hunter gene thrumming inside me. But the gift has already slipped away when she vanished into the night, leaving me with nothing but silence and the echo of her name.

I should hate her.

I keep seeing her across that dinner table, her laughter mingling with mine like we're just two strangers figuring each other out. I keep replaying the softness in her eyes before the mask dropped.

Why would she let me take her out? Why would she let me touch her, kiss her, breathe her in like she's just a girl and I'm just a man? She knew who I was this whole time.

Even after the glamour fell and I saw the centuries etched beneath her skin, the monster hiding in plain sight, she was still beautiful. She was even more beautiful than with her glamour masking her. And that, more than anything, terrifies me.

I stay sitting like this for the rest of the night, watching the sun rise over the buildings and bleed into my room. The shower hisses to life, steam curling around me like smoke as I step under the scalding spray. I press my forehead to the tile, willing the heat to burn her out of me.

But no matter how hard I scrub, her taste lingers on my tongue—sweet and sharp. Her scent clings to me, and worse, she's made me feel something I haven't felt in years.

Normal.

The mirror has fogged over by the time I step out, showing a vague ghost of my reflection. I towel off, dragging on a pair of striped boxers, and I'm halfway through convincing myself to forget when a knock sounds on the door.

"Come in." I call out.

Helen steps inside, sharp eyes scanning the wreckage of my room—sheets twisted, clothes scattered, the faint smell of perfume still hanging in the air. Her jaw drops, then curves into a grin. "A good night?"

I freeze for a heartbeat too long. How can I tell her the truth? That we've been hunting the enemy I just slept with. That I didn't kill her when I had the chance. That I didn't want to. Even as the silence stretches, even as Helen's grin deepens, I know one thing for certain: I'm not going to tell her. Not about this, not about her.

"You could say that." I say finally, tugging a shirt over my head and pretending the weight in my chest is nothing.

Helen arches an eyebrow. "What are your plans today?"

"I think I have a lead on the queen," I lie smoothly. "I'm going to check it out before working the bar tonight."

"Do you really think that's wise?" Her tone is sharp, skeptical, the way it always is when she smells a half-truth. I slip into my riding jacket, my fingers tight around the familiar curve of my keys.

"I think working the bar is the only thing keeping me sane. When this is over, when the world is safe, I want a normal life. A normal woman. A normal job. I've earned boredom."

Her smile is sad, cutting deeper than her words. "Killian...we aren't normal. We don't get rest. Don't let your false hope blind you to the mission. Duty above—"

"Desire." I finish for her, the phrase tasting bitter in my mouth. "I know the line, Helen."

"Good." She crosses her arms, hard where I am soft. "We've got a meeting tonight. I expect a full report on this 'lead.' Understand?"

I push past her, the weight of her eyes following me down the hall. The back door slams behind me as I straddle my bike. I need air.

I need her.

Pulling out my phone, I open the Temptr app. Sera's thread glares back at me like a wound I can't stop touching. My fingers move before I can talk myself out of it.

> **Me:** *Last night was fun, let's do it again.*

Her reply is instantaneous. Too instant. Like she'd been waiting.

Sera: *Which part, little hunter?*

I smirk.

Me: *Little? Come on…nothing about last night was little.*

Sera: *Careful. I spared you because I wasn't finished having fun with you. You're my pet, don't forget that.*

The words should burn, but they light something I hate to admit.

Me: *So take me for a walk in the park. Bring a ball. We can play fetch.*

Sera: *Funny. But I can't.*

Me: *Too bad. I'm busy today anyway. Stop being so needy.*

Sera: *You are so infuriating. I should have killed you last night.*

I grin, thumb hovering before sending the message I know will drive her mad.

Me: *Aw, you really do like me, huh?*

The phone buzzes in my pocket again and again, her fury flashing across the screen. I ignore it, twisting the throttle and cutting through the cloudy streets until I slip into the shadowed alley across from the club.

The bass hits first, a low thrum reverberating through the brick walls, shaking loose rainwater from rusted fire escapes. Neon bleeds across the slick pavement in violet and blue, breaking apart in puddles as fresh drops of rain begin to fall. I pull my hood low and lean against the wall, shadows swallowing me whole.

I stay fixed on the line forming outside the club. Drunk kids, tourists, predators dressed in silk and lipstick—all waiting under the wash of strobe lights. The hunter in me scans for tells: bouncers who aren't breathing, girls whose pupils gleam too wide with glamour.

But the man in me, the part I hate, keeps wondering if she'll come today.

The air shifts before I hear her. Perfume like smoke and spice wraps around me, cold and sharp, followed by the deliberate click of heels. She slides out of the shadows as if she were born from them, her arm brushing mine like she'd always stood there.

"You're like a jealous ex," she purrs, lips curling. "How long are you planning to sulk in my alley before working up the nerve to go inside?"

My jaw clenches. I keep my eyes on the line, noting a vampire angling a human boy from the queue with a smile too wide, too hungry. "Just making sure you bloodsuckers stay in line and hold up your end of the deal." I mutter absentmindedly to her.

"Mm." She giggles and the sound is like silk and a blade all at once. "I could say the same of your kind."

I turn around, despite myself, and my chest tightens when I see her standing there with her arms crossed. Her glamour is thin today, her skin pale beneath the clouds covering the sky, her eyes darker than the neon glow around us. She looks sickly, inhuman, otherworldly.

And yet...she's still devastatingly beautiful.

"Shouldn't you be inside?" I ask, distracting myself from pinning her against the wall right now. "Feasting on poor, innocent humans?"

"I was heading in." She says smoothly. "Not to feed, to meet my sisters. But then I saw you, and I just had to check on my favorite little hunter."

She brushes her knuckles across my cheek and I find myself leaning into her touch before shaking my head.

"I'm doing great." I growl, slapping her hand away. I pull my knife from my pocket. "About to kill the world's oldest evil and become a hero to humanity."

Her laugh is low, dangerous. "Careful, Killian. You're cute when you pretend."

That breaks something in me.

I lunge forward, my steel blade flashing as I drive it toward her throat. She twists smoothly, catching my wrist—the same wrist she broke last night. Pain flares and I wince, the knife clattering to the ground.

"Still trying to kill me after I gave you the best night of your life?" she teases, her lips grazing my ear.

A growl tears from my chest. I wrench free, yank another blade from my belt and slash. This time the steel grazes her arm, splitting fabric, drawing a bead of dark blood that shimmers like oil under the streetlights.

Her grin widens. "Good. I like it when you play rough."

She slams me against the wall, brick grinding into my shoulders. Her thigh presses into my hip, pinning me with her hand still locked on my wrist. She grabs my blade and lifts it above my head. The heat of her body burns through her dress, her lips hovering just above mine, her voice a ghost against my jaw.

"End it now, hunter. Show me your precious motto. Duty above desire."

I snarl, twisting hard and reversing the hold, shoving her against the wall. I grab the knife back and hold it to her throat—a single bead of blood wells beneath my blade. Her eyes glow faintly, and mine burn with conflict I can't hide.

She should be ash already. I should finish it, but I find myself hesitating. She sees it, and I find myself watching her lips as they curve up into a smile. Her hand shoves into my chest, sending me stumbling back. Her fist cracks against my cheek. Stars burst in my vision.

"Fuck you!" I shout, more in shock than pain.

"You're shaking." Sera smiles, stepping closer. "Is this the duty? Or the desire?"

Before I can answer, her arms wrap around my neck, her lips crushing against mine. My split lip burns, blood sliding onto her tongue. She moans softly as she feeds from it and I hate myself for the way my body responds, hardening at the sound of her feeding on me.

I shove her back against the wall, kissing her back, teeth clashing, my hands dragging down her body. Her dress is thin, every curve under my palms. She sucks my lip, drawing more blood, savoring me.

When she finally pulls away, her eyes rake down my body and she grins wide when she sees the bulge pressing against my jeans. "I have to go." She sighs. "Are you done trying to kill me, or should we reschedule this?"

My chest heaves, rage and lust choking me. "Why aren't you trying to kill me?"

She tilts her head, her smile soft for the first time. "Because I know what you are. And I don't want you dead."

Her words hit harder than her fist. My grip tightens on the knife, confusion flooding through me. "What am I? What—"

Before I can finish, she's gone. A blur of speed down the alley, leaving nothing but perfume, blood, and questions burning in my lungs.

I stand there trembling, blade still clutched uselessly in my hand, every instinct screaming I should've killed her. But all I can think is: what did she mean?

The hum of the bar hits me the second I step through the back door. Music spills from the jukebox, glasses clinking, laughter rising in waves. It's alive tonight, bodies pressed shoulder-to-shoulder, the kind of crowd that usually steadies me. But not tonight. Not with the weight of the alley still heavy in my chest.

I slip into the office to change into my work shirt, expecting the usual empty room. Instead, Helen, Eli, Bri, and Tommy sit waiting, their eyes sharp as blades.

"Hello..." My voice stretches thin as I scan their faces. No one smiles.

"We need to discuss the hunt." Helen's tone is flat, her arms crossed tight. "And you need to decide whether you're with us or still distracted."

Tommy leans forward, eyes narrowing. "Duty above desire isn't just some slogan for your love life, Killian."

I freeze mid-step, the words hitting harder than I want to admit.

"You're the boss," Eli adds, his voice quieter but edged with disappointment. "You brought us here. But lately...it feels like you've been somewhere else."

I blink at them, heat rising in my chest. "Somewhere else?"

My laugh comes out sharp and defensive. "I just came from the Crimson Court club. I'm the one who discovered the patterns. I'm the one who confirmed the queen runs that court."

"That's great." Helen snaps. "But since then? Dates. Disappearances. Nights hiding behind this bar. We see you, Killian."

"When was the last time you hunted?" Eli's voice cuts through, accusing, almost pleading.

The irony makes me laugh under my breath. If they only knew who I'm spending my nights with, they'd realize I'm hunting every damn second. Hunting her, failing to kill her.

I push the thought down. "Whatever. Let's talk about the game plan. We've got three hundred hunters arriving soon."

Finally, Bri speaks, her arms unfolding like she'd been waiting for the right moment. "Then we use them. All of them. We hit the club hard. Burn it down before they know what hit them."

Helen nods immediately. "Agreed."

"Agreed," Eli echoes.

Tommy's silence lingers only a heartbeat before he adds, "Yeah. Time to end this."

"Except..." The word slips out before I can stop it.

Helen rolls her eyes. "Here we fucking go."

"Except." My glare meets hers. "There are humans in that club. Tourists, students, innocents. We don't kill humans."

The rule. Our one unbreakable rule.

"The chance to kill the queen is bigger than one rule," Tommy says.

I stare at him. "What? You've always been the one screaming at us to hold that line. And now? A few acceptable losses are okay?"

"If a few innocents die to save the entire human race, then yes. It's worth it."

I feel my stomach drop. "I don't even know who you are anymore. Your travels changed you, uncle."

Bri's voice is softer, but no less dangerous. "What's so wrong with taking out a couple hundred bloodsuckers?"

"Oh I don't know." My voice rises, sharp and bitter. "Maybe retaliation? What if she isn't there when we attack? You saw how they had us in the hospital, we barely made it out of there with our lives. The queens will wipe out every hunter in this city for sport."

"Killian." Helen's eyes cut into me, sharp as broken glass. "We have a chance. We take it. Period. You can get on board, or you can step down."

The room goes silent. My hunters, my family, stare at me, waiting for an answer. For the first time, I realize the truth: I'm not stalling for strategy. I'm stalling because I want to find a way to save her.

Sera.

The plan is sound. It's our best chance. All I can think about is betraying it. Betraying them.

I force myself to nod. "I'm in," I say at last, but the words taste like ash in my mouth. "Of course I'm in."

Helen and Tommy exchange a look before finally easing back.

"Good," Helen says, the faintest smile tugging her lips. "Then let's begin."

I sit with them, but my mind is already elsewhere. On the music thumping as the bar comes alive with customers. On the vampire queen I should want dead. And the blood I know will spill soon.

Blood that might include hers. I have no idea which side I'll choose when the moment arrives.

17

Killian

It's been four days since I last saw Sera. What felt like never-ending rain finally turned to snow late last night, but it's early in the season and it's not sticking yet. The flakes melt the moment they touch pavement, leaving everything slick and gleaming. I've busied myself with the bar at night, preferring to sleep most of the day just to avoid thinking about her.

It never helps. I see her in my dreams too. I've refused to text her, and it would seem she feels the same way because as I stare at our chat thread, rereading our conversations and looking at her photos for the hundredth time, she hasn't sent me anything either.

Hunters are beginning to gather and I know it's only a matter of time before Eli and Bri make another attempt to attack. Luckily, I've been able to use the 'not enough are here yet' excuse to keep them at bay. The abandoned hospital has been our new meeting place, and it's getting packed more and more by the day. My attempt at keeping these kill-hungry hunters at bay won't be enough soon.

"Are you sure you're okay doing this alone?" I ask Alex while I grab my bike keys.

"I've done inventory with you so many times, Kil." She smiles. "I got this. You deserve a break."

I catch sight of my tired eyes in the mirror hanging in my office as I grab my coat—dark circles like bruises, stubble I haven't bothered to shave. "Is it that obvious?" I laugh.

"You look like shit, boss." Donovan laughs.

"Geez, thanks." I say.

My phone vibrates in my pocket and I can't help the smile that lights up my face. Even Alex and Donovan take note. I catch them sharing a knowing look as I read her message.

"Looks like she finally texted him." I hear Donovan laugh.

I ignore them. Let them continue thinking this is just another one-night stand gone bad. That my mood being shit lately isn't because of my need to be close to her again, to feel her, hold her, kiss her. I need her to know she's mine.

Fuck. No.

I need to kill her, make her suffer, end her entire monster blood-line, and give humanity the freedom to live on without fear of what's in the dark. That's why I smile while I read her message. An excuse to get her alone and finally make an end to the queen who lives in my mind day and night.

Sera: *I've missed you at the club, hunter.*

Me: *Sorry, who's this?*

I smile as I watch the typing bubbles on my screen.

Sera: *Funny.*

Me: *Are you going to tell me about what you meant in the alley? About why you won't kill me?*

Sera: *I'm not killing you simply because I enjoy playing with you too much. Remember Killian, you are my toy to dispose of whenever I choose.*

Time to set the bait.

Me: *Whatever. I need fresh air. I'm going to the trails.*

I grab my helmet while she types back.

Sera: *Don't be ridiculous. It's snowing. You can't go out on your bike in these conditions.*

I smile as I mount my bike, turning the key and feeling the familiar vibration rumble under me. I slide my helmet on and raise my phone to take a picture.

Me: *Don't tell me what to do. You aren't my queen.*

Sera may not be my queen...but she is mine. Even if she doesn't know it yet. Mine to kill, or mine to hold. I pocket my phone and take off down the road, ignoring the constant vibration of her messages as I imagine her pacing her hotel room, even throwing shit around.

The best part of Colorado is the views it offers. I turn into the park that I intend to get lost in for a few hours to clear my mind. I open my phone messages just to let Sera know they're read, but don't reply. I begin my ascent up the snow-covered trail and lose myself among the trees.

The air grows thinner as I climb, each breath sharp and cold in my lungs. Snow dusts the pine branches, making them sag under the weight. The bike's engine echoes off the rock faces, a lonely sound in the vast silence. Two hours in and I regret not grabbing my mask. I park the bike and set the helmet on the seat. The wind is brutal this high in elevation and though my thick jacket blocks most of the cold, my bones still feel the chill of the wind cutting through fabric. I'm starting to think it's time to head back.

A cold chill shivers down my spine as my hunter gene flares to life. Warmth floods through me, chasing away the mountain cold, along with every sense in my body becoming hyper-aware of my surroundings. I turn to find Sera with her arms crossed. She's wearing baggy sweatpants and a simple pink hoodie and the look on her face—fury mixed with something that might be worry only warms my chest more than my hunter's blood.

"Thanks for activating my gene." I smile, turning back around and continuing down the trail I've started on. "You can go now."

In a blur of motion, I'm pinned against the thick trunk of a tree, Sera's hand at my throat, though I note she isn't squeezing. Anger burns in her beautiful brown eyes and I can't help but get lost in them.

"Can you not reply to my messages?" she growls. "Is it that hard?"

"Messages?" I fake shock. "I never got any messages. Must be a bad signal at this elevation."

Sera leans closer and I feel the heat of her breath as she growls another threat at me, her words fogging in the chilly air.

"What are you doing out here? I told you not to get on your motorcycle in this weather."

"I needed air," I say.

"You'll risk your life just to get some air?" Sera asks. "As if you couldn't have just taken a walk around the damn block?"

I shrug. "How else was I supposed to get you alone?"

"I—" Sera hesitates. "What?"

She lets me go and I brush my jacket of tree bark remnants, the rough pieces falling to the snow-dusted ground. I turn to walk away from her, just to see what she'll do.

"Where are you going?" She yells after me.

"To kill a queen!" I yell back.

I feel her following behind me, though she keeps her distance. I move along the rocky uneven path quickly, boots crunching on ice and stone, knowing my destination is just up this hill. The trees open up to a rock jutting out the side of the mountain we've been climbing. It overlooks the entire city and I stand and stare in awe at the snowy view—lights twinkling like stars fallen to earth, the buildings small as toys, the world spread out like a promise.

"When I first moved here," I say to Sera who is standing in the tree line still, her pink hoodie bright against the dark pines. "I found this by accident after getting lost up here. It's my absolute favorite place in all of Colorado."

I turn around, pulling my knife from its leather sheath, I point it at Sera. She takes a step closer and smiles.

"Still playing this game?"

"I can't get you out of my head," I admit, my breath clouding in the cold. "You're consuming every waking thought I have."

My hand is trembling. We both know this is an empty threat, but I hold the blade out anyway. Sera takes another step closer, eyeing me dangerously. She licks her lips and I can't help but get jealous of her tongue.

"I have to kill you, Sera. I'm a hunter, it's in my blood. I was born to kill monsters. I was raised to find and kill one monster in particular."

Sera takes another step forward, snow crunching under her feet. "And now that you've found her? Got her up this mountain and trapped her on the edge of this cliff?"

I squint my eyes, praying my voice doesn't betray me as I growl, "I'm going to kill her."

"Then do it..." She whispers with a smile. "...little hunter."

I act as if I'm going to lower the knife, but then throw it at her with a grunt. She moves out of the way but it gives me the second I need to charge at her. I drop my shoulder and push her into the rocky mountain side. Sera wraps her arms around my torso and throws me back, twisting me as she does so that I spin in the air and land on my stomach, grabbing hold of a rock before I slip off the edge of the cliff.

Pulling myself to my feet, I grab another knife and run at Sera. She dodges my first two swipes, but I manage to slice her forearm on the third attempt and she hisses out in pain as I flip the blade in my hand and push it to her throat. I pull hard across her neck and slice the tender flesh. Blood rushes from the wound—dark and gleaming in the pale light. But she heals just as quickly as she's wounded, the flesh knitting back together like it was never broken.

I hold the blade out again, letting the hunter within me take control of my actions. Letting my duty as a hunter fulfill its one goal in this life. I push the blade to her chest and she freezes, seeing the look in my eyes must have given her enough reason to take this seriously because her smile fades and she holds her hands up in surrender. I push the tip of my blade into her chest and smile as she winces at the pain.

"Killian..." she starts.

"On your knees," I say.

"Okay. Okay." She breathes. "I'm doing it. I'm doing it."

I revel at the way she's repeating herself. Power floods me as I stare down at her on her knees in the snow. The blood still on her neck and pooling on her hoodie as my blade sinks even deeper into her chest.

"You win, Killian." Sera sighs.

I see her eyes begin to water and it breaks something in me. Even as I stare down at her, no glamour, just monster—pale skin too perfect, eyes too ancient—I only see the bright eyes of the woman who teases me. I hear the laugh of the girl who would get mad if I didn't call her on time. The way she handled herself during our first date of laser tag. My hand is trembling now and I let go of the blade before I do something I might regret.

"Get up." I say, defeated.

I turn and walk to the edge of the cliff, staring out at the city I've called home for three years. The city that's infested with vampires because of me. The city that's going to drown in its own blood...because of me. Because I can't kill the woman now standing behind me, staring at me. I let out a breath, willing the emotions that threaten to take over my heart to leave.

"Why did you stop?" Sera asks in a quiet, hesitant voice. "You had me." I hear her pick up my knife but I don't make a move to turn around.

If I turn around now, if I see the look in her eyes, I may become lost in them and never find my way out of their hold on me. I let out another breath. A silent apology to the city that will burn any day now...because of me.

"You need to go," I say finally.

"Look at me, Killian," Sera says. I only shake my head in response. "Look. At. Me."

I let out another breath. My final apology to the world as I turn and find Sera holding my knife in her hand. The same knife that I've used to kill countless vampires. The one Tommy gave me when I became the leader of our group. I take the blade from her and strap it back in place.

"Where can I go that will make you happy?" Sera asks as she takes another step closer to me.

"Back to my hotel?" Another step, her boots pressing prints in the thin snow. "Back to my court in Memphis?" Another step. "I could visit my courts in the United Kingdom?" Another step—she's inches from me and I want so desperately to take her, claim her, and make her mine. "How far should I go, Killian?"

"Anywhere," I say. "Away from here. Away from me. I have to kill you, Sera. Don't you understand that? You have to kill me and I have to kill you. Nowhere is far enough!" I realize I'm yelling now, my voice echoing off the rocks.

"There's nowhere you could go that would be far enough away! You haunt my every waking thought and fill my every dream! I can't sleep! I can't eat! I can't even fucking hunt! You have consumed me in ways that I don't even understand and yet the thought of hurting you brings me to my knees."

To prove my point, I fall to my knees in front of her, the cold snow soaking through my jeans. Letting my arms hang at my sides as I open myself to her.

"So kill me," I say. "Do your duty as a queen to your people and kill me. Because if you don't..." I pause, not sure where my mind is going. "...if you don't, I will never stop looking for you."

There's a long silence as Sera looks down at me. I close my eyes, waiting for her to make the killing blow and end the torment that is her consuming me.

"Then don't." I hear her whisper.

My eyes open.

"Don't stop looking."

I'm moving before my brain can catch up with what I'm doing. I crash my mouth into hers and wrap my arms around her in a need to touch her. She leaps into my arms and wraps her legs around me as I hold onto her and walk back into the forest until we crash into the trunk of a tree.

I feel her claws thread through my hair as she pulls my head back, forcing a grunt out of me. I begin to unzip my jacket and let it fall wherever gravity takes it, the cold air biting at my bare arms. Running my hands up her hoodie in desperate need to feel her closer. Sera lifts my shirt up and we break apart long enough to pull it off before I'm pinning her back against the tree.

"Are you cold?" Sera asks between kisses, her breath warm against my freezing skin.

"No." I gasp breathlessly. "Hunter's blood, remember?"

Sera drops out of my hold and makes quick work of stripping off the hoodie and sweatpants she's wearing. I stare in awe at her natural and raw form—pale as moonlight, impossibly perfect, ancient, and terrible and beautiful all at once. She begins working a glamour over her body but I press my hand to her arm.

"No," I say. "No glamour."

I see the hesitation in her eyes, but the glamour she was working on fades and I unbutton my pants and let them bunch at my ankles before stepping out of them. The snow crunches beneath my bare feet, the cold sharp but distant.

I lift Sera back into my arms and pin her against the tree again. She slides her tongue into my mouth and I welcome her completely. I feel her reach down and grab me, positioning herself at the tip of my cock before I loosen my grip slightly and let her slide down my body just enough to feel her take me completely.

"Fuuu..." Sera moans into my mouth.

I adjust my grip on her ass and begin moving her body up and down my cock. She moans into my mouth and it makes me hungrier for more of her.

"Are you okay?" I ask. "Does it hurt? Are you cold?"

"I need more." She breathes, resting her forehead on my shoulder. "More, Killian. Please."

I move her quicker, thrusting myself deeper and harder until she's a mess of moans and groans of pleasure, her breath hot against my neck.

"You're going to make me..." I begin but stop as I feel her tighten around me. I hold her in place, unable to do anything but release my finish into her, warmth flooding between us despite the cold.

"Yes." Sera smiles. "I want all of it."

I hold her in my arms and kiss her lips, shoulder, neck, and cheeks until I become soft enough to fall out of her. She gives a cute little squeal when I do and it only makes me want to kiss her again. I let her down and begin finding my discarded clothes, brushing snow off fabric.

Once we're dressed, I find myself staring at her in a whole new way.

"I should go," I say.

Sera smiles at me, nodding. "You're in no position to ride your bike. Especially now."

I shrug, making sure she sees the wink I give her. "So bossy."

Sera and I walk the trails back to my bike together. Not saying anything, just enjoying the comfort of each other's company. She slips back into the glamour I've come to know as we walk—the softness returning to her edges, the ancient weight lifting from her features—and for a couple of hours I'm just a man enjoying a cold-ass hike with a beautiful woman.

When I reach my bike, she gives me one final kiss and without saying anything else, she leaves. Disappearing into the sunset in a blur of supernatural speed, her pink hoodie the last thing I see before she's gone.

I am so utterly fucked.

18
Seraphine

The club is running smoothly. Advertising free drinks and discounted dances is attracting more humans than the four courts can feed on. Sitting on the balcony next to Amara, I watch as Morgana plays with a middle-aged woman's curly blonde hair, fingers threading through the strands with predatory affection. It's been two days and I can still feel his lips on my neck, his hands greedily grabbing for me, and the ghost of his breath on my skin.

I grin, watching Morgana lead the woman to the private rooms set up for feeding. Soundproof walls to dull out any screaming, as well as the loud constantly playing music in the club—bass thrumming through the floor, bodies pressed together in the strobing lights below. When we feed without killing, our saliva heals the bitemark we leave behind and the free alcohol helps our victims not remember anything for certain.

"I've enjoyed the last few weeks catching up, sister," Amara says to me, her voice smooth as honey over glass.

I smile, but don't take my eyes off the dance floor, following a man who's caught my interest—broad shoulders, dark hair, the way he moves, reminding me of someone I shouldn't be thinking about. "As have I. I'm glad we've settled our differences and can begin to have the relationship we should have always had."

"Where did you rush off to the other day in such a hurry?" Amara asks, her tone deceptively casual. "You ran out of the meeting hall so quickly, it was as if your life depended on it."

Because it did. Because some idiot hunter was going to get himself killed recklessly riding his motorcycle in the snow.

"Just out," I answer, waving down Marcella.

I point to the man I've been watching who looks eerily similar to Killian—same build, same swagger, a poor substitute but the best I'll find tonight.

"I will take him," I say with a sharp smile.

"I will make the arrangements." Marcella smiles, melting into the crowd.

The air around me shifts as she disappears into the heart of the club. I watch the man dance and my thoughts effortlessly drift back to the mountainside. He doesn't realize just how dangerous and powerful he truly is. As badly as he wants to kill me, something deeper is stopping him, stopping me as well.

I've known since the first time I fed on him and tasted his unique hunter blood that I couldn't kill him. That I didn't want to. My sisters are plotting something big, and I could use his power to my benefit if I play this right. At least that's what I keep telling myself.

I watch the humans below on the dance floor, Amara sitting next to me with her perfect calm demeanor, Rowena off who knows where—probably with this hunter she's been working with for some years now. But the truth is, I want Killian for more than his power. I want him for everything he does to me.

As if reading my mind, I feel my phone vibrate and I know it's him before I even open the notification.

Killian: *I need to see you.*

I read his message and lean forward. I have to calm myself before I take off after him, reminding myself I'm a queen to my people, and not just some lovesick girl pining for another taste of her man. And he is mine.

Me: *Busy, sorry.*

Killian: *Sera. Cut the shit. You are in danger, where are you?*

Ah, so the rumors of our gathering in the warehouse have spread to the hunters. I guess Rowena's pet is good for something after all. Now if only she would let us meet him, so we could share in his use to us.

Me: *It's cute to see you worry about me.*

Killian: *Sera. Please.*

Before I can respond, Marcella is at my side.

"Your room is ready." She announces with amusement.

Standing, I cross to the stairs and descend to the dance floor, quickly crossing through the press of bodies—heat and perfume and the sharp tang of sweat—and finding the private rooms in the back. When I push open the curtain, I find the man I've been eyeing leaning against the wall. His smile brightens when he sees me.

"They said you were someone important?" the man asks.

Taking my seat on the sofa, I cross one leg over the other and meet his eyes.

"Take off your clothes," I demand.

The man's smile falters, but then he begins unbuttoning his pants and tugging at his shirt. He stands there in only his black boxer shorts. His chiseled stomach reflects the dim lights perfectly. I can't help but notice the difference between this man and Killian—particularly when looking at the bulge growing in his boxers.

"Those too," I say.

The man hesitantly strips out of his boxers, standing in front of me with his hand covering his erection. I scoff. Killian would never be able to hide himself like this. I rub my legs together in an attempt to soothe the want for him.

I do love the way the humans have always obeyed everything I commanded, but tonight I can't help but think of Killian and how he defied me. I point to the man, then to the floor.

"I want you to crawl to me."

"I'm sorry, what?" the man asks. "You want me to—"

"Crawl." I interrupt. "To me. Now."

I see the hesitation in his eyes, and for once I almost relish the idea of a man denying my request. But just like all the others, he listens. With a grin on his face, he drops to his knees slowly, never breaking eye contact with me.

"You are one freaky lady," he says as he drops to his hands.

He moves slowly as he tries to look sexy while he crawls to me on his hands and knees. When he's close enough, I lift my foot and rest it against his forehead, my heel inches from his lips. I let my thighs open, revealing where I want him next.

He moves forward, my foot falling from his face as he moves closer and begins kissing my inner thighs. I open my legs wider, feeling the heat of his mouth as he moves closer.

A pleasurable sensation coils in my stomach as he begins working me. I run my fingers through his hair and guide him to the correct spot. This man is sloppy, missing the mark repeatedly. Once I have him where I need him, I lay my head back and close my eyes to enjoy the feeling.

Images of Killian flash through my head and startle me. His hot breath against my legs, the way he feels when he enters me. The feeling of him spilling into me as we find our release together. The image of his naked body flickers through my mind as I move against this poor man between my thighs.

Pulling him back, his mouth drenched with my desire—a desire not for him, I realize. Seeing him closer, I realize just how different this man looks from Killian. It disappoints me, and I no longer wish to play the game I started.

I stand, lifting him into the chair and sit back on his lap, facing him. I feel him throbbing against my leg, but he's already leaning his head back and waiting for me to do the work.

Typical.

I bare my fangs and attack, sinking them deep into his neck and holding him down when he fights back. His eyes have gone wide as he realizes the danger he's now in. His blood flows hot and rich down my throat as I drink him in.

A sudden cold chill hits my back as someone yanks the curtain back.

"Are you fucking kidding me?" his voice growls.

Before I can turn around to confirm, his hands are on me, pulling me back and slamming me against the soundproofing on the wall.

"Killian," I gasp.

His grip is tight around my wrist, and the naked man groans in the chair, pale from lack of blood, so close to being drained entirely. My attention snaps back to Killian as he thrusts me harder into the wall.

"Look at me," he says.

I am looking. The panic in his voice, the sweat on his forehead. The way his lips part just enough to invite me in. His heart is pounding against his chest.

"I race over here and you're fucking some random guy?" he says, accusation lacing his tone.

"Don't talk to me like that," I demand, returning his glare. "I didn't ask you to come here. I never said I needed, or wanted your protection."

Killian pulls a knife from his belt and holds the silver-tipped blade under my chin.

I roll my eyes, thinking these empty threats were done. "Gotta go for the heart." I tease.

"What heart?" he says.

I push him off me, tired of this little game. He stumbles back and I move forward to grab him by the throat. I lift him into the air and though he fights my hold, he can't get loose.

"Now you listen to me, Killian Blake," I growl. "We had our fun. You need to go before every vampire in this club smells you."

"You filthy bloodsuckers don't sense me." He smiles.

I loosen my grip and let him fall in front of me. Pushing him against the wall, I step closer, running a hand up his stomach and resting it on his chest.

"Do you know why that is?" I smile.

"Does it matter?" is his reply, staring at my lips. "It lets me kill you and that's all I care about."

My lips brush against his ear as I whisper softly. "You had your chance to kill me and couldn't do it."

For a moment neither of us moves. Killian's fingers trail softly up my inner thigh until he finds me, already desiring his touch. He slips two fingers inside me and I lean against him for support, a small moan escaping me.

"Killian." I gasp. "You're going to get yourself killed."

"You're right." He growls. "I couldn't kill you." He jerks his head to the man I was feeding on. "Because you're mine. Only mine. Mine to kill...mine to..."

He quickens his pace, curling his fingers inward and hitting a spot inside me that makes me gasp out a noise from somewhere deep in my throat. I want to bite him so badly, to mark him as mine but also to feed on him, to taste his blood on my tongue as he finishes me.

"Do it," he says, as if reading my mind.

I sink my fangs into his neck, savoring the vibration of his gasp as I feed on him. His fingers go deeper and deeper with every thrust. I breathe heavily through my nose as I continue drinking from him. I don't drain him like any other kill—I let the blood come out slowly, savoring the taste of him on my tongue.

The overstimulation is becoming too much. His fingers are rubbing against my most sensitive area, and I'm quickly approaching the peak of my satisfaction. I pull back, licking his bite marks so they heal. The warmth of my tongue pulls a satisfying groan out of him.

"You can kill me and be a hero to your people." Killian's voice is deep, the vibration of his words sending chills down to my core. "Or you can come for me like the good little queen you are."

"Fuck," I gasp, unable to resist anymore.

My core heats with pleasure as he continues sliding his fingers in and out of me. I kiss him deeply when he pulls out and fixes my dress. He brings his fingers to his mouth and sucks them in, breathing in my scent as he licks his fingers clean.

"They're coming for you." He says suddenly. "Hunters are gathering, and they plan to end your entire bloodline, Sera."

"I don't fear hunters." I breathe, still focused on his lips.

"They will kill you."

"They will try."

He pushes me again, harder this time, leaving his fists balled on my chest, the silver-tipped knife in his grip.

"Why are you so hardheaded? I'm just trying to—"

His words are cut short when my general, Vaelyn, bursts in and sees Killian's knife to my chest. He has Killian lifted into the air, his grip around his throat and his other hand holding Killian's wrist to stop him from bringing the blade down.

"Vaelyn no!" I command.

"You don't belong here, hunter." Vaelyn says, baring his fangs.

"I said knock it off! Drop the human, he isn't a threat to us." I try again.

"He is a hunter and he has threatened my queen." Vaelyn growls.

Everything happens too fast for even me to follow. Killian drops the knife, twisting to catch it in his free hand, and thrusts it up in a powerful plunge directly into Vaelyn's chest.

A scream tears from my throat as I watch one of my best and most loyal generals fade into ash, particles floating in the dim light like snow. Rage boils to the surface as I watch Killian stand and dust himself off, sheathing his knife.

"What did you just do!" I yell.

"Killed a vampire who was set on killing me." He says, with no regret in his voice.

"I was managing it!" I say. "You couldn't wait five fucking seconds for me to handle my own man?"

Killian stands tall, proud, as he steps closer to me. My fingers twitch with the desire to rip his throat out.

"I'm a hunter." He says calmly. "I may not want to kill you, but as I keep telling you—it's who I am, it's what I do."

I stare down at the ash still falling to the floor and then back at Killian. He's right—he was being threatened. Vaelyn did want to leave my court as well, so really the betrayal had been from him.

Killian had simply done me the favor of ridding me of someone who showed no more loyalty to me. Though he did just storm in here and protect me. This is all too much to process while Killian stands in front of me. Marcella will surely begin to get curious about my absence.

I stick my hand out. "Give me your knife," I say, leaving no room for argument.

Without questioning me, he hands me the knife he used and I walk over to the now-dead man slumped in the chair. I force his fingers closed around the hilt of the knife and turn to face Killian.

"You need to leave," I say.

"Come with me," he says back, stepping closer.

I back up, raising a hand to stop him.

"I am the Crimson Queen, Killian. I won't avoid a fight, and I don't need help from a hunter bred to kill me."

"Sera, please," Killian begs.

"Go. Now."

He hesitates, staring into my eyes with a desire I haven't seen in anyone since my first love. Saying nothing else, Killian turns and runs from the private room. I watch him head for the back door that will lead him to the alley when the curtain falls back in place.

Leaving me alone with my cold meal and dead general. A hollow ache in my chest that feels dangerously like regret. Not for letting Killian go, or not avenging my general's death. But for not following him, here and now.

I press my hand to the wall and steady myself as the weight of the moment crashes down. He warned me. He risked everything—his mission, his team, his life—to warn me. And I sent him away because I'm a queen. Because I have a duty to my people and because letting him in any further would destroy everything I'd built over the centuries.

But as I stare at the ash on the floor, particles settling like grave dust, I can't shake the feeling that I'd just made the worst mistake of my immortal life. What good is an empire if you're ruling it alone?

19

Killian

Hunters have gathered by the hundreds in the old abandoned hospital uptown. Eli and Helen think I've gone crazy after I spend the entire day talking them out of an all-out attack on the nightclub. Tommy returns from his shift watching the club and tells us that the vampires have cleared out, and that's the only reason we drop the idea of attacking.

Instead we focus our efforts on the information we got about a gathering at the warehouse across town. All four queens will be there, as well as their generals. We spend our days at the hospital going over mission details, listening to reports of vampire movements to help figure out our next move. The hospital smells of dust and decay, old blood stains still marking the floors despite our attempts to clean them.

It's been two days since I found Sera with another man in her club. Eleven messages remain unread. Sera is clearly ignoring me, and I'm sure me killing her general didn't help any.

I spend my nights in the bar keeping myself busy so I don't think of her. It isn't working. Between each drink I make, every order I take, and each table I wipe off, I still look for her in the crowd. After

I close the bar and go upstairs, I still imagine her waiting for me in my bed.

I know these are crazy thoughts to have. Learning how to hunt vampires was my upbringing. I can clear an entire pack without raising any suspicion. So why is it that the very moment the person I've trained my life for shows her face...I hesitate.

Even now, when I think about her, my blood boils with the desire to kill her, but something deeper refuses. It's frustrating to be constantly at odds with myself.

"Killian." Helen says, pulling me from my thoughts. "What do you think?"

"Of?"

She rolls her eyes at me, annoyed with my distracted mind lately. "We're moving on the warehouse."

I look at the map spread out on the counter, edges curling with age, marked with red circles and arrows. If the four courts are really gathering, it will be the perfect opportunity for us to end the war before it starts. We have the upper hand here, and it's time to put her out of my mind and think like a hunter again. Maybe I'll get lucky and someone else will make the killing blow.

"I like it," I say. "It's our chance to get the true queen and end this nightmare."

"He's back!" Eli laughs, slapping my shoulder hard enough to sting.

Tommy and Bri are giving me smiles of admiration for my sudden declaration of going to war. But Helen sits back in her chair and watches me with curious eyes. She's smiling, but something in the way she looks at me makes me feel exposed, like she can see right through me.

"If we're done here," I say, standing. "I'm heading to the bar to begin inventory."

"Need any help?" Helen asks.

I look at her cautiously. "You want to help me with the bar?"

"I don't want you to be alone while there are so many vampires out to kill us," she says.

"I'll be fine," I say. "I want to be alone."

The bar is quiet. I flip on the jukebox and dance to the beat of the music as I write down my inventory, meticulously cataloging each bottle of liquor and each box of food in the freezer. The frigid air bites at my skin when I step into the freezer, my breath fogging in the artificial chill. When I step out, I hear the floorboards overhead creak under the weight of someone walking.

I set down the clipboard, open the compartment under the counter, and pull a machete and pistol out. I slowly make my way up the stairs, checking corners before fully turning and keeping an eye behind me in case anyone wants to sneak up.

When I reach the top of the stairs, I move through my living room and pause when I hear another creak in the floorboards, coming from the bedroom. I make my way cautiously across the room, leaning my head on the door and listening for the sounds of movement.

Holding my gun against the door, I push it open and charge in.

A hand shoots out, grabs my gun before I can fire. They pull it from my grip and throw it across the room. I bring my machete up, swinging at my attacker. I bury the blade into the shoulder of whoever is in my room. A loud yelp of pain follows and I freeze.

"Sera!" I gasp. "What are you—"

She pushes me away and pulls the blade out of her shoulder, blood staining her dress before the wound heals. "What is with you stabbing me!" She yells.

She rolls her shoulder as the wound knits together, flesh closing like it was never broken. Her eyes are full of rage as she tosses the machete aside. Pulling out the knife I left with her at the club, she tosses it to me.

"I was returning your damn knife, hunter." she says.

"My knife?" I ask. "Sera, where have you been? I've been messaging you!"

She crosses her arms. She's wearing a black dress with a ruby red pattern stenciled on it, and a slit in the leg that runs up her thigh. It allows her to move freely and I stare at her, taking in every inch as she stands there. Finally, she huffs and relaxes her arms.

"I wanted to come to you that night," she admits.

I take a step closer. "Then why didn't you?"

"Because you're a hunter!" she yells. "You are *the* vampire hunter. You are more dangerous to me than any other hunter on this planet. You are my enemy, Killian."

"I would never hurt you." I say, shocked at how easy it is to finally say it aloud.

"I'm the queen of the Crimson Court, Killian," she says. "My loyalty is to my people."

"And I would never hurt you," I say again.

She holds my gaze a little longer before taking another step closer.

"I'm here to kill you."

I smile. "No. You aren't."

I don't know what gives me so much confidence to say this, but something tells me I'm right. Sera and I are destined to kill one another, and yet even after multiple attempts, neither of us could do it. I knew with confidence that just like I wouldn't kill Sera, she won't kill me.

She holds my gaze for a moment too long before looking away. "But I should. You have a duty to hunt and kill me. This isn't a game, Killian."

I shrug, taking my shirt off. "It sure feels like one to me. I'm done pretending I want to actually hurt you. So if you aren't going to kill me, and you don't want to tell me why you're actually here...there's the door."

Silence follows me as I pick up the knife I used in the club, I brush the silver tip with trembling fingers before setting it on my dresser.

Sera finally lets out a defeated sigh. "I'm not going to kill you."

"I know," I say. "So, would you like to leave now? Or after we shower?"

"Awfully bold of you," she says from behind me.

I shrug again, indifferent. "I'm taking a shower and then taking a nap." I close the bathroom door and finish undressing. As I turn the water on and wait for it to heat, steam beginning to fog the mirror, I notice my hunter blood has left me. I'm surprised because I was sure she would have stayed.

Maybe I read the room wrong. Maybe it's for the best. Tomorrow is going to be hard enough without mixing in my personal emotions. Better to leave the feelings here above the bar, for good.

Stepping into the water, I let the heat wash the smell of her from my skin—vanilla and smoke, blood, and something uniquely her. I grab my soap and begin rubbing small circles across my chest when I feel the pressure change in the bathroom. I smile to myself as Sera opens the foggy glass door and steps in with me.

"Shut up." She whispers, trying to hide her own smile.

I grab her waist and pull her into the water with me, kissing her deeply under the heat of the shower. I feel her tongue slip into my mouth as I begin washing her body. This feels right—not like I'm kissing the enemy or showering with a vampire, but like I'm having an intimate moment with someone I care about. Someone who deserves to be taken care of.

"The hunters are going to be slaughtered tomorrow." She says, still so close that our lips are touching.

"Your vampires are going to be slaughtered," I say back, kissing her again. "You need to stay out of that warehouse."

She steps back, keeping her arms wrapped around my waist. "You know I can't do that, Killian."

"You're a stubborn woman." I grab the shampoo bottle.

Sera laughs, taking the bottle from me and pouring a glob into her hands, turning me around. "I'm the queen of vampires. Obviously I'm stubborn."

She begins massaging the soap into my hair. The feeling of her nails on my scalp feels heavenly. I feel chills going down my arms at the simple pleasure of someone taking care of me. It makes me realize just how touch-deprived I've been.

I turn around, rinsing the soap out of my hair and eyes. Blinking the water free, I grab the shampoo. Sera's hand shoots out, stopping me.

"It's not a hair washing day," she says.

What the fuck does that even mean?

I notice her hair in a tight bun, still dry. Somehow she kept her hair out of the water while we kissed.

"What?" I ask.

She reaches around me and turns the water off. "You need more women in your life." Sera hesitates for a second before quickly adding, "platonic women."

Smiling, I shake my head and grab the extra towel I keep in the cabinet above the toilet and hand it to her. She looks at me like I just spit on her, and something in me tells me she'd like it if I did. I just laugh and begin drying off.

"Sorry, your majesty. We don't all live a life of luxury in penthouses and five-star accommodations."

She grins, drying herself off before dropping the towel and walking past me, deliberately swinging her hips as she does. Shaking my head, I drop my towel and follow her to the bedroom.

"You got your wish," Sera says. "We showered together."

"Sure did," I say.

Her eyes are burning into me, and I can feel my desire radiating off my skin. The air around us is charged with the tension building, set to explode.

"I guess I should go now." Her eyes on my lips. "I have a war to prepare for. Hunters to kill."

"Yes," I say absently. "And I have a cold-hearted vampire queen to kill. Humanity to save."

We stare at each other in silence, her eyes locked onto mine as the air thickens in anticipation. Finally, like a storm cloud releasing its heavy rains, the tension breaks when I lunge at her and together we fall into bed, limbs tangling as our lips find one another in fiery desire.

My hands trail down her hips, pushing apart her thighs and sliding two fingers over her entrance. I feel her hand wrap around me, tugging in the same slow rhythm that I rub her with. My tongue slides into her mouth and finds hers eagerly waiting for me.

"Sera," I breathe between kisses. "You are so beautiful."

I kiss down her chin to her neck, finally finding her collarbone. She pushes me off, getting on top of me as she kisses me deeply. I see the same heat in her eyes that I saw at the club and it ignites something in me.

"I never got to taste you." She breathes against my chest, kissing a trail down my body. When she reaches my nipple she licks her tongue across it. The sensation brings an unfamiliar, but amazing, feeling that shoots down my spine.

"Because I want to make sure you're thoroughly taken care of." I manage between my own heavy breaths.

Her breath is hot against my skin as she moves lower. Her kisses finally reach me, and I find myself gripping the sheets while I wait in anticipation.

"My turn." She smiles against my cock. I feel her lips brush against the underside of me. Then her tongue is running up the length of me until she reaches my head. I feel her thumb brush the precum building on my throbbing tip before she takes me completely into her mouth.

"Oh, fuck." I can't help but moan. "Sera." I gasp. "Fuckfuck-fuck."

I fight against the urge to thrust my hips up, wanting her to do whatever will make her the most happy. Her fingers thread through mine and I loosen my grip on the sheets and hold her hand as she takes me deeper into her throat.

"You need to stop." I gasp. "Sera. I'm going to come."

She pulls off and laughs as she climbs up my body, straddling my hips and grinding against my rock-hard soaking-wet cock. My hands trail up her hips and I find my hold on her and rock her back and forth. She adjusts herself, lining up on the tip and slides down my length with a shaking breath.

"Fuuuuckillian," she slurs her words as she loses herself in the pleasure of it all.

I can't help the smile that spreads across my face. She begins to bounce on my lap. I watch her breasts bounce perfectly to the rhythm we're moving in and I work my hands up her body and take them into my hands, pinching her nipples softly in my fingers and rolling gently. She throws her head back and screams out a moan.

"You are so fucking beautiful, Sera." I tell her, meaning every word. "You take me so well."

Her mouth is open in a silent scream as she smiles down at me. "Say that again."

I lift her off me, holding her weight so that I can thrust harder and deeper into her. "You were made for my cock. You take me perfectly."

I quicken my pace, trying to match my speeding heartrate as I chase after my orgasm. I'm on the edge of finishing but I want to wait for her to finish first. The sounds of our bodies together echo in time with our breathing—a melody no jukebox could ever play so beautifully.

She collapses onto my chest, thighs shaking, tightening around me as the heat of her release drives me mad with desire. I feel the mess we're making together leaking down my thighs but I keep thrusting into her.

"I'm...so...close..." I breathe.

Her fingers find my hair and pull, grabbing onto any leverage she can find as she breathes heavily onto my chest. Her hot breath only serving to give me that final push over the edge.

"Do it, little hunter." She moans and I feel her smile. "Come for your queen. Come in your queen."

I don't even get the chance to argue with her about not being my queen before I'm growling out in satisfaction. I stop holding her weight off me and let her crash down, taking me fully as I fill her with every hot pulse of my finish. My legs are shaking and I'm slightly aware of my nails raking down her arms.

I turn my head to find her arm next to my head—she's supporting herself as she leans on my chest. I bite her wrist, licking, sucking, and grinding my teeth through the rest of my finish. Sera falls off me, her arms resting on my chest, sweat-drenched hair spilling over her face. She breathes through the strands, laughing when I roll to my side and brush it behind her ear. Her face is flushed and her cheeks rosy red.

"I'm sorry I bit you." I chuckle.

She shakes her head, still trying to catch her breath. "It was hot. Fuck, it was all so hot."

We lie like this together, limbs tangled in a mess, in silence for what feels like forever and not long enough all at once. I run a gentle finger down her cheek and she startles back awake. She'd been falling asleep in my arms, but now she's smiling at me with sex-drunk eyes.

She scoots closer, burying her head into my chest. "Sera..." I start.

"Please don't ruin this moment," she says.

I smile, but need to try one last time to convince her not to go to the warehouse. "Don't go." I beg, running my fingers down her back.

She sits up suddenly, anger back in her expression. "What would you have me do, Killian? Turn my back on my people? Send them into a slaughter while I run away with a hunter?"

I sit up with her. "Are you not the happiest you've ever been right now? In this bedroom with me?"

She looks at me, and I see the struggle she's having between her two worlds. I can see the war in her mind playing out. Finally, she picks her side and swings the metaphorical dagger across my throat.

"You're just a hunter, Killian." She growls, standing and walking to her dress. "You're fun, and you're a distraction. I feed on hunters after using them for my own needs, so consider yourself lucky that I'm sparing you today."

"Why are you pretending this—"

"Pretending?" she cuts me off. "You really think I would fall in love with a hunter? One who has caused the deaths of so many of my people? One who just killed my most trusted general?"

She pulls the last strap of her dress onto her shoulder and slips back into her heels. She turns for the bedroom door and her hand pauses on the handle.

"Sera..." I try one last time. "...please don't go. Fine, we can't be together. Fine, you'll never want me the way I want you...but please don't go...not today. Spend the day with me. Let me convince you that this can work. Please...Seraphine."

There's a silence that hangs over the room and a heavy weight that presses down on my chest as I wait for her next words.

"If you're at the warehouse tomorrow, you will die with the rest of the hunters." Is her response. "War is coming. And there can only be one of us walking away."

Before I can say anything, she's gone. I'm left in the bed, staring at the open door and the ghost of her still in my sheets. I run my fingers gently across the indent still in my pillow from her head.

Then something shifts inside me.

Maybe it's the hunter gene fading again, or maybe it's her words echoing in my head. But my chest cracks apart and hardens into something new.

She made her choice. She chose her crown over me. Now it's my turn to choose.

I stand, pulling on my clothes with mechanical precision. Each button, each lace feels like armor going back on. The man who held her, who begged her to stay, is being buried beneath the hunter I've been trained to be.

If Seraphine wants a war, she'll have it.

And she's right. Only one of us can walk away.

20
Seraphine

I cross the city in a blur of movement that no human eye could follow. My chest aches with a desire to stop running, turn around and go back to him. Throw myself into his arms and hide away for the rest of the day. I hate myself for saying what I did to him, but the truth is tomorrow our people go to war and only one side can walk away victorious.

I reach my room and begin stripping off my clothes. I go to the bathroom sink and splash cold water in my face in hopes to clear my mind of him. My room smells faintly of polished wood and expensive soap—lavender and something citrus-clean that does nothing to erase the scent of him still clinging to my skin. I look around at the freshly made bed, perfectly folded towels, and my closet full of dresses and other clothes that have been organized for me.

I have everything I could ever want for my life, a thousand years of building my court into something I'm truly proud of. I have thousands of vampires who are loyal to me and even my sisters and I have grown back to being closer, on the surface at least.

So then why do I still feel like I'm missing something? Deciding it might be best to work out some of this mess in my mind, I get dressed in some leggings and a tank top and make my way to the door. When I open it, I'm met with General Casen standing stoic as ever, his hands behind his back.

He takes a quick step back. "My Queen. I was just about to knock."

"I was about to go spar. Care to join?"

Casen's lips curve into a smile, but the look in his eyes is sharp. "I would be honored. But I came only to inform you that the warehouse ambush is being moved to tonight."

I stare at him, refusing to let the panic and worry show in my face. Not for me or my people, but for the stubborn hunter who I know is walking into a death trap.

"What's the point of an ambush if we move the date of our 'meeting' time?" I ask.

"Rowena and Morgana are tired of waiting." Casen explains. "Rowena has told her hunter pet to attack tonight so they can be done with this and move on from the city."

I can't help the curious eyebrow lifting. We were just discussing plans to build a combined court here for mutual meetings and now they want to get out of here? Something isn't sitting right about this change of plans, but I can't let my sisters see my confusion. I fix my face into one with no expression.

"Ready the men then. I'll be down shortly to join my sisters."

Casen nods and turns to leave. I close the door, already stripping out of my clothes in order to change to my battle armor. I don't even realize I have my phone in my hand until I'm pulling up the Temptr app and messaging Killian.

Me: *I'm sorry.*

His reply takes a minute, and instead of relief that he actually answered me all I feel is anger and frustration.

Killian: *You made your choice, Vampire. This ends tonight.*

Me: *You stupid hunter. You are walking into a trap set by my sisters! She's working with one of your hunters.*

Killian: *And this is your problem, how? You made yourself very clear when you left here.*

I nearly snap my phone in two.

Me: *You are a fool. A stubborn human fool!*

Killian: *I'm not afraid of your kind. And these twisted feelings I have for you won't stop me from killing you and your sisters.*

I read his message twice, unable to help the smile playing on my lips. I bite my lower lip and respond.

Me: *I wish things were different. I wish I could be with you, Killian. Honest.*

Killian: *Duty Above Desire.*

My nails dig into the phone's case, the material cracking beneath my grip. He's spouting his hunter motto to me in order to deflect, but I can't blame him after what I said to him earlier.

Stupid, stupid human. Idiot. Brave, maddening fool. He's going to get himself killed. I slide my phone back into my pocket, grab my weapons and steel myself. As I dress in my armor, my mind is running through my options of how tonight could go and how I could possibly save the crazy fool's life without my sisters finding out.

The power in his blood started as the reason I wanted him left alive. But as I tighten the last strap in my crimson armor, even I have to admit it's become more than just how I can use him to benefit my court. I want him alive because he makes me feel more myself than I have felt in many, many centuries.

And it might be time to risk it all to ensure I get what I want.

I step out of the hotel lobby into the night air, and there are my sisters, armored and waiting.

Rowena stands like a shadow given shape, her black leather combat gear fitting close to her body, every seam designed for speed and silence. Across her shoulders, segmented plates flare outward like ghostly wings, each piece catching the light in a sheen that makes them appear half-smoke, half-steel. Holsters line her thighs and hips, knives and short blades glinting at the ready—a walking arsenal disguised in elegance.

Beside her, Morgana looks carved from winter itself. Her armor mirrors Rowena's form-fitting style, but where Rowena's whispers of shadow, Morgana's gleams like frozen death. Blue-black leather hugs her frame, her shoulder guards jutting in jagged, crystalline points like shards of living ice ready to pierce. Even the faintest movement shimmers cold light across the edges, as if frost crawls with her wherever she moves.

Amara, ever the bold one, wears white into battle. Her sleeveless leather top gleams like ivory, stark against the darkness of the night. No heavy plating covers her arms. Instead, pale, bone-like ridges curve up her collar and spread across her shoulders in a pattern that looks both delicate and lethal. Where our sisters embody shadow and ice, Amara is the pale fire before the kill—unyielding, blinding, merciless.

And then there is me. Crimson from crown to heel, I step forward in my blood-red leathers, every inch designed to command. Rubies studded in my chest piece catch the stray light of the streetlamps and throw it back in shards of fire, in a pattern that resembles fresh blood dripping from my throat. My shoulder guards layer thick, designed for both protection and intimidation. I designed my pants for agility, and included hidden compartments in the pattern, each of which conceals a blade, a stake, or something sharper. I've braided my hair back tight, winding it into a tight crown.

We look like death given form—royal, ruthless, terrible to behold. Centuries of battle have carved us into weapons sharper than any steel we carry. The night itself seems to step back as we stand together, four queens forged in endless war.

I give a simple nod, the signal that binds us, though I keep my face carved from stone. Inside, the fire of anticipation curls hot in my chest. Hunters have come to the city, arrogant enough to think they might strike first. With the whispers of our human pawns guiding them straight into our jaws, they will not leave tonight alive.

The warehouse reeks of rust and stale oil, the sour stench pressing at my temples until it pulses like a headache. Moonlight spills through shattered windows, broken beams of silver striping the concrete floor. Dust drifts in the stagnant air, stirred only by the scrape of boots and the hiss of blades being drawn.

The hunters are close. I can feel them in every heartbeat, every breath, every gene in their blood straining awake at the scent of us.

The warehouse doors open, iron screaming against the hinges as they file in. Hundreds of them, armed and grim, their faces pale in the moonlight. They think themselves predators, but they are lambs walking into the slaughter we have set for them.

I can't help but compare this feeling to the first time we faced this group of hunters—at the hospital when we overwhelmed them with our numbers and could have, should have, ended them at once. We wait until the last one crosses the threshold.

Then I watch as the shadows come alive.

My sisters and I surge forward, our courts at our heels, fangs flashing, blades ready. To human eyes, it would have looked like a vanishing act—here one moment, gone the next. But these aren't ordinary humans.

Hunter's blood ignites, sharpening their reflexes to match our own. Steel clashes against steel, sparks flying, the sound of battle ricocheting off the cavernous walls. Screams, snarls, the wet crunch of bone—chaos painted in red.

Rowena darts through the melee, knives carving arcs of light before she sinks her fangs into a throat. Morgana strikes like an avalanche, each blow shattering hunters as though they are brittle twigs. Amara is ghost-white fire, merciless, precise, her claws tearing through flesh and armor alike.

I wade through with purpose. Every strike I deal is precise, every death a promise. My crimson leathers gleam in the dim light, jewels flashing like embers, blades cutting through hunter after hunter. The air grows thick with blood, copper sharp on my tongue.

That's when I see him.

Killian.

He fights with a reckless abandon that infuriates me. He is brutal, stubborn, and worst of all—relentless. His blade carves a vampire to ash, the dust spiraling around him like smoke in the moonlight. His hair is damp with sweat, his jaw set, and his eyes fierce.

And he's still too slow.

Darren, Amara's favored general—a butcher centuries in the making—is behind him, axe already raised. The weight of the blow will split him in half before he even turns.

My breath catches.

There's a moment where time stands still as I watch Darren bring down his axe. I should let it happen. His death will end this dangerous game I've been playing with him. One mortal life snuffed out, and the chains binding me to him will be broken. But as Darren's blade inches closer and closer, I realize I'm moving before my mind catches up with the decision.

I fling the drained hunter I had in my hands away and cross the floor in a blur. My hand locks around Darren's wrist, twisting sharply.

"No," I hiss, my voice feral and unrecognizable to me.

Darren's eyes flash, confusion sparking into fury as I seize his throat. I feel his pulse hammering against my palm, and with my free hand I yank a knife straight from Killian's belt and drive it straight into Darren's chest.

The general gasps, body locking as the ash consumes him from the inside. In moments he is nothing but ash collapsing at my feet. When the air clears, Rowena's grin gleams like a blade of triumph—but not for me. Amara's face is worse. Betrayal burns in her eyes, and hatred is etched so deep that it can never be undone.

The fight rages on around us, but I feel the shift. My sisters saw, my generals saw, and the hunters saw me save Killian Blake's life.

I killed one of my own...for him.

Killian spins, blood streaking his cheek, breath ragged. "What the hell was that?" he snaps, voice sharp with disbelief.

I have no answer.

The battle presses on and I keep him in my orbit, protecting him whether I want to or not. My sisters' fury presses in on me. And then I see it.

Amara.

Her white armor gleams in the chaos, trapping Killian against the warehouse wall. I try to move, but Rowena and Morgana bar my path.

"Not this time, sister." Rowena smirks, her hand clasping down on my shoulder like iron.

"You made your choice." Morgana says coldly. "And chose a human once again, history repeating itself...Now watch him die."

They part just enough for me to see Amara pin him, claws raised high. Killian ducks at the last second, her talons screeching against the steel wall, sparks flying. He twists, shoving her back, and in one fluid motion draws a blade from beneath his coat.

He drives it deep between the bone plating of her armor. The sound that leaves her throat freezes the entire warehouse—a gasp, ragged and furious, as ash devours her from the wound outward.

Amara, Queen of the Ivory Court, collapses into nothing.

The silence that follows is total. Then the chain reaction—the one we have spent our entire lives trying to hide from the hunters, the truth of what happens when a queen dies.

One by one, every vampire bound to her line convulses, ash pouring from their eyes, their mouths, their skin. They crumble in waves, their centuries of existence erased in seconds. The floor is carpeted in ash, the air thick with the death of an empire.

I stand rooted, my chest heaving, my mind reeling. Amara is gone. Her court is gone. My sister's eyes are knives in the dark.

Even so, it's not finished.

A hunter's arm snakes around my throat, dragging me backward. Cold steel kisses my ribs. I haven't even raised a hand to fight back—shock has stolen my body.

"It's time you monsters left this world for good." He spits.

"Eli!" Killian's voice cracks across the room. "No! Not her!"

He sneers at him. "Yes, her! The fact that you're defending her proves it. Tonight, she dies. Tonight, they all die."

He lifts the blade and I close my eyes. I know I could twist out of the man's grip and slice his belly open before he could react. I know I should feel terrified at the thought of my life ending so brutally and publicly like Amara's. But all I feel is...empty.

Empty because of the loss of my sister. Empty with the knowledge that I'll never get the chance to be with Killian. A thousand years of life, wasted with ruling and gaining power. Power that, in this moment, feels so minimal and useless. In the span of seconds it takes for Eli to lower his blade into my chest I imagine a thousand lifetimes with Killian at my side.

I imagine how happy I could be if he were to join me in my court and rule at my side. Would he even want that? I imagine he would, and I imagine he would rule with mercy and grace as a true king should, not with tyranny. I'm tired of all the violence my sisters and I have done, and it would be nice to rule next to someone where we could build something more than just war and death. I inhale for a final time, a smile on my lips as I imagine Killian and I standing in front of our empire, ruling together.

A gunshot rings out, snapping me from my final dreams with Killian.

Killian's gun is pointed at me, but the shot wasn't meant for me. The bullet slams into Eli's sword and knocks it off course with a sharp clang. He charges, tossing the weapons aside and tackles Eli to the ground. They struggle, Killian's knife flashing, Eli's blade straining against him.

"Run!" he roars. Not at Eli.

At me.

For one heartbeat I freeze, torn between the queen who demands I stand and fight, and the woman who wants to obey him. His eyes meet mine—raw and unguarded—and I see the weight of his choice.

Once again, he chose me. But this time, I chose him back. This warehouse is a grave, the ashes of my sister cling to my skin, her court reduced to dust at my feet. I turn, choking on grief, and flee into the night.

The chains of betrayal drag behind me. Mine against them, theirs against me. And I know that there is no going back.

21

Killian

The weight of what I did hasn't fully landed yet. My body moved before my brain could catch up. I pinned Eli down, knife pressed to his throat, while Sera slipped into the shadows and vanished. My chest heaves, eyes flicking back to the spot where she stood only moments ago.

It's empty now, like a stage after the actress has stormed off, leaving only the echo of her presence. My heart twists, caught between relief and dread. Then I look down at Eli.

His gaze cuts into me, sharp as any blade—full of betrayal, fury, and confusion all tangled together. Only now do I realize my hands are shaking, the knife still hovering at his throat. Gods, what the hell am I doing?

I loosen my grip, shame creeping in like icy water seeping under a door. Slowly, I push myself off and help him up, the weight of my choice pressing harder against my ribs.

Two queens remain, their crowns aren't gold or silver, but something far more terrible—authority etched into the way every vampire in the warehouse bends toward them. They stand untouched at the heart of the chaos, pale faces watching me as if I'm nothing more than an amusing insect crawling across the floor.

I grin and wipe the ash from my shirt, flipping my knife in my hand and masking my unease behind bravado. I meet the two queens' eyes, struggling to find a way out of this mess I created when I chose Sera over my own hunters.

"So..." My voice cracks before I steady it. "There's more than one original queen?"

The words taste like rust. Hunters have always believed there is one true vampire queen, the mother to them all. The end boss. The monster you never really wanted to meet. The world tilts sideways at the thought that there's more than one original monster.

Every vampire's gaze swings toward us. Only a handful of hunters remain, scattered and bloodied. Helen drags herself into view, limping, blood soaking her pant leg, but alive. My eyes scan desperately for Tommy.

Nothing.

"I want his head!" The queen in black's voice cracks like a whip. Her long, skeletal finger stabs toward me. Her tone is ancient and cold, carrying the authority that can make an army obey without thought.

Helen moves faster than thought, pulling her gun and firing three clean shots. The bullets split the air, but the black queen slips past each one with impossible grace. Still, it's enough to break their rhythm, enough to buy us a heartbeat of hesitation from the horde.

"The queen falls, and every vampire they sired falls with them." Bri's smile is grim, teeth clenched as she shoots me a glance that's both question and challenge.

One queen down. Three to go.

I nod, forcing a crooked smile. "Guess we've got work to do."

Everything explodes into motion. We raise our weapons and empty our clips. The warehouse thunders with gunfire, each bullet a desperate prayer. Vampires hurl themselves into the line of fire, flesh turning to ash mid-leap, the air filling again with choking clouds of dust.

My lungs burn with it, throat raw, eyes stinging. I chose not to wear my hunting mask tonight so that Sera could pick me out easily among the army of hunters, but now I regret it.

Eli's shots find the blue queen, piercing her pale skin, but none stick true. They're too shallow, and she's too lucky. Her body shudders but she doesn't fall.

Both queens unleash a sound that splits the air—an unholy shriek that stabs into my skull like knives. I drop to one knee, hands clamped over my ears, vision swimming as the scream rattles my bones. Around us, every surviving vampire scatters, retreating like shadows at sunrise, dragging their queens into the dark.

I lift my head, heart pounding as the hunter gene—that primal instinct in each of us—has gone quiet. I feel empty of purpose as I look around and meet the eyes of each hunter that remains standing.

The fight is over, but the war has just changed. For the first time, I understand: the throne isn't built for one. It's built for many.

"What the fuck, Killian?"

Helen's voice is a growl, low and jagged, the kind that carries more than anger. The words cut deeper than any blade. I lower my head, shame heavy in my chest, throat thick with words that refuse to form. I have no good answer, no defense that won't sound hollow.

I have no regrets about saving Sera. I have no intention of apologizing for that. But as I look at the hunters around me, particularly my own team, I am sorry for ruining the trust my team has established with one another.

"I... I'm sorry," I whisper.

Helen's boots scuff against the ash-coated floor as she takes a step toward me. Her eyes burn, glassy with fury. "We had her! The queen we've hunted our entire fucking lives was in our grasp, and you stopped it! Why?" Her voice cracks at the end, but the hate in her stare is steady and merciless.

My mouth opens before my brain catches up. "Sera—"

"What?" Eli groans nearby, wincing as he tears strips from his ruined shirt and wraps his bleeding arm.

"Her name is Seraphine," I say. "She's the girl I've been seeing these last few weeks."

The silence that follows is brutal.

Eli freezes mid-motion, his bloodied hands still pressing fabric to his wound. I expect to find Helen glaring at me, anger in her expression as she prepares to rip me a new one. However, she's picking at her nails like she does when she's bored. I can't help but give her an annoyed glance—she started this ass-chewing and now she's utterly checked out of it.

Shame burns through me when I meet Bri's angry glare. Her arms are crossed and I can feel the disappointment radiating off of her. I don't regret that I saved Sera, even now as my hunters express their disappointment.

"I didn't know who she was at first." My voice cracks. "I swear I didn't."

Bri's glare is fire. "When did you find out?"

I exhale a long and slow breath. "A few days ago. That date I went on...it was her."

Her jaw drops, and her breath catches as if someone struck her. "You not only let her go... but you slept with the queen of fucking vampires?"

The words echo louder in my skull than in the warehouse. Eli raises his hands, bloodied palms open, trying to ease the storm. "I'm sure he has a reason, babe. His instincts brought us here, uncovered truth we never—"

"I don't have a reason." My voice cuts him off, harsher than I meant. His sigh as he lowers his hands carries more disappointment than words ever could.

I drag a hand through my hair, ash sticking to my fingers. "Not one I can explain, not fully."

I catch Helen looking up from picking at her nails, her lips curve up in a smile but she says nothing.

"Everything in me wanted to kill her. Gods know I tried. But when the moment came... when I had the chance... I just couldn't."

"Killian..." Eli's voice shakes, fury laced with grief. "You are our leader. You let down this entire team. Tonight's fight...everything...was for nothing!"

The words hit me like a punch, but anger rises to meet them.

"Nothing?" I snap, stepping forward. My voice echoes off the warehouse walls, raw and cracked. "We discovered there's more than one original. I killed one of them! I wouldn't exactly call that nothing!"

The hunters around us murmur uncomfortably, some nod with agreement while others scoff their obvious disagreement. Ash crunches under my boots as I turn, rage boiling too hot to stay. I storm toward the double doors, my hands trembling around the hilt of my knife before shoving it back into its sheath.

I pause at the threshold, the ruined warehouse stretching behind me in silence. "If you haven't noticed...one queen is dead. Her entire line of vampires with her. Not to mention the rest we put down tonight and the intel we got. I fucked up, yes. But don't you dare call this a loss."

My voice breaks on the last word, but I don't wait to see their faces. I push through the doors into the early morning light, lungs sucking in cool air sharp with pine and smoke.

My bike waits a few hundred feet away, chrome shimmering in the dawn. I swing onto it, the leather seat cold beneath me, fingers trembling as I jam the key into the ignition.

The engine roars to life beneath me, drowning out the silence of betrayal that still rings in my ears. Gravel sprays from my tires as I tear down the dirt road, the morning air biting cold against my face. Every second I put between me and that warehouse only sharpens the anger boiling inside.

Bri's words, Eli's disappointment, Helen's disinterest after stirring the pot—they all replay in my skull like broken glass grinding together. Can't they see? Can't they fucking see the good that came out of tonight? One queen dead. One entire bloodline gone. We gained more than we lost, but all they see is my failure.

By the time I hit town, the rage has crawled up my throat, hot, and suffocating. I pull into a shadow-drenched alley, kill the engine, and shove the key into my pocket. My boots scuff against the cracked pavement as I pace, fists clenching and unclenching.

Heat burns in my chest like a furnace I can't shut off. I grab my helmet and throw it at the brick wall as hard as my muscles will allow. A scream tears from my chest. I need an outlet. Something to bleed this anger onto. This would be the perfect time to have a vampire show up.

That's when I stop pacing and smile to myself. A thought, sharp and vicious, cuts through my mind as I think of where I can go.

The club.

Leaving my cracked helmet on the ground, I start the bike and pull back onto the main roads with a grin stretching across my face, humorless and feral. By the time I roll up on the club, the hunter gene that lives under my skin pricks to life inside me. That electric hum I can never mistake sizzles as my muscles coil tight, senses sharpen and every shadow shifts. A shiver runs down my spine, goosebumps prickling my arms as anticipation bites into me.

I kill the engine and dismount, rolling my neck until it cracks. My shoulders loosen, my knife heavy and familiar in my palm as I stalk toward the entrance. The moment I cross the threshold, the mask slips. The vampires' glamour peels away like cheap paint, revealing pale and monstrous faces that no human would ever see. Ash still clings to my blade from the warehouse fight, and it feels right.

"Hey!" A burly vampire snarls, pointing at me with claws curling at the ends of his fingers. "You don't belong here!"

"You shouldn't have come back here," I growl.

Two other vampires flank me, sprinting forward.

Good.

The first swing comes fast, but I'm faster. Ducking low, I drive my knife up through the burly bastard's throat. Yanking the blade free, I drive it deep into his heart. His eyes go wide for a heartbeat before his body collapses into ash. Screams erupt from the humans who haven't realized where they'd been drinking. Bodies surge toward the exit in a panicked wave.

I pivot, blade gleaming as I slash at the second one. He dodges, lunging in close, fingers tangling in my shirt as he snarls. The stink of rot and old blood hits me, and my grin spreads wider.

I grab his wrist, twisting until the bones crack with a wet snap, and yank him down. My knee comes up hard, smashing into his forehead with a satisfying crunch. He stumbles back, dazed, his heel skimming the sunlight creeping down the street. His survival instincts scream louder than I could, holding him just shy of the burn.

I don't give him a choice.

I sprint forward, leap, and drive both boots into his chest. The impact sends him reeling backward into the dawn-lit road. He screams—high and short—before his body erupts in fire and ash. The scent of burning flesh hangs in the air as his scream cuts off.

The last vampire freezes, shock painting his twisted features. For half a second, he looks like prey.

I don't wait.

Knife in hand, I sprint. He turns, panicked, trying to flee. I flip the blade, catch the edge, and hurl it. The steel whistles through the air before sinking deep into his back. His body jerks, stumbles, and bursts into a cloud of ash before he even hits the ground.

Silence falls heavy after the chaos, broken only by the distant sound of humans running, their screams fading into the city. I stand in the middle of it, chest heaving, ash coating my boots, the taste of victory bitter on my tongue.

The rage inside me hasn't cooled, not even close. But at least for a moment, it has a direction.

I step back inside the club and shut the doors before locking them. Turning to face the vampires that stand waiting for me, their fangs bared and claws extended. Their eyes are a mixture of red, blue, and black—all three courts present. With a wide smile and emptiness in my eyes, I attack.

The nightclub pulses with the remnants of screams and the metallic tang of blood in the air, bodies strewn across the dance floor like discarded toys. I'd lost myself in the frenzy, my silver blade slicing through vampire flesh with ruthless precision, each strike a release for the rage boiling inside me. My heart hammers in my chest, sweat and blood mixing on my skin as I stand amidst the carnage, breathing hard, the world a blur of red.

My chest heaves as I take a deep breath. Staring at the ash covering the club floor, I sheath my blade and turn for the doors.

I freeze.

Sera is standing with her arms crossed, wearing the same battle armor she was in hours ago at the warehouse. Crimson leather gleaming in the dim light, rubies catching what little illumination remains.

"What are you doing here?" I ask. "I told you to run."

"I'm not leaving without making sure my people are safe, Killian." She replies. "You should know that."

I gesture at the ashes on the floor. "Are you mad?"

Sera laughs, the sound rich and genuine. "I was going to kill them myself. Honestly, I enjoyed watching you fight. It was hot." She winks at me.

I raise a cautious yet curious eyebrow, ignoring the heat that floods my chest when she winks at me.

"Rowena and Morgana sent these men to find me," she explains.

"We should keep running." I say before I can think. "Together."

Sera steps closer, her hand resting gently against my cheek, her skin cool against my overheated face. "I'm not running from my sisters."

"Then what are your plans?" I ask, wrapping my arms around her waist and pulling her close. The heat of her skin warms something in my chest.

"Crimson Court is confused," she answers, brushing her thumbs over my lips. "The generals I brought with me to this city need to be told why I did what I did."

"That you chose me," I breathe.

She leans into me and brushes her lips against mine. "Yes, Killian. That I chose you. But I also choose them too."

I smile at her, hearing her confirm it aloud brings more warmth to my chest. We kiss again, and again. Her hands trail down my body and work my belt loose.

In the corner of my eye, I see the shadows stir. We aren't alone in the club. Sera feels it too as my hunter gene flares to life, electric and sharp. My muscles tighten under her palms as she lifts my shirt up.

I swing around defensively, stepping in front of Sera and pulling my blade as a woman steps out of the shadows with unnatural calm. A smile plays on her lips as she approaches us.

22
Seraphine

From the shadows steps Marcella, my oldest and most trusted friend. She doesn't flinch at the sight of Killian and me embracing, his pants unbuttoned and his shirt halfway off, fabric hanging open to reveal the planes of his chest. Killian doesn't hesitate—he pulls his knife in one fluid motion and lunges forward, the blade catching the dim light.

I grab him, halting his advance with both hands on his arm. "Killian, no!" The words tear from my throat. "She's with me."

Killian stops mid-strike, muscles coiled beneath my grip as he looks back at me. His jaw ticks, a muscle jumping beneath the stubble. He's searching my face for any sign that this is a trap, that I've betrayed him, that everything between us has been a lie. When he finds none, the tension drains from his shoulders. He sheathes his knife with a sharp click and buttons his pants, then extends his hand to me. I take it, unable to hide the smile that tugs at my lips as I step to his side. I'm a little hurt that Killian hesitated to trust me after everything, but he lowered his blade for me.

My heart tugs at the sight of him still positioned in front of me, his body a shield between Marcella and me. His protectiveness isn't an act or some calculated move. It's instinct. It's unthinking and automatic, the way fire rises and water flows. He's ready to fight for me, ready to bleed, and as much as I would love to see him go against one of my strongest Crimson warriors, something in Marcella's eyes gives me pause. A flicker of urgency beneath her calm exterior.

"What is it?" I ask, my voice dropping.

"Rowena and Morgana have called a meeting with the remaining generals. They are planning something."

"Aren't they always?" The sigh escapes me before I can stop it.

"I have clothes for you, my Queen." Marcella's voice is steady as she holds out a folded gown, the red fabric draped across her arms like an offering.

Killian laughs, the sound rough, and disbelieving. "My Queen? You really have these vampires worshipping you."

Marcella's eyes snap to him, her fangs descending in an instant as she spits at his feet. "We serve her, human, because she saved every one of us. Gave us eternal life when we had nothing but death waiting, and has led us for millennia through wars you can't begin to imagine."

Killian raises his hands in mock submission, though his grin remains.

"You will be smart to remember just how old and powerful the Crimson Queen truly is." Marcella adds, each word dripping venom.

I let out a laugh, breaking the building tension that crackles between them like static. "Now, now. I have to go. Will you be okay?"

Killian laughs again, but this time there's an edge to it. "I will be fine. I need to report back at the bar anyway. Not that those bastards deserve anything from me."

Before he can leave, I catch his wrist and pull him back to me, my fingers circling the warm skin. I stare into those beautiful green eyes, wanting nothing more than to stay here in this club with him, to forget thrones and courts and the weight of centuries pressing down on my shoulders. "No more killing my vampires." The demand comes out softer than intended.

His answer is a kiss. Slow at first, almost tender, and then deeper as his hand cups the back of my neck. His tongue slides past my lips, and heat blooms between us again, spreading through my chest like wildfire. I wrap my arms around his waist and pull him close, feeling the hard planes of his body against mine. His arousal presses against my stomach, unmistakable and insistent. When he finally pulls back, his forehead comes to rest against mine, our breath mingling in the small space between us.

"Be safe." The words are barely a whisper.

My chest tightens painfully. For someone who was born to kill me, bred and trained for that singular purpose, his words sound too much like a lover's plea. I step back, the cool air rushing between us, and nod once to acknowledge what he's said. I watch as he runs toward the exit, boots pounding against the floor, the heavy metal door slamming shut behind him with a finality that echoes through the empty club.

Marcella steps forward, placing the dress in my arms. The weight of the fabric grounds me. Her presence is a reminder of who I am, what I was before Killian, what I'll be after. I smile at her, nodding my appreciation.

"Let's go. I don't want to be late to my own coup."

The weight of the throne room presses down on me the moment I shove open the double doors, the wood groaning against my palms. Silence sweeps over the chamber like a blade cutting through whispered conversations. Every crimson general turns as one, their eyes sharp with suspicion, waiting and watching. The air smells of smoke and candle wax, heavy with the metallic tang of too many vampires in one space, the scent thick enough to taste.

Rowena and Morgana sit poised on their thrones beside mine, their gowns trailing like rivers of shadow across the stone. Their faces are masks of marble, beautiful and cold, but their stillness is the calm before a storm.

"How nice of you to join us finally, sister." Rowena's smile curves, though it doesn't reach her eyes. "Tell me, are you done running at the command of your hunter?"

The jab slides into my ribs, sharp and deliberate as any dagger. But I refuse to let her see blood. I cross the chamber with measured grace, each step echoing off the vaulted ceiling, and climb the dais.

I lower myself into my throne, and the velvet cushion meets my back like a reminder of duty, of power, of everything I stand to lose.

"Last night," I say, my voice carrying across the cavernous space, "proved just how dangerous these hunters have become. The boundaries are drawn. It is time we return to our land and defend it."

Morgana's smile curves, all teeth and venom like a serpent preparing to strike. "Bold words, sister. And what of Amara's lands? Because of you, she is dead. Gone to ash and memory."

I snap my gaze toward her, fire scorching through my veins. "Me?"

Rowena answers instead, her voice velvet wrapped over steel. "You had chances to end this hunter long before last night. But you would not. Or could not." She pauses, letting the accusation hang in the air. "Because of your weakness, Amara is ash. Worse still, he exposed what should have never been revealed—that each of us rules a lineage of our own."

"And when he called, you ran." Morgana finishes, rising from her throne like a predator scenting blood on the wind. She takes a single step toward me. "So tell us, Seraphine...why should any general bend the knee to you?"

The chamber breaks into whispers, the sound of rustling cloaks and shifting boots echoing like a tide of doubt threatening to drown me. My eyes sweep the crimson ranks—faces I have forged into soldiers over decades, allies I've bled beside, and even family I've chosen when blood failed me.

"I am your Queen." The words ring out clear and undeniable. "I have placed no one above this court or its duty. Not my sisters. Not the hunters. Not even him."

For a moment, silence holds the room in its grip. Then, one by one, the generals drop to their knees, red capes brushing the marble floor in a wave of loyalty that swells my chest. Relief flares hot and bright—

Until I see the hesitation. The wavering in certain eyes, the fractional delay before they kneel.

Several generals tear their crimson capes from their shoulders and let them fall like discarded skin, the fabric pooling at their feet. The sound of it hitting the ground is louder than thunder in the hushed chamber. They cross the floor, boots clicking against marble, and stand behind my sisters with new allegiance painted stark on their faces.

Betrayal burns hotter than any flame I've ever known. Standing, I step forward, descending one step from the dais as I memorize each face turned against me. Their treachery will not be forgotten. It will be carved into my memory like scars on flesh.

Rowena's slow clap shatters the moment, each impact of her palms deliberate and mocking. She stands, her gown whispering over the steps of the dais as she descends toward me.

"Well, well. It seems your own people don't want you anymore, sister."

Rage boils in my veins, fists curling so tight my nails dig crescents into my palms hard enough to draw blood. I turn back to the remaining generals, trying to steady my voice against the fury threatening to crack it. "We have set the boundaries—"

"About your boundaries," Morgana cuts in, gliding down the steps to flank my other side. Her grin is serpentine, cold-blooded. "Rowena and I no longer align with a queen who can't even choose her own kind over a human hunter."

They strike at once, moving with coordinated precision. Icy hands clamp down on my arms, their fingers like iron manacles holding me fast before I can summon my strength or call on the power thrumming beneath my skin. Two of my own generals—traitors wearing my colors—step forward with cuffs that glow a dim, sickly yellow. I feel the magic buzzing from the shackles before they even touch my skin, a wrongness that makes my teeth ache.

The metal clamps around my wrists with twin clicks that sound like coffin lids closing, and suddenly I am drained of every ounce of strength in my body. My knees buckle.

I drop hard, a grunt of pain forcing past my lips as I fall forward. The impact jars through my bones. I hear my sisters laughing behind me, the sound high and cruel. I mean to stand, to fight, but my legs won't obey. I stumble further down the steps of the dais until I'm lying in a heap on the cold floor, the marble pressing against my cheek.

The generals part down the center of the chamber like a curtain being drawn, and through that divide steps a figure—a man I have seen before, his face familiar in a way that makes my blood run cold. My breath stills in my chest.

"I've seen you." I snarl, trying once again to stand but only managing to lift my head, neck straining with the effort. "You're Killian's uncle."

Tommy smiles down at me, the expression never touching his eyes as he climbs the dais with calculated ease. "I am."

"Where is he, Thomas?" Rowena asks, her voice sharp with command.

"I lost him during the fight." He bows, the gesture practiced and empty. "But I intend to find him, with your permission."

Rowena glares down at me with a smile on her face that twists a knot in my stomach, pulling tighter and tighter until I can barely breathe. She shares a look with Morgana, something passing between them in that glance, and I brace myself for what she's about to say next.

"I have a better idea." Rowena's voice is silk and poison. "Take a group of Sera's generals. End him and bring me his head."

"No!" The word rips from me before I can stop it, raw and desperate. "Tommy, he is your family! You can't!"

Tommy looks at me, no emotion flickering in his eyes. Nothing. Not even a trace of the man who should care about his own blood. Rowena cups his cheeks with both hands and diverts his attention back to her, and I let out an exhausted sigh of defeat, the sound scraping from my throat.

"I will, my Queen." Tommy bows again before turning on his heel and leaving, his footsteps fading into nothing.

Morgana crouches at my side, her fingers wrapping around the shackles at my wrists. She pulls me up so that her lips are brushing against my ear, her breath cold against my skin.

"We don't have to kill you, Seraphine. But if you won't stand with us, then we will cage you until you do."

A wave of armored generals surges forward, hands grabbing at my arms and legs. They drag me through a pair of doors in the back of the ballroom, my heels scraping uselessly against the floor. Down a stairwell that stinks of damp stone and betrayal, the air grows colder with each descending step. There is a prison in the basement of the hotel. My sisters had built a prison, planned this coup, turned my throne into a trap meant for me.

The cell swallows me whole, its iron bars humming with runes carved deep into the metal to sap my strength. They keep me bound in the shackles, leaving me helpless on the cold tile floor, my cheek pressed against the filth. Alone, with only my fury to keep me company in the darkness.

But my thoughts turn to Killian despite everything. He is walking into a trap, blind to the danger. The hunters have turned on him just as my vampires have turned on me. Killian is blinded by his pride for his hunters, his loyalty to people who don't deserve it, and it will be the death of him. Betrayed by his people...and his own family.

The runes carved into the iron bars pulse faintly in the dark, a sickly red glow that crawls over my skin like fire ants, burning without consuming. Every time I try to heal, reaching for the power that has sustained me for centuries, the symbols burn hotter. They leech my strength away, drinking it down like blood. My ribs throb with every shallow breath, each inhale a struggle, the taste of copper thick and cloying on my tongue.

Rowena comes first after what feels like hours, though time has lost all meaning in this place. She crouches before the bars, her shadow stretching long and distorted against the tile. Her fingers are cold, bony, and possessive as she traces the glowing runes as though admiring fine embroidery, her touch almost loving.

"Beautiful, aren't they?" she purrs, her voice a caress.

Then, without warning, her fist shoots through the bars, striking my ribs hard enough to splinter bone. The crack echoes through the cell. Pain lances through me white-hot and blinding, forcing a cough that rattles my entire chest and brings fresh blood to my lips.

"You know..." She whispers, leaning closer so I can see every detail of her cruel smile. "The witch made them for us."

"The witch..." My voice comes out as a rasp, barely recognizable. "...is dead."

Rowena's laugh is soft and poisonous, like silk drawn slowly over a blade. "Oh, is she now? Just as the original hunter bloodline ended?" She tilts her head, watching me with predatory interest.

Her words sink into me like ice water poured over my head, shocking and impossible. For a heartbeat, I forget the pain splintering through my ribs, forget even the bars caging me. If she speaks the truth, then everything I have believed—the balance, the sacrifices, the history carved in blood and bone—is a lie.

My head falls back against the floor, too heavy to hold upright, but my mind is a storm of questions and fury. Rowena leans closer, her eyes glinting with cruel delight as she drinks in my shock. "It seems even the witch has grown weary of her own games. The same games that birthed us, birthed him. Now she wants both of you erased from existence."

I spit blood at her feet, the droplets spattering across her pristine shoes. I force the words past swollen lips. "If I die...we all die."

"Yes." Her smirk widens, feral and satisfied. "There is that." She taps one sharp nail against the glowing runes, listening to the hum as if it were music. "But the witch is clever. She is already finding ways around that little...inconvenience."

She stands with a graceful rustle of silk, brushing imaginary dust from her gown. Then she kicks me square in the stomach without warning. Air tears from my lungs as white-hot pain rips through my body, tearing a strangled sound from my throat. Rowena only smiles at the noise, pleased with herself, then drifts back into the shadows. Her laughter lingers like smoke long after she's gone.

My eyes snap open at the sound of rustling in the cage next to mine, fabric dragging across stone. I crawl to the bars separating us, my palms scraping against grime and dried blood, trying to peer over into the darkness. But it is no use. The sounds of heavy breathing, like someone huffing and puffing with exertion or pain, fills the basement with an unsettling rhythm.

"Hello?" I ask, my voice cracking. "Is someone there?"

No response comes for a long moment, just that labored breathing continuing in the dark. Until the faint sound of laughter begins. It is a dark and wicked laugh, a whisper echoing off the walls that sounds something close to: "Soon, Seraphine. Very soon."

A chill runs down my spine despite the stale warmth of the basement.

I'm not sure how long has passed since I saw Rowena or since I fell asleep from exhaustion. My ribs no longer scream with every breath, the bones knitting back together in the slow way the runes permit. I have a grimy feeling in my mouth like I'm long overdue to brush my teeth, the taste of old blood and neglect coating my tongue.

Morgana emerges from the dark like something summoned, her movements slow and serpentine. Her smile is the kind that promises ruin and enjoys every moment of it.

"Seraphine, Seraphine, Seraphine..." She croons, each repetition dripping with venom and false sweetness. "How you disappoint me."

"You'll get over it." I growl, mustering what defiance I have left.

She paces before me like a predator circling wounded prey, her eyes bright with something ugly and hungry. "Do you remember what it was like before? When we were still human?" Her voice drops, becoming almost wistful. "I wanted to be you. I worshipped you. Every laugh, every step, every smile—you were the sun, and I was only a shadow trailing behind, desperate for your light."

Her hand reaches through the bars, a long finger trailing down the front of my torn dress. The touch makes my skin crawl. Her nail splits the fabric with an effortless flick, exposing pale skin beneath and leaving me more vulnerable.

Then, her worship turns to fury in a heartbeat.

She balls her fist and strikes, again and again, knuckles cracking against my face, my ribs, my jaw. Each impact sends fresh explosions of pain through my skull. Blood fills my mouth until every breath becomes wet and ragged, bubbling past my lips. The runes throb hotter with each blow, eating at the edges of every wound, denying me the relief of healing, and keeping the pain fresh and sharp.

"These marks," Morgana hisses, gesturing at the glowing symbols with something like reverence. "Designed to strip you of your gift. Isn't it exquisite? I can break you, sister, and watch the wounds fester. Watch you rot, powerless and pathetic."

She laughs, the sound sharp and cruel as breaking glass, and with one last contemptuous kick sends dirt scattering into my face. The grit stings my eyes and coats my bloodied lips. Her shadow slides away, leaving me gasping and broken in the glow of the runes.

Alone. Broken. Forgotten.

As she passes the cell next to mine, the one where the dark laughter came from, she kicks at the bars hard enough to make them ring. She spits through them.

"Filthy fucking dog." She growls before fading into the shadows, her footsteps echoing away.

Time bleeds together in the darkness, minutes, hours, or days all bleeding into one another. Until footsteps echo again—measured, deliberate, and familiar in a way that makes my heart leap.

I smile despite the pain as they approach the cage.

Marcella.

She appears at the bars, her eyes gleaming with quiet amusement and something softer beneath. "Seems you've fallen from grace, my Queen."

"How many of my people?" I manage, my throat dry from thirst and hunger.

"All of them." Her answer is flat and unflinching, no attempt to soften the blow.

My heart twists painfully in my chest. "And you?"

Her lips curve faintly, the ghost of a smile. "I recognize only one true queen. We have stood together since the fall of England's king, through wars and plagues and centuries of darkness, and I have no plans to turn on you now."

Relief loosens the tightness in my chest, allowing me to breathe more fully. I wasn't abandoned. Not entirely. Not by everyone who mattered. Marcella unlocks the door, the mechanism clicking open, her dagger slicing through the bindings and breaking each rune with practiced precision. I feel my strength already returning as my bruises fade like watercolors washing away, and the worst of the pain leaves me in a rush that makes me dizzy.

She presses a cup of human blood into my trembling hands, still warm, and I drink greedily. The warmth surges back through my veins like fire, reviving me, making me whole again.

"I've cleared a path." She says softly, watching me with concern. "You've been down here for three days."

Three days. The revelation hits me hard.

I rise steadier now, my legs remembering their strength, gratitude swelling in me until I think I might burst with it. On impulse I embrace her, pulling her close, and she returns it without hesitation. She brushes a strand of matted hair from my face with a sisterly tenderness that almost breaks me.

"Killian?" I ask, my voice barely above a whisper.

"They have just finished plans to capture him. They mean to attack tonight." Marcella gives me a tender smile, sad and knowing. "Go to your hunter."

I nod once, understanding everything she's not saying. Then with a burst of speed that sends my hair whipping behind me, I vanish into the night. Racing through shadows and alleyways, following the pull in my chest that leads me toward Killian. Toward the truth I can no longer deny myself, no matter what it costs.

23

Killian

The wind feels good on my face as I ride my bike through town, the rush of air cutting through the humid evening. Three days since I left Sera in that club and I haven't stopped worrying about her safety since. Every message I've sent has gone unread, the little checkmarks mocking me from my phone screen, and although I feel like I'm starting to go a little crazy, another part of me doesn't give two fucks because her safety means more than my own sanity.

My phone buzzes against my thigh and I pull over to check it.

Tommy: *Hey kid, you going to be at the meeting today?*

Me: *I'm headed there right now. Not that I really should.*

Tommy: *Knock it off, Kil. You made a mistake and have spent every day since making it up to your team. The other hunters are leaving soon so they won't matter in the long run. Keep your head down and it'll get better.*

I read the message once, twice, and a third time. Each passover I roll my eyes harder and harder until I'm practically glaring at the screen. A mistake? If saving the woman I love from being murdered was a mistake, then I really need to rethink my line of work and the company I keep.

Similar thoughts have been plaguing my mind since the warehouse, circling like vultures I can't shake off. My feelings for Sera have become undeniable, a constant presence beneath my skin, and I don't want to feel any other way. I chose her, and she chose me. The nature of my hunter gene demands justice for the humans, screaming in my blood for vengeance. I feel the urge to kill every vampire I could reach, including Sera, especially Sera. In the same breath, the thought of raising a knife to her makes me sick to my stomach, bile rising in my throat.

It's been a couple of sleepless nights to say the least, hours spent staring at the ceiling while my mind wars with itself. But I have decided to take a step back from the hunters, hence why I find myself pulling up to the abandoned hospital to meet with the remaining hunters, to announce my step down.

Approaching the hospital carries a different weight now, the crumbling brick facade looming like a judgment. I feel eyes on me from every window, dark shapes moving behind grimy glass. Walking through the lobby and past the groups of hunters who'd fought beside me, their judgment pours out of them in waves as I pass. Conversations die mid-sentence. Heads turn. Eyes follow.

To them, it doesn't matter that I fought beside them, bled alongside them in a dozen battles. It doesn't matter that I killed an entire nest at the club, bodies piling up under my blade. It doesn't matter that I have a unique gene that gives me an upper hand, making me more lethal than any of them could dream of being. It doesn't matter that an entire line of vampires is dead because of me, their ashes scattered to the wind.

To them, I am the hunter who saved a vampire.

A traitor.

I walk into the room that has been where we've conducted meetings, the familiar space now feeling foreign. A few days ago this room would have been packed with every hunter in town trying to get their two cents in, voices overlapping in heated debate. Now, the room feels less full, emptied by death. Too many hunters were taken out during the fight at the warehouse, their chairs standing vacant like grave markers.

Helen sits at the table in the front of the room, her eyes tracking me as I enter with a smile on her face that doesn't quite reach her eyes. I notice her eyebrows raise slightly, and I can't help but feel she's reading my thoughts, like she sees straight through my skull and knows exactly why I'm here. Eli leans in, his broad shoulders casting a long shadow as he speaks to the room in hushed tones. Bri's pen clicks against her notebook with restless irritation, the sound sharp and repetitive.

Silence falls across the room as I approach the table to confront my team and let them know my choice. I do a quick scan of the faces, noting that Tommy isn't present.

Bri doesn't look up from her notepad, a pissed off expression etched into her features. "Oh look. The vampire lover shows his face."

A ripple of laughter follows, cruel and pointed. My jaw tightens but I force a smile, refusing to let them see the sting. "Okay. I deserve that." No I don't.

"You deserve worse." Someone behind me scoffs, the voice male and familiar.

"Fucking traitor." Another voice, female, yells from the back of the room.

Eli stands, raising his hand before the room of restless hunters can escalate anymore, his palm out like a traffic cop. "What are you doing here, Killian?"

"Where's Tommy?" I ask, ignoring his question entirely.

"No one has seen him since the warehouse." Helen answers with amusement threading through her tone, like she finds something funny in his absence.

I glance at her, trying to figure out why she's acting the way she is. Ever since the warehouse she has been all smiles and giggles, a complete shift from her usual sharp demeanor. I catch her constantly watching me when she thinks I'm not looking, and she's even kept quiet during our meetings, which isn't like Helen at all. Helen never keeps her opinion to herself.

I pull my dagger out of its sheath, the blade sliding free with a whisper of steel. I hold it out in front of me, admiring the intricate design etched into the metal, the leather wrap on the handle worn and formed over time to fit perfectly in my grip. The same knife

I've used to attempt to kill Sera, the edge still sharp enough to split a hair. The same blade that I was given when promoted to leader of my crew, a ceremony that felt like a lifetime ago. The same dagger that now makes my skin crawl when I touch it.

"Killian..." Helen's skeptical tone draws me out of my thoughts, pulling me back to the present.

I set the dagger down on the table in front of Helen, Eli, and Bri with a deliberate clink. The message is simple, unmistakable.

"I'm done."

"Done?" Eli asks, disbelief coloring his voice.

Bri scoffs, her pen finally stopping its incessant clicking. "You're giving up your title as leader for a fucking vampire? A vampire who will be dead in less than twelve hours."

I look at her, trying to decipher the meaning of her words, the specific threat hidden in that timeline. When Helen stands, the chair scraping back, I turn my attention to her. "You aren't stepping down as our leader...are you?"

I shake my head slowly. "I'm stepping away from being a hunter."

Eli slams a balled fist into the table hard enough to make the wood groan. "You can't!"

The whispers and the murmuring around the room as hunters make their judgments does nothing but confirm my decision. This is right. This is what I need to do.

"You fuck one filthy blood sucker and you lose sight of what truly matters?" Bri spits, her words like venom.

I glare at her, holding her angry stare with one of my own. But I refuse to let her bait me into an argument. My mind is made up. Nothing they say will change it.

I turn to leave, boots echoing on the concrete floor.

"She will be dead by morning," Helen says from her chair, the words casual but loaded.

I pause mid-step. Turning to see Eli and Bri smiling at each other, a shared secret passing between them.

"What?"

"We are attacking the Ayrshire Hotel. Ending the remaining three queens once and for all," Eli explains, his voice taking on a proud edge. "We could use our leader at our side when we win this war."

"You can't even look at me without seeing me as a traitor." I laugh, the sound bitter in my throat. "But you want me to join you in a fight against the vampires tonight?"

"You'll be a good distraction for that Crimson Bitch," Bri says simply, her smile cruel, and I have to make a conscious effort not to wrap my fingers around her throat and squeeze.

"Fuck all of you," I say, the words cutting and final.

I'm halfway to my bike again, anger burning hot in my chest, when I feel my phone vibrate. I pull my phone out in a hurry, heart leaping with hope, needing to tell Sera what the plans are and get her out of this town before it's too late.

It's not Sera.

To my utter shock, it's Melissa. The one-night stand who blocked me minutes after our hookup, deleting me from her life without explanation. I tap open her message thread, confusion replacing my urgency.

Melissa: *Hey, so this is awkward…*

I type back as I start my bike, the engine rumbling to life beneath me.

Me: *Hey back.*

Melissa: *I'm just so lonely, and wanted to know if you wanted to hang out? See where things go?*

Me: *I'm headed to the bar to open it. Feel free to come by and hangout.*

I slide the phone back into my pocket and pull on my riding gloves, the leather familiar against my palms. I know what her intentions are, and can read between the lines easily enough, but my thoughts are for someone far more dangerous than a woman who can't even communicate herself. Though I will admit, after Sera has practically gone off the grid for the past three days, I can't help but wonder what that meant for us. What we even are. I could use a human distraction.

No hunters. No vampires. Just fun.

Bad Habits smells of beer-soaked wood and lemon cleaner, the scent hitting me the moment I walk through the door. Donovan is stocking bottles behind the counter with methodical precision, Alex is swearing at the broken jukebox and kicking its side, and the usual pre-opening chaos buzzes around me like white noise. Jumping in without thinking, I start hauling crates from the storage room, wiping tables with quick efficient strokes, fixing bar stools with screws that never quite fit right no matter how many times we replace them.

The mindless, normal work keeps me from thinking too hard about blood and fangs, about choices and consequences. The bell above the door chimes and I don't even need to look to know who it is, the sound distinct and familiar. Though I can't deny the pit that opens up in my stomach when it's not Sera walking through that door.

"Hey Melissa!" I call across the bar. "Pull up a chair."

I check my phone as she makes her way across the bar, heels clicking on the worn floor. Tommy is asking me if I was at the bar. Before I can set my phone down he replies again, the message appearing instantly.

Tommy: *Stay put. Need to see you.*

Melissa is wearing a short, tight skirt and a tank top with no bra, the outfit leaving little to the imagination. The outline of her nipples is obvious under the thin shirt, pressing against the fabric. She takes a seat at the bar, her hand finding my arm as she tugs on me lightly, fingernails brushing my skin.

"I was thinking we could go upstairs? Talk a bit?"

I look at her, then at Donovan and Alex who are both suddenly very interested in their work.

"Hey guys, I'll be back down in five."

Donovan laughs, the sound knowing. "Just five, huh?"

I roll my eyes, but begin to climb the stairs, Melissa right behind me. She falls on the leather couch with a shy smile and the tension between us is awkward, charged with unspoken expectations. My phone vibrates and as I pull it out to check, Melissa clears her throat and distracts me before I see the name of who messaged me.

She had somehow slid past me while I was in the kitchen getting us a drink, moving with surprising stealth. She is now standing in my bedroom doorway, completely naked. Not a stitch of clothing on her body. She crooks her finger at me seductively, urging me to follow her as she turns and goes further into the room, hips swaying deliberately.

I follow her, not to act on what she wants—though my body is begging me to, blood rushing south despite my reservations. I am already trying to find a polite way to turn her down, not in the mood for anyone other than the one person I can't have. The one person who hasn't answered my messages in three days.

She is sitting on the edge of my bed, her legs open in clear invitation, her arms resting behind her for balance. On any other night, the sight would have driven me mad with want. She is completely exposed, offering herself without hesitation. Her breasts are full and ready to be kissed, nipples hardening in the cool air.

"Melissa—"

"We can be quick. I'm so horny, Killian."

I run my hand through my hair, clearing my throat around the words I need to say. "It's just that I'm kind of seeing someone."

She stands up, a wicked smile curving her lips as she walks over to me with predatory grace. "I don't see anyone here, do you?"

She kisses me suddenly, catching me by surprise. Her lips are soft and insistent. Her hands trail down my chest as she drops to her knees and works the button of my pants open with practiced fingers, shimmying them down my thighs.

"Melissa, I'm not interested in doing this."

"You sure look interested." She giggles, her eyes dropping to the evidence contradicting my words. She grabs me in her hand, warm and confident. The warmth of her tongue sends an involuntary moan from me, the sound escaping before I can stop it.

"You sure taste interested." She smiles up at me.

I find my hands running through her hair despite myself as she opens her mouth and takes me deep, the warmth of her wrapping around me as she works me into the back of her throat with practiced ease.

I try not to enjoy it, try to imagine it's Sera instead. I should stop her, and make her leave before it goes any further. But fuck...it feels so good. It's not as if Sera and I are actually together. After all, she is my mortal enemy. I am meant to kill her, and she me.

I did just leave my family for her though. I chose Sera because I love her, not that I will ever tell her that. I know the way I feel though, know it with a certainty that terrifies me, and I definitely have a love for Sera. I feel my hips rocking as I feed my cock deeper into Melissa's throat, chasing the sensation.

Fuck. No. I don't want this. I want Sera.

I grab a fist full of her hair, meaning to pull Melissa off me and make her leave. In a blur of movement, Melissa is no longer in my hands, her warm mouth no longer wrapped around my cock. I open my eyes, not even realizing they were closed, and my heart stops dead in my chest.

Sera has Melissa by the throat, lifting her off the ground effortlessly. Her fangs are sunk deep into her neck, draining the life out of her in seconds as Melissa kicks and scratches uselessly at Sera's arms. The scream never leaves her throat as Sera drains the life from her, drinking deep. I watch, frozen in shock, as life leaves Melissa's eyes, the light dimming until there's nothing left but emptiness.

Sera's rage-filled eyes flick to me next, burning crimson and feral. She throws Melissa's body across the room like a ragdoll, the body landing with a hard thud on the floor, limbs at unnatural angles.

Her fangs are still bared, still covered in Melissa's crimson blood dripping from the points, her chest heaving with a feral rage that makes her look more monster than woman. She stalks toward me like a predator fresh from its kill, her hand reaching out and gripping my throat with bruising force.

It's only when her hand tightens around my neck, cutting off my air, that I feel the hunter gene inside me come to life at the threat of a vampire. The instinct roars through my veins, demanding I fight back, demanding I kill. I make no move to defend myself as Sera pins me against a wall, my pants still undone.

"What. The. Fuck." She hisses. Her breath is hot with rage, smelling of copper and fury.

"It's not—" I start, but the words die on my lips. There is no excuse. No explanation that will make this better.

"You think you can bury yourself in some human and just forget about me? Like I wouldn't find out?" She growls, eyes burning red with betrayal and possession.

Shame sears through me harder than the lack of air from her choking me, hotter than any flame. My voice cracks, raw and desperate. "I wasn't trying to forget you. I was trying to stop her."

She laughs, no amusement behind it, the sound sharp and cutting. "Yes, Killian. It looked like you were putting in a ton of effort to stop her."

"You didn't have to kill the girl!" I argue, anger flaring despite the hand around my throat. "She didn't deserve death."

Her grip loosens suddenly, fingers uncurling. I drop back to the floor and gasp for air, rubbing my throat where her hand left marks. I see something softer in Sera's eyes before anger replaces it again, shuttering the vulnerability.

"You already chose me, Killian." She smiles, but there's no warmth in it.

"I did." I nod, meeting her gaze.

Her eyes darken suddenly, narrowing.

"DO!" I correct, the word coming out forcefully. "I do choose you."

The sound of gunfire erupts downstairs, multiple weapons discharging at once. My attention snaps to the stairs. Pulling my pants up and quickly buttoning them with fumbling fingers, I run to the bedroom door before Sera's hand clasps my shoulder, stopping me cold.

"They're here. Let's go."

"What?" I'm desperate for answers, my mind racing. "You don't get to just kill her and then order—"

Her fangs flash, startling me into silence. "Now!"

"Killian, are you up there?" Tommy's voice calls from down the stairs, familiar and wrong all at once.

My heart starts pounding and I freeze, every muscle locking. "Tommy?"

"Killian, no!" Sera growls, pulling me to the bedroom window as she checks around the alley for a way out, scanning with predatory focus. "He is here to kill you. Let's go."

"What?" I ask again. I'm so stunned at everything happening right now, I'm not sure where to put my focus. "Tommy would never—"

Her snarl cuts me off, animalistic and urgent. In one motion, she wraps me tight against her chest, her arms like steel bands, and launches us through the window. Glass explodes around us in a shower of glittering shards, and the night air bites my skin as she carries me in a blur across the street. My stomach lurches as we slam against the brick of the apartments next to the bar, the impact knocking the air from my lungs.

I cling to her as she scales the wall with inhuman grace, muscles bunching and flexing beneath her skin. My heart tries to rip free of my chest, pounding so hard I can feel it in my throat. I force a look back at my window, shards still falling like rain, catching the streetlight. Tommy steps through the shattered frame, gun raised and ready. Flanking him are two figures in red cloaks, their pale faces twisted in hunger, their eyes burning crimson like hot coals.

No.

I refuse to stitch the truth together, refuse to accept what I'm seeing. My uncle, my brother in arms. The man who raised me after my parents died. Standing shoulder to shoulder with the monsters we hunted, the creatures we swore to destroy.

The vampires argue with him, gesturing wildly, but I can't hear over the ringing in my ears, the roar of betrayal drowning out everything else. Then Tommy lifts his gun and aims straight at me, his face set with determination.

The world stops.

The crack of bullets split the night, sharp and deadly. Muzzle flashes light on his face—hard and determined, not a hint of hesitation. No doubt. No mercy.

Sera dodges with serpentine precision, leaping higher and twisting between shots with impossible speed as the rounds spark against brick, leaving pockmarks in the wall. My body jerks with every pull of the trigger, as if each bullet hits me anyway, tearing holes in everything I thought I knew.

Why, Tommy?

We reach the roof, my feet hitting solid ground again. I stagger back, lungs burning, chest heaving, the weight of what I've seen crashing down like a building collapsing. Sera releases me and straightens, her expression softening for the first time since she appeared.

"Are you okay?"

I nod mechanically. She's asking if I've been shot, checking me for wounds, but my mind is still trying to process the events of the last few minutes. Melissa dead on my floor. Sera covered in her blood. Tommy is trying to kill me.

"Let's go." Sera orders, her voice leaving no room for argument.

Behind us, claws scrape on brick with a sickening rhythm. Red cloaks appear at the roof's edge, vampires hauling themselves onto the rooftop in pursuit, their movements fluid and hungry. I should have been running, should be moving, but my legs won't obey. Everything feels like it's unraveling too fast, the world spinning out of control. Melissa's blood is still sticky in my mind. Sera's hand is still ghosting my throat. Tommy's betrayal cracks something deep inside me, something fundamental and irreparable.

I turn, meeting Sera's crimson gaze. She looks like damnation incarnate—beautiful and terrible, a nightmare and a dream. And some part of me, gods help me, wants her never to let me go.

A gunshot rings out again, but this time closer and sharper. I spin just in time to see Tommy vault onto the rooftop with athletic grace, his gun tracking me, steady and unwavering.

He isn't aiming at Sera. He's aiming at me.

Grabbing Sera's hand, our fingers interlocking, we run. And as we flee into the night, my world burning behind us, I realize the truth with crushing clarity.

Everyone I've ever trusted has betrayed me.

Everyone except the monster I am supposed to kill.

24

Seraphine

Killian and I barely hit the next roof before another volley of shots cracks through the night, the sound sharp and unforgiving. Sparks burst against brick in bright orange flashes, and the sound echoes like thunder between the buildings, bouncing off glass and stone.

I can feel the panic rolling off him in waves, tangible as heat. It shows in the way his every step falters, his breath ragged and uneven, even the confusion eating at his instincts like acid. He's drowning in it all. In the blood still sticky on his hands, the betrayal carving holes in his chest, and the impossible truth of his own family hunting him down like an animal.

Despite that, underneath it all, I can feel his hesitation to follow me. The same hesitation that made me want to rip his throat out for what I found him doing with that human, her mouth on him like she had any right. The scent of her flesh still stings my nose, cloying and wrong.

I shouldn't have killed the girl, and I know it was wrong. It was just another thing added to all the other stuff we were already dealing with tonight. I regret what I did, but right now my focus needs to be on keeping Killian alive.

"We can't keep this up!" Killian shouts, ducking as another bullet whines past his head close enough to feel the wind. "We need to lose them, or fight."

"He's here to kill you, Killian. Not talk." My voice is sharp, cutting, but my grip on his wrist betrays the fear I feel clawing at my ribcage.

"That doesn't change the facts, Seraphine!"

Facts. The word sours in my mouth like spoiled wine. What facts matter when death is breathing down his neck when bullets are singing his name? Still, I see the stubborn fire in him, burning in his eyes despite everything, and know I can't drag him forever. I give a single nod, sharp and reluctant. His idiotic choice will be honored. For now.

We leap across the alley, the gap yawning beneath us for a breathless moment before we land hard on the gravel roof below. Pebbles bite into my palms as we roll, the sharp sting barely registering as we slam into the shadows behind two hulking AC units. Killian's breath comes fast beside me, his knife already in his hand, knuckles white around the hilt like he's holding on for dear life.

Sven leaps first, in a blur of red cloak and claws extended like blades. I meet his strike mid-air, the crack of bone-on-bone reverberating across the rooftop loud enough to wake the dead. Aiden is already there, flanking me with predatory precision, his nails raking across my arm before I twist and carve my own claws down his cheek. Blood sprays hot and crimson, sizzling where it strikes the gravel like acid eating through stone.

Killian twists the hilt of his knife with practiced ease, and it expands into a medium-sized staff, twin blades carving silver arcs that catch in the moonlight like falling stars. Amanda darts for him, faster than any human eye can track, but he expects her movement and catches her wrist mid-swipe, crushing bone with a sickening crack and pushing her back. Her shriek tears through the air, sharp and agonized. He drives his boot into her chest with brutal efficiency, sending her skidding across the rooftop in a shower of gravel.

Gunfire cracks again. Tommy's shots sing like commands, every one aimed at Killian with ruthless precision.

My chest seizes at the sound, knowing he isn't holding back. No mercy. No hesitation.

"Tommy, stop!" Killian roars, barely diving behind the cover of the AC unit as bullets punch holes in the metal.

"Orders are orders." Tommy laughs, the sound cold and devoid of love. "You should know that better than anyone, son."

Killian's jaw ticks, a muscle jumping beneath his skin. "I'm not your fucking son!" He lunges from behind the unit, dual-bladed staff whipping in a storm of silver, forcing Tommy back step by step.

I barely hear them. My focus locks on the others—the faces of their betrayal burning into my memory. Sven and Aiden, brothers I turned in 1824, Sven begging me on his knees to save Aiden from the grave, tears streaming down his face. Amanda, who once laughed with me while we outran police sirens in '29, giddy with stolen jewels and money, the world ours for the taking.

Each memory stabs fresh, their loyalty twisting into daggers aimed straight at my heart. Sven comes again from behind, claws flashing for my spine. I spin, my talons ripping through his throat with savage precision. His eyes go wide as he chokes on his own blood, the sound wet and desperate. Aiden slams into me before I can recover, driving me down into the gravel.

"Traitors!" I spit, kneeing him in the ribs hard enough to crack bone. "I made you. I gave you eternity!" My claws tear into his chest, ripping through flesh and muscle, flinging him aside like he weighs nothing.

"I went west, like you told me." Tommy's voice cuts sharply across the chaos, clear despite the violence. "I found more than just vampires. I found purpose. I found love. But most importantly, I found my queen—Rowena."

A laugh rips out of me, bitter and sharp as broken glass. "Rowena? My sister? She's no queen of love. She'll bleed you dry and smile while she does it."

"Not when she found me!" Tommy snarls, eyes alight with fanatical devotion. "You don't know a damn thing, little blood queen."

The insult strikes like a slap across the face. I lunge, rage blinding me, but Killian's arm catches me, halting me mid-strike. His chest heaves, his face torn with pain that has nothing to do with his wounds. I press my back against his, feeling the rapid rise and fall of his breathing, to watch the others—Amanda and Aiden help Sven from the wound I gave him, which is slowly healing with supernatural speed.

"So that's it?" Killian shouts at Tommy, voice cracking with emotion. "All those years of raising me after my parents died, teaching me everything...you just throw it all away for some vampire you barely know?"

For a heartbeat, I look at him. The hurt in his voice, the betrayal carved in his eyes like scars—it twists something inside me, something I thought had died centuries ago.

Was that what I am to him? Just another vampire?

Tommy answers with steel and blood. He parries Killian's strike with the butt of his gun and drives his fist into Killian's ribs with brutal force. Killian doubles over, the air forced from his lungs, but his blade still sinks deep into Tommy's shoulder. Blood sprays in a crimson arc and Tommy's roar shakes the rooftop, primal and furious.

"Still think of me as family?" Killian spits, wild-eyed and desperate.

For the first time, Tommy's mask cracks. His voice drops low, almost tender, the way it might have been years ago. "Family isn't blood, Killy. It's loyalty. You chose the wrong queen."

I swing around as he levels the gun at Killian's forehead, the barrel gleaming in the moonlight.

"NO!"

The word rips from me, tearing my throat raw, and my body doesn't hesitate. I swing wide and grab Tommy's wrist, twisting with all my strength as he fires. The bullet grazes Killian's temple, tearing skin and ripping apart the top part of his ear—close enough to taste death, close enough to steal him from me. He staggers, dazed and bleeding. I slam my fist into Tommy before he can fire again, my claws shredding his chest as he pushes me back with hunter strength that shouldn't be possible.

Tommy spits crimson, his grin wolfish through the blood coating his teeth. "Rowena was right. You're weak, Seraphine. Both of you." His eyes gleam with hate and certainty, burning like coals. "But don't worry...she'll finish what I started."

Then, the rooftop erupts in chaos and violence.

Sven lunges, his claws flash for my throat like striking snakes. But I am ready this time. My hand snaps up, catching his wrist mid-swipe. I twist until bone cracks like breaking branches, the sound distinct and nauseating. His howl tears the night apart, echoing between the buildings. Dragging him into me, I bury my fangs deep into his jugular. His hot blood floods my mouth—copper, fire, and betrayal—before I rip free, taking half his throat with me.

He reels, staggering backward, and I don't waste the moment. I tear Killian's knife from his belt and drive it straight into Sven's chest with all the strength of centuries behind it. His red eyes go wide with betrayal, with the realization that this is the end, before his body dissolves. He breaks apart into drifting ash that vanishes into the wind like he never existed at all.

"SVEN!" Aiden's roar splits the night like thunder, raw with grief and fury. Rage pours off him in waves as he slams into me, the force hurling us both into the AC unit. Metal shrieks and crumples under the impact, pain tears through my ribs like fire spreading through dry wood.

Killian is a blur in the corner of my vision, steel flashes as he holds off Amanda and Tommy both, not worried about the wound to his head still bleeding freely. Tommy has burned through his bullets, thank the gods, but he wields a short sword with the stubborn precision of a man who trained Killian himself, who knows every move before it happens.

My hunter is holding his ground, but barely. Sweat and blood mix on his face.

Aiden's claws lash at me, a storm of steel and fury that tears at my clothes and skin. I duck low and roll beneath him, coming back up behind him with predatory grace. My fingers seize his collar, my other arm hooking his waist. With a snarl that comes from somewhere deep and primal, I lift using every ounce of vampiric strength, and slam him into the roof.

The shingles crack and buckle under the impact, fragmenting like a spider's web. The knife glitters in my hand as I straddle his chest, pinning him. "Go join your brother in hell, traitor."

My voice is bitter, shaking with emotion I can't afford. My hands shake as I plunge the blade into his heart. His scream is cut short as his body dissolves to nothing but ash and regret, scattering in the night wind.

I don't allow myself to breathe. I can't. Not with Killian still fighting for his life.

He moves like a man possessed, sweat and blood slicking his face, matting his hair. Amanda darts in circles around him like a shark, while Tommy jabs with his short sword in sharp, precise strikes meant to kill. Amanda lunges low, sweeping at Killian's legs with clawed hands, but he leaps just in time, bringing his blade down and skewering her shoulder. She groans but doesn't falter, the pain only making her more dangerous. Snarling, she grabs the blade, yanking Killian closer for the kill, fangs bared.

I'm already moving.

My hand tangles in her hair, fingers gripping tight. I yank her back with vicious force, baring her chest to him. His eyes meet mine for only a heartbeat—a moment of understanding passing between us—before he adjusts his grip and rams the blade home. Her gasp is sharp, guttural, and her eyes—once loyal, once filled with laughter—dim to nothing as her body breaks to ash that coats our skin.

Killian rips the weapon free, his breath ragged and labored, and turns to face Tommy. He's smiling, almost looking proud despite the blood running from his wounds.

"You really have grown in the last five years, son."

Killian freezes, his knuckles bone-white on his blade. I can taste the storm building inside him—rage, grief, and disbelief all warring for dominance.

"I don't know who the fuck you are anymore." Killian says, voice breaking on the words. "But you aren't my family."

For the first time, Tommy falters. His smirk wavers, though he tries to cover it with bravado. "You'll see it my way. Rowena will see to it."

Rowena. The name cuts sharper than any blade, deeper than any wound. My sister's shadow reaches even here, stretching across rooftops and bloodshed, a reminder that my crown is slipping while I play soldier in the dark with Killian.

Duty screams at me to finish this quickly, to focus on the war ahead, on the throne I'm losing. But another part of me—a part that has watched Killian bleed and laugh and fight like he belongs at my side—burns hotter than duty ever could.

Before Killian can answer, my hunger and fury blur my vision red. I lunge for Tommy, and Killian is right behind me, moving in perfect synchronization. Tommy, ever the veteran, slides low and escapes, springing to his feet with a cocky shrug.

"Going to have to be quicker than that." He gloats.

Killian reacts without thought, hurling his double-edged staff. Tommy ducks and the blade bites deep into the twisted metal of the AC unit, embedding itself. Before he can recover, I charge, leaping and driving both heels into his chest. The impact cracks bone beneath my feet, the sound distinct and satisfying, and sends him reeling backward straight into Killian's weapon still buried in the unit.

The blade spears through him.

Tommy's eyes go wide with shock and pain. He claws at the staff in his chest, but his strength is gone, bleeding out with every heartbeat. His gaze locks on Killian's, his voice rasping like torn paper. "She'll come for you. Both of you. You won't survive her."

"Then let her come." I snarl, the words a promise and a threat.

Killian steps forward, his face a mask of controlled fury, twisting the staff free before collapsing it back into its knife form with a practiced flick. Tommy staggers, gasping for breath that won't come, before slumping lifeless to the rooftop. His blood pools beneath him, dark and spreading.

The silence afterward is unbearable.

Only Killian's ragged breathing breaks it, and the hot stench of blood hangs heavy in the air like a shroud. Tommy—his mentor, his family, the man who raised him—is gone. I killed three of my generals tonight, people I turned, people I trusted. Betrayals and victories blur together until all I can taste is ash coating my tongue.

My crown weighs heavier than ever, pressing down on my skull like a physical weight, yet here I am, standing beside a man I'm not supposed to care for, whose grief is breaking him before my eyes. Killian's face is pale, streaked with sweat and tears he's trying to hide. His blade trembles in his hand. His eyes when they meet mine show he is torn between horror, hatred, and something that terrifies me more than any battle.

Something that looks like love.

"We should go." He whispers, voice breaking on each syllable.

I nod, forcing my voice steady when my heart isn't, when everything inside me is chaos. "I know a place." I offer him my hand—not a queen reaching for a subject, not a vampire claiming a hunter, but a woman reaching for a man she's grown to care for despite every reason not to. "Let's go."

He stares at my hand for a long moment, and I wonder if he'll take it, if this is where it ends. Then his fingers wrap around mine, warm, human, and alive. Together, we leap from the roof into the waiting shadows as the night swallows us whole. Behind us, the ghosts of his mentor and my traitorous generals cling like chains, weighing us down. A reminder that neither of us can ever run far enough from what we've done, from what we are.

From what we're becoming.

25
Killian

After hours of ducking alleys and slogging through the stinking maze of sewers, Sera finally raises a hand for us to stop. We crouch in the shadows of a narrow alley at the edge of the city, our bodies pressed against crumbling brick. Across the cracked asphalt, an empty field stretches toward the tree line, tall grass swaying in the pre-dawn wind. The national park looms just beyond, its silhouette waiting like a promise of escape, dark and infinite.

"I don't think anyone followed us." She murmurs, her voice steady but low, barely audible over the distant hum of the waking city. "We should stay here until sunrise. Safer to be sure."

The word sunrise makes me snort. I press harder against the makeshift bandage on my head, trying to slow the blood seeping through the fabric. The wound throbs in time with my heartbeat, a splitting ache that blurs the edges of my vision with each pulse. My ear burns where the bullet has shattered it—pain I should've healed from already, pain that should be a distant memory by now. The hunter gene dulled it, but it didn't erase it. Not this time.

"If we're waiting for sunrise, you'll be ash by morning." I say, sliding down the wall of a boarded-up pharmacy until I'm sitting on the cold concrete.

"For someone so determined to kill us, you really know little about us." Sera laughs, the sound rich and unbothered as she settles across from me, her back against the opposite wall. Moonlight paints her skin in silver, catching on the dried blood at her temple. Her smile is sharp and unbothered, like she hasn't just killed three of her own people.

"I know how to kill you." I smile through the pain. "That's enough."

I tug the bloody cloth from my head, wincing as it pulls at the wound, and open my phone to flick on the camera to check the damage. Black screen. Dead battery. Go figure. I catch the reflection of my face in the cracked screen anyway—skin pallid and waxy, blood streaked across my temple like war paint. I mutter under my breath, "why the fuck isn't this healing?"

"Question." Sera says, her tone shifting to something more curious. "How did you think I went on that date with you in the middle of the day?"

I pause, considering her question. The memory of that afternoon comes back—sunlight streaming through the laser tag building's windows, warming her skin. "Hm. Never thought about that."

Sera laughs, and I can't help but smile at seeing her beauty despite everything, despite the blood and the death and the impossibility of us. "My sisters and I can be in the sunlight. That little curse didn't start until we started turning humans."

I open my mouth to ask more, curiosity sparking despite the exhaustion, but the pain in my head distracts me and I go back to inspecting the wound with my fingers, feeling the jagged edges.

"Nature always finds a way, Killian. Balance." Sera raises an eyebrow at me, studying me with those ancient eyes. "You've never laced your weapons with mountain ash?"

"Mountain ash?" I repeat, the words unfamiliar on my tongue.

She rolls her eyes, pushes off the wall with fluid grace and crosses to me. Her dress whispers against the gravel, tattered and stained but still elegant somehow. When she sits close enough, her perfume cuts through the stink of blood and sewer water—something floral and dark. I hate how it pulls me in, how much I want her at this moment. Bruises and all.

"How are you a leader of hunters," she asks, tying her hair back with deliberate calm, fingers working through the tangled strands. "And know nothing about your lineage?"

I smirk, though my head pounds with every heartbeat, making it hard to think straight. "I'm good at what I do. Instincts better than most. My genes let me push further than the rest. History lessons weren't exactly part of the training package."

Her brow arches, skeptical. "And do you know why that is?"

Something in her tone makes my stomach tighten, a warning bell ringing somewhere deep. I swallow hard. "No. Tommy..." The name snags in my throat like barbed wire, the image of him falling flashing behind my eyes. "...he never gave me that. Just drills, fights, orders to find the queen. To find you."

Her eyes narrow in suspicion, studying me as though weighing the truth of my words, searching for deception. I tilt my head back against the brick, giving her a tired grin despite the pain. "Well...found you."

Her laugh is sharp, almost unwilling, escaping before she can stop it. "Idiot."

I open my mouth to toss something back, but she cuts me off.

"Mountain ash," she says, slipping into lecture mode, her voice taking on that professorial quality. "Is from the Rowan tree. Its flowers, ground into powder and blessed, strip away magic. That's why your healing has stalled. It's a leash meant for us."

I frown, trying to piece it together. "But I can still see behind your mask. I still feel the gene working in me."

Her gaze softens, though only slightly, something almost tender crossing her features. "That's because you come from the bloodline of the Original Hunter." She lets the words hang, like a knife left hovering above my chest.

I blink at her, trying to process the weight of what she's saying. Original hunter. The phrase lodges in my skull, heavier than the pain buzzing in my ear. Before I can push for more, demand answers, a clatter snaps through the alley. A stray cat darts past, knocking over a glass bottle that rolls noisily across the pavement, the sound echoing off the walls. Both of us are instantly tense, scanning rooftops, corners, even the sky above. Only silence answers, pressing down like a weight.

Sera tears a strip of fabric from her dress and presses it to my forehead. Her hands are steady, clinical, though the heat of her skin lingers against mine.

"Your healing will catch up soon." She breathes, her face close enough that I can see the flecks of gold in her eyes. "Until then, keep it wrapped. We'll talk about the rest later once we've eaten. Once you've bathed. You stink, little hunter."

I nudge her hand away, managing a weak grin. "Speak for yourself, your majesty."

She doesn't answer. Her eyes flick down to my face when I brush dried blood from her lip with my thumb, the touch lingering. For a moment, the space between us feels too close, charged with something dangerous. I lean in, she leans back.

"I'll check the perimeter." Sera says, rising in a blur of movement. "We head for the forest. My safe house will be a haven for us."

Before I can reply, she's gone. Her speed tearing her into the night faster than my wounded eyes can follow. I sag against the wall, blood still trickling down my temple despite the fresh bandage, the words 'original hunter' rattling around my skull like a curse I can't shake.

Minutes later, Sera slips back into the alley, crouching in front of me with that infuriating grin tugging at her lips.

"Ready to run, or do you need your beauty rest?"

I huff out a laugh, gripping the wall as I push myself upright, my legs protesting. "Can't get much prettier than this, Sera."

She rises with me, her hand catching mine. It's cool and steady, grounding even when everything else feels like it's spinning out of control. Then we run—down the cracked main street, past the broken lamps and shuttered storefronts, vaulting over the stone barrier that marks the city's edge. The sky bleeds orange behind us as the horizon ignites with dawn, painting the world in fire. Shadows give way to the trees, thick and endless, swallowing us whole.

Sera moves like smoke, slipping between trunks, twisting around branches at speeds that make my head spin and my lungs scream. My lungs burn, my wound throbs with each jarring step, and yet she never slows, dragging me through turns without warning until the forest finally breaks open into a clearing.

I freeze.

A waterfall thunders before us, crashing into a crystalline pond that spills into a rushing river cutting through the rocks. Jagged rocks rise around the pool like guardians, moss glistening under the thin veil of morning light filtering through the canopy.

"This...is beautiful." I manage, bent over and panting, hands on my knees.

"You aren't going to like this next part." Her grin widens as she steps close, scooping me into her arms effortlessly and yanking the wrap off my head before I can protest. Before I can curse, she's sprinting straight at the falls.

The roar swallows everything. Water slams into us with bone-crushing force, a curtain of liquid stone that feels like a thousand fists pounding. My skull feels like it splits in half, white-hot pain tearing through the wound. I scream, though the sound drowns instantly in the thunderous cascade, and then we are through.

Sera sets me down on smooth stone. I collapse forward, clutching my head until the world stops exploding behind my eyes, stars bursting across my vision. When I lift my gaze, I almost forget the pain.

The cave is enormous, its walls carved with ancient runes that pulse faintly in the dim light, glowing with some inner power. Soft lamps glow across designer furniture—leather, velvet, and silks in deep jewel tones. Shelves of antiques line the walls: blades that look like they've seen centuries of war, portraits of people long dead, relics that must have witnessed history unfold. Beauty and menace twine together, just like her.

And there she stands, smiling at me like she didn't just try to drown me.

"Did you stop in the waterfall?" I snap, water dripping from my hair.

Her grin sharpens, pleased with herself. "I thought if I washed the wound, it would heal faster." She twirls, graceful and infuriating. "I was right."

I touch my temple, realizing the bleeding has stopped. The wound is sealed, though the top of my ear is gone, scar tissue carving a jagged line down the side of my head. The pain is gone, but the anger lingers, hot and sharp.

"That fucking hurt."

"I think you mean thank you." She teases, her smile widening.

"Thank you...but fuck."

I walk deeper into the cavern, letting my fingers trail over relics and paintings, feeling the age in them. But before I can sink onto the velvet couch, her voice snaps like a whip.

"No sir. Shower first."

I turn, incredulous. "What about you? You're just as filthy as I am."

"My cave, my rules, hunter." She smirks, smug and untouchable.

Rolling my eyes, I mutter a curse and follow her directions down a stone hall that curves naturally through the rock. The shower is built into the cave wall itself, water streaming from a steel fixture into a wide basin with a simple drain carved into the floor. Towels sit folded neatly on a stone bench, soft and white. I strip off my blood-soaked clothes and step under the spray.

The water is hot, merciful, washing away hours of grime and blood. I close my eyes, letting it wash away the night's grit, feeling the tension start to drain from my muscles. That's when I feel her presence. A shift in the air, unmistakable.

"Are you going to watch?" I ask, not bothering to open my eyes. "Or join me?"

Her reply comes in a blur. Suddenly she is here, naked, slamming me against the stone wall. Water cascades down her body, her mouth crushing mine with desperate hunger. Her legs wrap around my waist, and I pull her close, tasting her moan as she melts into me.

When she slides down, turning her back, I press in behind her, lips brushing her throat, tasting the water on her skin. Steam curls around us, her skin slick under my hands.

"Help me wash my hair."

I reach for the shampoo, lather my fingers, and work it through her dark strands. She moans softly, tilting her head back, and the sound punches heat straight through me. My hands roam lower, soap sliding over soft curves, tracing every inch I can touch.

She turns, returning the favor. Her fingers work the suds into my hair, then down my chest, gentle and thorough. Her eyes lock on mine, the fire there undercut by something more raw, more vulnerable.

"You tried to replace me with a human." Her voice cracks at the edges, the hurt too real to hide beneath her usual armor.

I swallow hard, shame burning through me. "No one can replace you." I cup her face, forcing her to look at me. "I just...wanted to feel normal. My team doesn't trust me. I don't trust myself. I thought...if I slept with someone else, it would prove you don't have power over me."

Her touch trails down my ribs, slow and deliberate, but her eyes stay sharp, searching. "Did it work? Do you feel normal?"

I hesitate, staring at the water swirling down the drain, then meet her gaze. "No. Not even close. All I could think about was you. Even when I hated you for killing the girl, some part of me was just glad to be near you."

Her lips soften into something rare. Something vulnerable. She rises on tiptoes, kissing me—not with hunger this time. Something quieter. Something terrifying.

A kiss that says more than either of us dare speak.

Steam still clings to the air as Sera reaches back and twists the water off with a sharp click. Droplets cling to her skin, catching the cave's golden light, and for a moment I just watch her—the sharp angles and impossible softness all at once. We each grab a towel, the warmth fading quickly from our bodies as the cool cavern air wraps around us.

"What do you know about the hunter gene?" She asks casually at first, though I catch the way her eyes linger on me. She's curious, but weighing how much to reveal.

I drag the towel over my hair and think back on every lecture Tommy has given me, every drill, every scrap of information that boils down to little more than tactics and kill methods.

"Honestly? Not much. I know it sharpens my senses, gives me strength beyond normal humans. Lets me see through the mask you all put on. But mine's...different. I can hide my scent and wounds close in seconds." I gesture to my ear, or what's left of it. "Mostly."

She smirks, but there is a glint in her gaze that isn't amusement—it's knowing, ancient.

We pad barefoot to the bedroom. The space smells faintly of lavender and old leather, a strange blend of the ancient and the modern. She opens the dresser, pulling out an oversized gray hoodie with 'BITE ME' scrawled in crimson across the chest. I raise an eyebrow.

"Subtle."

"Don't flatter yourself." She tosses it aside and sifts through more drawers until she finds a pair of black sweats and a white hoodie, both soft and worn.

I get dressed, trying not to think about the fact that she has clothes that fit me in her hideaway cave, and follow her back into the main living area. Her leather sofa gleams, worn but luxurious, the kind of piece that whispers of centuries and money. We sink into it together, the tension of running and fighting bleeding off in the stillness.

She draws in a breath, slow and deliberate, her fingers tracing light lines up my arm as if deciding how much of herself to give away. Finally, she exhales, and her voice softens.

"In the year 1054, Lucien served as a personal guard to the king."

The words hit me like freezing water. "You were alive then?"

She chuckles, low and melodic, as though the question amuses her more than it should. "Born in 903, turned in spring 927." Her lips curve into a smile. "Do the math."

I stare, my mind trying to wrap around the number. "You're...one thousand years old?"

"One thousand, one hundred and twenty-two." She corrects, precisely.

"Damn." It slips out before I can catch it.

Her brow arches. "Careful." But the smile in her eyes betrays the threat.

I laugh and pull her closer until her slight frame folds against me, fitting perfectly. Her skin is cool, the scent of rain and old stone clinging to her, grounding me in the impossibility of her presence.

"Tell me your story." I smile, running my fingers through her damp hair. "Tell me all about your sisters and how you became the most dangerous creature to walk this earth. Tell me about this love of yours and how hard you fell for your knight in shining armor."

Sera shifts in my arms, laughing. The sound vibrates against my chest. "I never said I loved him."

"Oh come on." I squeeze her playfully. "I know how these stories go. Star-crossed romance, doomed passion, tragic heartbreak. Spare me the clichés, queen."

Her laugh softens into something quieter, more vulnerable. She nestles deeper against me, her voice lowering to a whisper.

"Actually...it was the exact opposite."

I go still, sensing the weight of what is coming, the truth she's about to share.

26

Seraphine

The road to Eoforwic, now known as York, gnaws at us. Winter bites deeper each day, the winds tearing through fur and flesh alike until our bones feel brittle as frost. My sisters huddle close in the carriage, wrapped in pelts so heavy their small frames nearly disappear beneath them, only their pale faces visible in the dim light.

Rowena murmurs prayers to a god who has long since turned his face from girls like us. Amara stares out the frosted window, her breath fogging the glass, always dreaming of something beyond our reach. Morgana plucks stray threads from her cloak with restless fingers, her mouth twisted into the same half-smile that promises trouble.

I sit with the king's sister pressed against my side, warming her with my own body heat. She trembles, soft and fragile as a bird, every shiver a reminder of the life I have been born into: servitude. Our futures tied to those who rule, our desires shackled to theirs like chains we can never break.

Two endless months later, York's gates loom before us. The city is a beast of stone, its walls streaked black with soot and weather, rising against the gray sky like teeth. Crowds press against the gates, Danes with eyes like wolves, craning for a glimpse of their new queen. Their jeers and cheers mingle, a coarse thunder rolling through the air that makes the carriage shake.

I shake the princess awake, her head lolling on my shoulder. "We are here, my lady."

The guards fling open the carriage door, and the cold rushes in, cutting like knives against exposed skin. She steps down first, regal in her composure despite the journey's toll. I follow, my sisters at my back, heads bowed in submission as the crowd devours us with their stares. Their eyes crawl over us like insects, assessing, judging, dismissing.

Life within the walls blurs into routine. A marriage sealed, alliances forged in blood and gold, the princess crowned a queen. We live in peculiar comfort. Fed, clothed in garments finer than most servants dared dream of, silk against our skin instead of rough wool, and yet we are invisible until needed.

On quiet days, when there are no orders barked at us, we drift into longing. Rowena and Amara whisper of other lives, of castles of their own and men who might worship them instead of commanding them. Morgana drapes the queen's jewels around her throat when she thinks no one is watching, staring into the mirror as though willing her reflection to change into someone who matters. I listen, half in silence, half consumed with thoughts I dare not voice.

What I want couldn't be spoken aloud. What I want is power.

"Off to see that witch again, dear sister?" Morgana teases one evening, her smirk sharp as glass, cutting through the dim candlelight.

I pull my cloak tighter around my shoulders. "Mind your tongue. I'm going to find a better life for us."

The Danes revere their witches. Seers who whisper futures into the ears of kings, who bend fate with their gnarled hands. Rumors say some hold power more primal. Older. A witch like that has found me in dreams, her voice threading through my sleep, and once seen, I couldn't look away.

Her hut stinks of rot and herbs when I push through the door. Smoke curling in thick, choking ropes that burn my lungs. My throat burns, bile rising, but I press forward into the gloom, refusing to show weakness.

"Do you have what I asked for?" Her voice slithers from the shadows like a serpent. Then she emerges, stooped and crooked, hair tangled as brambles, her skin parchment-thin and crawling with veins like worms beneath the surface. Her eyes, though, are alive. Too alive, burning with an intelligence that makes my skin crawl.

I draw the queen's brush from my satchel, my hand shaking despite my best efforts. "I do."

She snatches it, stroking the polished wood like a lover, pressing it to her nose, and inhaling deeply as though smelling something precious. Her mouth splits into a grin that shows every rotten tooth. From her cloak she produces five vials, glowing faintly in the fire's half-light. Blue, white, black, red, and gold. The witch holds out four of them, slipping the fifth into her sleeve with practiced ease.

"As promised." She rasps, pressing the four into my palm. They're warm, pulsing with something that feels alive.

"And the last?"

Her grin widens, skin pulling taut over her skull until I can see the bone beneath. "In due time. These will make you strong and unbreakable. For one day."

The floor tilts under me, the room spinning. "That is not our deal."

Her finger wags, crooked and accusing. "Do one thing for me, and it becomes permanent. True immortality. Fail, and the gift rots you from within until there's nothing left but ash and screaming."

"What thing?" My voice trembles despite my attempt at strength.

Her eyes burn brighter, flames dancing in their depths. "Kill the Danish king." The words leave her lips like a curse, settling into my bones, and her laugh claws at the walls until I flee.

I burst back into the queen's chambers, chest heaving, clutching the vials against my chest. My sisters swarm me at once, their faces eager and desperate.

"Well?" Rowena demands, grabbing my arm.

The words tumble out in fragments, but they barely listen. The vials gleam in my hands, catching the firelight, and greed lights their eyes like fever. Before I can stop them, before I can warn them of the cost, they pull the corks. Liquid spills down their throats.

Rowena swallows black, Morgana tips back the blue, and Amara drinks the white.

"No! Wait!"

Too late.

Their bodies convulse, backs arching, then straighten. Beauty blooms like poison flowers across their features. Skin turns luminous, hair thickens and darkens, their eyes burning with strange fire that makes them look otherworldly. The surrounding air seems to hum with power.

My envy is a living thing, clawing at my chest. My fingers close around the red vial. I uncork it and drink.

It's like swallowing fire and frost together, warring for dominance in my throat. Pain rips through me, tearing at every nerve, but then vanishes like it was never there. My spine lengthens, bones knitting stronger, muscles taut with new life that thrums beneath my skin. Hunger surges inside me, fierce and insatiable, but not for bread or meat. Something darker coils in my belly, demanding to be fed.

Rowena's laughter rings out, sharp and wild, echoing off the stone walls. "Do you see? We are gods now!"

"Everything is brighter, and I feel alive!" Amara gasps, spinning in delight, her movements impossibly graceful.

Morgana's nails rake my arm as she clutches me, drawing blood that wells in perfect crimson beads. But the cuts seal at once, flesh knitting together. Her smile widens, feral and hungry. I step back, the weight of the witch's warning heavy in my chest.

"This...isn't forever. Unless we kill the king."

Silence falls like a blade.

Rowena's lips curl into something cruel, Amara's eyes glow with sudden understanding, and Morgana bares her teeth in silent agreement.

"So, we kill him."

Dusk bleeds across the sky as we cross the courtyard, painting everything in shades of blood. The air is sweet with blossoms, but beneath it I can already smell blood, metallic and promising. My hand trembles when I knock on his door.

"Enter." Comes his gravelly call.

We bow low, four shadows with sharpened smiles.

"The queen has sent us, my lord." Morgana purrs, her voice honey and silk. "To tend to you."

He waves us away with a dismissive gesture. "I have no need for you."

Rowena steps closer, her voice honeyed venom dripping from every word. "But my king...we need you."

Then we strike.

Nails tear flesh, ripping through muscle. Teeth crack bone with sickening snaps. His cry is strangled in his throat as his blood sprays the walls in arterial bursts, painting them crimson. The scent hits like thunder, drowning us in copper and salt. The hunger roars free and I bury my mouth in his flesh, drinking greedily. His warmth slides down my throat, filling every vein with fire, with power, with something that feels like finally coming home.

With every swallow, my body twists. Teeth lengthening into fangs, sharp and deadly. Nails sharpening into claws that could tear through anything. My sisters feed beside me, their eyes glowing with savage delight, lost in the same ecstasy.

When at last he lies still, a hollow husk drained of everything, we rise. Blood drips from our mouths, staining our dresses, our chests heaving with something like ecstasy. The room reeks of iron, thick enough to taste, and for the first time in my life, I feel powerful.

We flee into the night, but it's no longer dark. The stars burn like torches overhead, so bright they hurt. The world feels too sharp, too loud. I hear everything from the flap of an insect's wings to the snap of a branch miles away, to the beating hearts of sleeping villagers. At the tree line, she stands waiting. The witch. Smiling, her teeth wet with shadows.

"You four are beautiful." She smiles, pride in her voice. "Now go. Roam the world. But tell no one what you are."

The darkness swallows her whole, and we stand transformed. No longer dreaming of better lives. We have become nightmares.

-Summer, year 1054-

For over a century I have sharpened myself into a weapon in the shadows. Gathering warriors, bending noble whispers to my will, weaving threads of influence over England like a spider's web. And yet, every time I try to slip into the ear of the young prince, I find myself thwarted by the same man.

Lucien.

The prince's personal guard is small in stature, but persistent as a gnat and twice as irritating.

"Again, Seraphine?" His voice carries across the marble court before I've even reached the dais, his boots clicking in a rhythm that already grates on my patience. His dark brows knit into a permanent scowl I've come to know too well.

"I only want to introduce myself." I purr, tilting my head and letting a smile sharpen the corners of my lips. My cloak spills around me like a pool of blood against the stone.

He folds his arms, unimpressed by my beauty or my power. "Introduce yourself to his jugular, more like. You'd poison his ear before his father's corpse is cold."

How infuriatingly right he is. Not that he needs to know this. He herds me out, ushering me past the gaping courtiers who whisper behind their hands. As the great doors slam shut behind me, the echo reverberates in my ribs. My fingers curl into fists, but I force a smile instead. My eyes lift to the windows cut high into the court's walls.

Stone yields to my claws as I leap, scaling the wall with ease. My cape whips behind me like a banner of defiance as I slide through a narrow balcony window, emerging into the crowd once more.

I stand tall, red cloak flaring, and wait until the prince's gaze lands on me. A hand closes around my shoulder. Lucien's grip is firm, his sigh louder than the crowd's whispers.

"If you wanted my attention, Seraphine, you could've just asked."

I let a low chuckle roll from my throat, slow and smoky. "I don't think you'd handle rejection well."

"Funny." He bites back, though his eyes flicker with something more than annoyance. "How did you get back in?"

I lean close, lowering my voice so only he can hear, my breath against his ear. "Wouldn't you like to know?"

His hand tightens, but I twist, driving my palm into his chest. He skids across the floor, crashing into the stone wall hard enough to rattle the sconces. Gasps ripple through the court, courtiers pressing hands to their mouths in shock.

I merely shrug and turn, cloak sweeping the marble like a curtain drop, leaving him to gather his pride from the floor. Months bleed together, and still Lucien bars my path at every turn. Every whisper I try to plant in the prince's ear, he uproots. Every door I slip through, he's waiting on the other side.

Until one winter night.

The castle reeks of smoke and spilled ale, the aftermath of victory's celebration. Guards slump in alcoves, wine staining their lips, their snores rattling against the stone. Their snores rattle against the stone as I glide past unseen.

The prince's door stands ajar, firelight flickering within, casting dancing shadows. My pulse quickens with anticipation as I push it open.

And freeze.

Lucien leans casually against the mantle, shadows bending around him like obedient dogs. His grin is sharper than any blade I've ever seen.

"You never give up, do you?"

I inhale through my nose, forcing my smirk back into place. "I prefer persistent. It sounds less... desperate."

His chuckle is low, humorless. "You have plans, Seraphine. Plans I won't let crawl into the light."

The fire throws his shadow long across the wall, stretching him into a giant he isn't. I step deeper into the room; the rug muffles my footsteps.

"Why do you refuse me, Lucien?" My voice drips honey, sweet and poisonous. "You block me at every turn, like some little knight desperate to prove himself."

He doesn't flinch. "Because I know what you are."

The words root me mid-step.

"You... what?"

His eyes burn steadily on mine, unwavering. "I've heard the stories of the Dane King. The massacre in York. The portraits I found... they were of you."

I let a slow smile curve my lips, trailing my fingers over the back of the couch. "Could've been my grandmother. Strong bone structure runs in the family."

"It wasn't." His voice is iron.

I circle him, my cloak whispering against the floor like a warning. "Then what a wasteful death this will be."

I lunge. My claws slice air, but he ducks fast, faster than any human should. A flash of steel catches the firelight as he draws his blade, cutting a line across my arm. Pain hisses through me, sharp and stinging.

"Ow," I growl, baring fangs. "Rude."

His grin widens, infuriatingly smug. He lunges again, knife flashing. I catch his wrist, ready to snap it like kindling, when a second blade buries into my stomach. My breath escapes me in a sharp gasp as I stagger back.

I yank the blade free, dropping it to the rug, already feeling the wound knitting shut. My eyes lock on him. "What are you?"

"A man," he says simply, straightening his tunic. "But one who wants to be more."

I tilt my head, studying him, seeing him clearly for the first time. "You want to be a vampire?"

"Not under you," he shoots back quickly. "I want to stand with you. I've trained my whole life for this. The witch will make me immortal through magic, not through a bite. I want to rule by your side."

The words root deeper than I expected. Forty years after changing, my sisters and I had splintered and gone our separate ways, pulled apart by power and ambition. Loneliness had followed me like a shadow ever since, constant and cold.

He must see it in my face because he softens, just slightly. "I've been watching you. You aren't like them. I want to be your equal. Not your prey."

I circle him again, slower this time, weighing the sincerity in his gaze, searching for lies. Finally, I stop in front of him, my lips curling.

"Then deal. But you leave with me tonight. No crown. No prince. Only me."

His grin is unwavering. "Deal."

He strips the royal armor from his body, letting it crash into the stone. The sound echoes like a vow, like a promise being sealed. And for the first time in decades, I'm not sure if I'm still playing the game or if the game is playing me.

-*Fall, Year 1058*-

We have been chasing shadows for years; rumors of the witch who had once made me what I am. Every tavern, every battlefield, every backwater village tells a different story. Some swear she burned long ago, others that she wanders the wilds, waiting for desperate souls. Most nights, it feels hopeless. And yet, traveling with Lucien hasn't been wasted time. Our love has grown in the dust and blood of the roads, forged in firelight and sharpened steel. We have become inseparable. We are partners, lovers, and conspirators.

That night, the village sleeps uneasily on edge from whispers of an oncoming army. Boys too young to die stand guard, clutching spears with sweaty palms, their eyes darting at every sound. Lucien and I watch them from the shadows, laughing softly at their trembling bravado. The sound of his laughter and warmth pulls me close. For a fleeting moment, I let myself believe forever could be ours.

Then I catch the scent. Herbs. Charred sage. A curl of something darker, acrid, and sweet. It's like stepping back through time to a century gone in a single breath. My steps falter. At the edge of the square, tucked behind crooked beams and dangling with bone charms that click in the wind, stands a crooked hut, the chimes whispering in the night air.

"Lucien," I whisper, my chest tightening. "She's here."

We enter, the air thick with smoke and rot, every surface littered with jars, feathers, and half-burnt scrolls.

"Show yourself," I growl, closing the door behind us.

From the shadows, the witch emerges, her body bent but her eyes sharp as blades. "The years have been kind to you, Seraphine," she rasps, her lips splitting into a grin.

"We want forever," Lucien blurts, too eager, stepping forward. "I want you to make me like her so that we may rule together."

The witch's eyes flick over him, hungry, amused. "Forever wasn't enough, was it? You had to go and fall in love." Her laughter cracks like ice.

"Will you help us?" he presses.

"Of course," she purrs, gesturing for us to sit. "This I will do for free."

We gather at the fire, its glow throwing shadows across her wrinkled face. From her robes she pulls a vial; golden, shimmering like sunlight trapped in glass. My breath catches.

"That's the fifth vial," I whisper. My sisters. The four of us had sworn never to spread her gift further, and yet one by one we had broken the rules, creating chaos, creating monsters. And now, this.

The witch only nods. Lucien hesitates, the vial trembling in his hand. "Why so freely?" he asks, his voice edged with suspicion.

"My reasons are my own, boy." Her smile is sharp. "Drink it or give it back."

I should have stopped him. I should have torn it from his hands. But I see the fire in his eyes. It's the same fire that has warmed me, the same fire that promised I'd never be alone again, and I can't move.

The cork pops. He drinks deeply. His heart thunders, pounding so loudly I can hear it in my skull. Muscles tense, cords of power tightening across his frame. His pupils dilate until the blue I love is swallowed whole. My lips part, a warning on my tongue, but the witch is already laughing.

"You four could never listen," she hisses. "Always spreading, always defying. So eager to play gods."

"What are you—" I begin, but Lucien's hand is already at my throat.

The world blurs. My back hits the wall. His grip crushes my windpipe, fangs bared, eyes burning with something I don't recognize.

"Lucien..." I gasp, clawing at him, my voice raw.

"I told you not to share my secrets," the witch goes on, her laughter filling the room. "And now, I will end the lot of you."

"What... did... you... do?" My words crack through the choke of his hand.

"I gave him what he wanted," she says sweetly. "Immortality. But his blood will always hate yours."

He drops me, and I collapse, coughing, scrambling back, only for the gleam of his knife to arc toward my chest. The blade catches the light, and I barely deflect it with a desperate strike. My heart shatters with every swing of his arm. This isn't him. This can't be him.

"Lucien, stop!" I scream, my voice breaking. But his face, once tender and once mine, twists with pure hunger, rage, and betrayal.

I can't kill him. Even as steel carves through the air, even as fire licks my veins with every wound, I can't raise my hand to end him. I love him too much. Instead, I stumble toward the door, blood slick at my ribs.

"I'll be back for you," I hiss at the witch, my voice low, trembling with venom.

"I'll be waiting," she croons.

I flee into the night, Lucien's footsteps pounding after me, his speed matching my own. The witch's laughter chases us into the dark, a sound that will echo in my skull for centuries. A curse, a dirge, a reminder of what love has cost me.

304

27

Killian

I sit with her curled against me, her voice low and steady as she unravels the centuries that have shaped her. Her story paints itself across my mind in dark strokes: the witch's hut swallowed in smoke and rot, the blood on her hands still fresh after a thousand years, the shadow of Lucien chasing her through time like a ghost that won't rest. When her words finally trail off, the silence is heavy, almost suffocating, pressing down on us like a physical weight.

I lean forward, tightening my arms around her and forcing her eyes to meet mine.

"So, what happened?" I ask, need threading through my voice. "Did he find you? Did you take his life? Did you find the witch?"

She laughs softly, the sound fragile as spun glass. "So many questions, Killian."

"Well, you ended the story like it just...stopped there. As if the last thousand years don't matter." I try to smile, but impatience creeps in, sharpening my tone. I need answers, but more importantly I need to know where this leaves us.

Sera leans back into me, her finger tracing idle patterns across my thigh, slow and absent, like a memory she isn't ready to let go of.

"We spent four centuries chasing each other across the world." She says finally, her voice is quieter now, almost a whisper. "I wouldn't kill him. Not at first. I thought if I kept running, if I stayed ahead, maybe I wouldn't have to. But shadows never stop following, Killian. Eventually...I was tired. Tired of running and tired of always looking over my shoulder. So, I ended it. With the help of my sisters, we killed him."

The pause that follows is sharp enough to hurt. I can feel the weight of what comes next pressing on her tongue before she speaks, heavy as a stone.

"And then we hunted down his bloodline. Every single person. Or so we thought." Her nails graze against my leg, the tension bleeding through her touch. "But hunters still exist. Which means we missed someone, or the witch made more."

I run my fingers through her hair, combing gently and grounding myself in the silk of it. My chest tightens. "Do you think there is a connection between Lucien's bloodline and mine?"

"I don't think, Killian. I tasted it the night you let me feed from you. I know." Her words are calm, but the certainty in them hits me like a blade sliding between my ribs.

I swallow hard, my throat suddenly dry. "So, what does that mean?"

Her eyes lift to mine, and in them, for the first time, I see something dangerous: hope.

"It means we can survive this."

A frown tugs at me. "What do you mean?"

"The last part of the story. The promise the witch made me when I spared her life."

I shift, turning so I can see her face, every flicker of emotion that crosses it. Her beauty sharpens in moments like this, not soft or romantic, but carved from steel and fire.

"In 1587, I found her again. I wanted to gloat, to remind her she had failed. More than that, I wanted her dead." Her lips pull into a small but bitter smile. "I had her in my grip, her throat trembling against my hand. Then she made me an offer."

I huff a laugh, trying to cut the tension that has settled like a storm cloud. "Two powerful beings cutting deals. What could go wrong?"

Her chuckle is low; humor edged with old rage. She lightly smacks my arm, but when she speaks again, fury threads her voice.

"She told me my sisters were plotting to kill me, to take the court I had just built. She said the only way to outlast them is with the bloodline of the hunter."

My stomach drops. "What the fuck does that even mean? The hunters are all dead at this point, right?"

Sera's gaze doesn't waver.

"No, they had come back into the world, but they were weak. Washed out copies of what we took out all those centuries before. They weren't a threat to us. The witch said if one of us could take the heart of the one born to kill us...if the bloodlines of a queen and hunter were joined, something new would be created. Something stronger. Not prey, not predator, but something new. Rulers."

I stare at her, trying to make sense of it, but the words tangle in my throat. "I...I don't understand."

"What's not to understand?" She snaps, frustration bleeding through. "The hunters want us dead. My people want us dead. But together, Killian, we could actually survive this."

"Or." I say softly. "We can run."

Her body goes rigid, her anger surging fast and sharp. "I will not spend another lifetime running!" Her voice cracks like thunder, echoing through the cave. "I'm done hiding. Done waiting for the next knife in my back. I choose to fight. I choose..." She turns, eyes burning into mine, voice trembling now. "I choose you, Killian. Not as my enemy, not as my hunter. As my...I choose you."

The weight of her words strikes me like a physical blow. Hearing her confirm the same feelings I have been feeling for her tightens my chest and warms something low in my belly. I cup her face, my thumb brushing her cheek.

"From the first night, I knew I couldn't harm you. I tried to convince myself I could. But I can't." My voice breaks, softer than I want. "I want a life with you, Sera. I choose you, too."

Her lips part, her breath catching like she hadn't dared to believe it. "You do?"

I lean closer until our lips brush, the faintest ghost of a kiss. My heartbeat pounds, steady and certain, as I whisper the words I know will bind us both.

"I stepped down as a leader, for you. I left the hunters, for you. I choose you, Seraphine. From this breath until I take my last, I choose you."

I press my lips to hers, a kiss that ignites like a spark to dry tinder. Her mouth opens eagerly and our tongues tangle in a fierce dance that sends electricity racing through me.

Without breaking the kiss, I slide my arms around her waist and lift her effortlessly, her body light in my grip. She wraps her legs around me, her breath hot on my neck as I carry her across the cave to a large king-sized bed, the soft furs piled high and inviting us in.

I lay her down gently, my eyes roaming over her form, already imagining the feeling of her skin under my hands. "You're mine now." I whisper, my voice a low growl, the words laced with both command and tenderness.

I stare at her neck, trailing kisses down her throat, feeling her pulse race beneath my lips. My fingers find the hem of her hoodie, and I tug it up slowly to reveal the curve of her breasts.

She arches her back, helping me strip it off, her eyes gleaming with a fierce passion I crave. My fingers hook into her sweats and pull them down her legs, exposing her completely.

I brush my lips over her stomach, licking my way down her body as Sera arches her back in want. She opens her legs for me, the smell of her desire filling my senses and driving me mad with my own need for her. I kiss her thigh, letting my tongue slide across the sensitive spot that drives her crazy.

Sera bucks her hips, her fingers threading through my hair as she grinds eagerly against my mouth. I breathe through it, catching quick breaths where I can. Letting her use my tongue however she needs to find her release.

Her fingers tighten in my hair as she holds me still, grinding harshly into my face as her thighs begin to shake. Warmth floods my mouth as I continue to devour her, listening to her moans echo off the cave's stone walls.

She pushes me back and then pulls me onto her body as if I weigh nothing under the strength of her vampire blood. I feel my throbbing tip against her drenched center. I position myself but stop before thrusting inward. Her eyes glare into mine.

"Don't stop," she begs. "Please, Killian, don't stop."

I kiss her, my tongue sliding into her mouth. She moans as she tastes herself on my lips and I trail down her neck and then up to her ear.

"Bite me," I whisper.

"What?" she breathes, bucking her hips to get me to enter her.

"Feed on me," I demand again.

She lets her glamour falter as she bares her fangs. My hunter's blood reacts to danger, and I wince as she bites down on me. At the same moment her fangs penetrate my neck, I thrust into her until I'm buried fully. I feel her spread apart to make room for me.

"Oh, fuck." I gasp.

Her moan vibrates against my neck as she feeds on me. The feeling of blood loss while thrusting into her is one I could never put into words. It feels heavenly with each stroke I make. The dizzying feeling of being drained only makes me push harder and deeper.

I know Sera won't harm me, and the rush of danger mixed with my hunter blood demanding I defend myself mixed with the pure exotic pleasure of burying myself into the woman I was falling in—

"You're going to make me finish again." Sera moans, drawing me out of my own thoughts.

"Do it." I growl, thrusting one last time as my own release begins.

She tightens around me, thighs shaking with pleasure as she moans out my name. "Good girl." I smile, my hot release filling her at the same time. My neck heals the instant she pulls her fangs free.

"That's it." I say. "Just like that."

We collapse together onto the bed, panting with pleasured exhaustion. For the first time in longer than I can remember, I feel...unguarded. Exposed in a way that has nothing to do with being naked. She turns her face toward me, damp strands of hair clinging to her temple, and smiles.

"Hi." I whisper, still half dazed, grinning like an idiot.

Her laugh comes soft and melodic, her eyes rolling as though she wants to hide the warmth now spreading across her features. "Hiya back."

I pull her tighter into me, but it isn't enough. Even with her body pressed against mine, skin to skin, I ache for her to be closer, as though I can fuse us together if I only hold on hard enough. She must feel it too, because she burrows deeper into my chest, her breath feathering against my collarbone, her hand curling possessively against my ribs.

Her body softens in my arms, her breathing slowing as sleep tries to claim her. And I just lay there, watching her, memorizing the way she fits against me, the way her warmth anchors me to something I haven't let myself believe in for years. For the first time, the thought of forever doesn't feel like a threat. It feels like a promise.

I run a lazy circle down her arm. "I want forever with you."

Sera shifts, looking up at me with surprise brightening her eyes. "Forever is a long time, Killian."

"I don't think forever will be long enough with you, but it's a good starting place."

Tears well in Sera's eyes, and I lean in to kiss her gently. "Would you let me turn you, Killian?"

I shrug. "I'm telling you I want to spend forever at your side. Yes, I want you to turn me."

Sera sits up abruptly, and instinctively I follow her, placing a gentle hand on her thigh to calm her. I can see the panic rising in her eyes, fear warring with hope.

"I'm not Lucien, Sera." I say softly but firmly. "I will never harm you. I will never run from you. If you'll have me, that is..."

I hold a breath, waiting very impatiently for her to respond.

"I want you to be at my side, Killian. Not as my subject, but as my equal." Sera smiles, leaning in to kiss me. "I can't bear the thought of losing you."

I wrap my fingers around the back of her neck and deepen the kiss, pouring everything I feel into it.

"I'm going to go get us something to drink." I laugh, standing and running to the entrance of her room. "It's not every day you become a king to all vampire kind."

Sera lets out a laugh and throws herself back on the bed, her hair spreading across the fur. "You are such an idiot."

I smile, warmth flooding through me. "An idiot you are madly in love with."

Her eyes widen, but I run before she can say anything back. Once in the kitchen, I rummage through drawers and eventually the fridge. Finding an array of food and one bottle of wine that hasn't been opened. I'm so focused on the food I find, wondering when she had time to stock the fridge, since the food is still in date.

I don't even hear the footsteps from across the cave until I'm turning around with arms full of snacks and drinks.

I freeze. My jaw drops.

Everything I'm holding in my arms drops and shatters on the floor as I stare in utter shock at the woman in front of me. I hear Sera running down the hall from the room, her footsteps rapid and concerned, and I'm already moving instinctively to be at her side.

It's only then that I realize we are both still naked and covered in evidence of sex when I run into Sera and put her behind me as we face the woman who simply stands in the middle of the living room with a dark smile on her face, her arms crossed.

"Who are you?" Sera yells. "How did you find this place?"

I'm too stunned to say anything as the familiar woman takes a few steps forward and laughs, the sound cold and amused.

"Oh, come on, Seraphine. Has it been so long that you don't recognize your creator?"

Sera gasps, but I gasp even louder.

"Helen?" I ask, my voice cracking. "You created vampires?"

"You're the witch?" Sera asks, disbelief and rage warring in her tone.

314

28

Seraphine

Again, I find myself behind Killian as he stands in front of me, using his own body as a shield to protect me. The woman I recognize from Killian's bar is standing with her arms crossed, a grin on her face that spreads too wide, too knowing. Once she reveals her true identity, it's as if her own glamour slips just enough for the truth to shine through, like light through a crack in a wall.

It's in her eyes that I notice the similarities to the witch who made me. The same calculating gleam, the same ageless malice. A long silence holds in the cave, finally broken by Killian taking a step forward.

"What did you do to Helen?" he asks, his voice tight with barely controlled anger.

She rolls her eyes. "I am Helen, you fool."

"Rowena told me you were still alive." I say, stepping beside Killian, refusing to hide behind him any longer. "That you were meddling once again."

The witch—Helen—only smiles in response, the expression dripping with satisfaction.

"Watching you over the last few decades has truly been the most exciting part of this game."

"Game?" Killian asks, tension threading through the single word.

"Oh, yes, boy." Helen coos, her voice sickeningly sweet. "A game that was started long, long ago. When a desperate girl from nothing came to me and begged for more in life. Desperate to be given the chance to rise above her station in life."

The words sting, carrying the weight of truth. I was that desperate girl once.

"So why do you now want the game to end?" I ask.

"End?" Helen looks shocked, her hand pressing to her chest in mock offense. "I don't want it to end, silly girl. It's just now getting to the good part!"

Neither Killian nor I say anything, only share a single look before Helen continues, her eyes dancing with dark amusement.

"I promised you a way to protect yourself against your sisters. I told you they were rising against you, and now you see for yourself that I was right." Helen smiles, satisfied, curving her lips. "The original hunter, and the original vampire are two very powerful magics when combined. They will create something new. Something...more."

"Like what?" Killian asks.

"All in time, Killian." Helen says with a smile that makes my skin crawl. "You have both chosen each other. Against nature and against everything and everyone opposing it, you both found a way through it."

Helen takes two more steps forward, and I fight the urge to step back. "Love is powerful magic. Love creates, love destroys, and more importantly to our current topic...love changes."

"You are talking in riddles." I growl, frustration sharpening my voice.

Helen crosses the room, sitting on the island in the kitchen and grabbing a banana. She peels it slowly, lost in her own thoughts before looking up at us.

"War is coming." Helen says, her voice dropping into something darker, more ominous. "The time of vampires versus hunters is coming to an end and it's time the two of you choose your side. Rise above and become what you are meant to be or fall with the rest of your kind."

"What is this more you keep talking about?" Killian asks. "What happens when we mix our blood?"

"I have waited generations for Lucien's bloodline to resurface. Both of you stand on the threshold. That is all you get for now. The choice is yours to make."

"What's in it for you?" I ask, suspicion threading through every word.

"Balance." The witch says simply, as if that explains everything.

Helen stands and turns to make her way to the entrance of the cave. Killian and I stay put, not wanting to be anywhere near that crazy woman. When she turns back to look at us, there is darkness in her eyes that makes my ancient blood run cold.

"Step through with me," Helen says. "Join me at the top of the world. Fate is at your fingertips; all you have to do is grab it."

With those ominous last words, she turns and walks away. Disappearing into the shadows of the caves and leaving Killian and I alone with our thoughts.

"She didn't even eat the banana," Killian says.

I can't help but laugh at his ludicrous timing of what he chooses to focus on. I take his hand and lead him back to bed, we have much to discuss, but I don't care to be vertical while we do it.

"It doesn't change anything," Killian says for the fifth time since we laid down.

We've been in bed for hours, discussing everything Helen said. Her warnings and their meanings, the possibility of what mixing our blood will do, and every step of the way Killian has reassured me that it doesn't matter.

"How can you say that?" I roll my eyes.

"Because it doesn't." He shrugs, the gesture casual despite the weight of what we're discussing. "I want to be with you. We have spent months fighting each other. Fighting against the feelings that we both feel for one another, and now we have the opportunity to be together, and you want to let Helen ruin that."

"She isn't ruining anything." I argue, pulling back to look at him. "But we would be fools not to consider her words carefully before recklessly making a choice that may be for the worse."

"Reckless?" He asks, hurt flashing across his face.

"I didn't mean—"

"No, I heard what you said." Killian cuts me off.

I sometimes forget that he is so young. Though we are similar in age, looks wise, I have centuries of knowledge and watching the world change, empires rise and fall. Killian is but a baby in the grand timeline.

"Let's get some sleep. Nothing needs to be decided tonight, Killian."

Killian grabs me, pulling me into his arms and holding me against his skin. I can't help the smile that spreads across my face. The way I mold perfectly against his body, as if I am made to be right here, in his arms, forever.

He's right. The choice for us to be together forever is one that has already been made, long before tonight. Helen giving us ominous warnings means nothing to me. I chose this man to be mine knowing the danger of him being an original hunter. I still choose him knowing we might create something new in this world, knowing the dangers that could come from it.

If we create something that destroys the world, at least we will be together while it all ends. Something about watching the world burn with him at my side brings another smile to my face. Killian must see my smile and know I've made up my mind to turn him.

He leans into me and presses a kiss against my forehead. I lean into his touch, savoring the warmth of it.

"It's you, Sera. Always." He smiles at me.

"You." I agree.

I push him onto his back and crawl on top of him, straddling him just perfectly as I look down into those beautiful green eyes of his. I feel him press against my thigh and I can't help the smile that tugs at my lips.

"We just finished." I laugh.

"I can't help what you do to me." Is his response and damn him for it.

I roll my hips, giving him friction and watch as his lips part in a gasp. Heat builds in my core, and I adjust to feel him rubbing against my clit as I rotate my hips.

His hands wander up my thighs until he's holding my waist and helping me rock in a steady rhythm. Without much effort, he slips into me and I gasp at the feeling of him sliding his full-length in.

"Fuck." He moans. "How did I get so lucky to deserve such a beautiful queen."

My eyes go wide when I hear him call me his queen, it's the first time he's done it without it being a joke. It twists something in my chest that makes me bounce harder for him. Though, I can't help but tease him just a little.

"Your queen, huh?"

"My queen. My woman. My every breath." Killian moans.

He pushes me off, and rolls on top of me. I follow his lead, lost in the lust of it all when he pulls my hips up, my head laying against the bed as he lifts my ass in the air. I'm on all fours, exposed and vulnerable to him, but I feel nothing but safe as he positions his tip behind me and thrusts back into me.

"Fuck!" I gasp.

His hands trail down my back as he moves. The sound of the bed rocking, the headboard slamming into the stone wall echoing in rhythm with our moans. His hand wraps around my neck and he lifts my head up; the arch it puts in my back allows him to thrust deeper and it makes my toes curl.

"Look." Killian moans.

He doesn't say any more, but I know he's meaning in the mirror that hangs on the wall by my closet. The same one that is currently reflecting the both of us in bed right now. The angle I'm in shows me on all fours for him, but cuts most of his body off, all I manage to see is him thrusting in and out of me in hard powerful thrusts.

"I want you to watch me fuck you." Killian growls. "Watch as the hunter born to kill you, chooses you over and over again. Watch as every breath I take, and every thrust I make is for you. Only you. Forever, my queen."

"Killian!" I gasp. "Fuckfuckfuck."

I squeeze a fist full of the sheets as my orgasm rockets through my body, sending sensations from the top of my head down to the curl of my toes. Listening to him talk me through it only heightens the orgasm, and I refuse to look away from the mirror. I watch as he chooses me repeatedly. My name in every breath he takes.

He collapses on me, the heat of his body covering me as he pulses his release into me. I feel every throb of us finishing as he stills behind me. The muscles in his core are flexing as I milk every drop out of him.

I wake to an empty bed. I throw the covers off me and follow the smell of food being cooked in the kitchen. The clock mounted in the living room tells me it's three in the afternoon. I've only been asleep for four hours, and my body is screaming at me to go back to sleep.

"Killian." I say, my voice is softer than I have heard in a long time.

Killian is at the stove, dancing to music that is playing. I stare at his cute little butt shaking to the beat as he sings into the spatula he's using to stir something in a pan. I decide to sit on a barstool at the island and watch him some more, not bothering to announce myself.

He sticks the spatula in a second pan that I didn't notice at first. I realize now that he's making pancakes and eggs and the smell in the air must be the bacon he has in the oven. He tosses the pancake in the air and catches it with a skill that honestly takes me by surprise. He is a fascinating man, and I'm beginning to see how he runs such a successful bar. He's a showman at heart.

"Killian." I try again. This time he hears me.

He turns around with wide eyes. An apology in his eyes. "Did I wake you?"

I shake my head with a laugh. "I rolled over and you weren't there."

"I didn't go anywhere." Killian smiles, grabbing a paper plate from the counter. "I wanted to bring you breakfast in bed."

"You are too cute." I say.

"I'm still going to." Killian says, his expression is serious. "Get your ass back in that bed or so help me..."

He lets his threat end there, but I'm already standing with my hands raised in surrender. "As you wish."

I barely get laid down before he's bringing in three plates of food and a pitcher of orange juice. Pancakes, bacon, eggs, and hashbrowns get laid down in the middle of the bed. He plops down on his side of the bed and presents me with a fork.

"Breakfast is served." Killian smiles.

I roll my eyes and take a fork, gathering some scrambled eggs and hashbrowns and taking a bite.

"Holy shit!" I gasp. "This is fucking good!"

Killian raises an eyebrow. "Did you doubt me?"

I'm too busy stuffing my face with more of his cooking to answer, but finally I swallow and give him a shrug.

"You live off fried food and beer. You are the literal poster child of a stereotypical man."

He holds a hand over his heart. "Ouch. You hurt me. Right here." He taps his chest dramatically. "Right in my heart."

"Should I kiss it better?" I ask sarcastically.

He wiggles his eyebrows. "In that case, my heart has relocated to my dick."

A laugh leaves me before I can stop it.

"I hate you."

Handing me a glass of orange juice he smiles. "No, you don't."

No...I don't.

"So, after we eat. Then what?"

"We go back to sleep." I suggest.

"Deal. But then what?" he asks.

I can't help the smile that plays on my lips. He is good at hiding it, but his nerves are getting the best of him the closer we get to the inevitable conversation of turning him into a vampire. I've kept my glamour on as to not trigger his hunter gene, in hopes it helps keep his mind clear of his desire to kill me.

But he is nervous, and it's cute to see him try and keep it hidden from me. His disguises of cooking and trying to get me to bring it up first would normally work...if I was any other woman.

"You become a vampire, and we possibly end the world together." I say.

"Wow." He says through a mouth full of pancakes. "You really know how to wine and dine a man."

Once again, I find myself laughing with him.

I shrug. "Helen wasn't very clear on the details. But we know it's going to be something new."

"And we will face it together." Killian says without hesitation.

"Together." I agree.

29

Killian

I wait for Sera to fall deep into sleep before slipping out of her arms, careful not to wake her. I slip back into the sweatpants that Sera had picked out for me and creep out of the bedroom as silently as the cold stone floor allows.

The cave stretches before me; a secret world suspended in time. Shadows cling to the walls like living things, flickering across centuries of paintings, sculptures, and relics that have witnessed empires rise and fall. The air is thick with the scent of aged parchment and candle smoke, mingling with something older, something indefinable that speaks of magic and memory.

I run a finger along the surface of a painting of a famous king, feeling the ridges of brushstrokes worn smoothly by centuries of existence. Memories of history lessons and the war he lost, the empire that rose in its ashes flash through my mind. I never cared much about school, but seeing the past portrayed on the walls of this cave, knowing Sera had been around for all of it, makes me wish I had studied harder.

Passing a statue of a woman holding a baby to her bare breast, I keep thinking how soon I'm going to be a part of a world beyond mortality. One day there might be a cave full of historical relics that I've lived through, artifacts that carry my fingerprints. Fear of the unknown should have clenched me, should have frozen me in place, but it doesn't. I have been a hunter and a predator, but for her, I want to be more.

I cross the cave to the reason I find myself still up so late, or early depending on how you look at it. The past few days in the cave have been amazing, a stolen moment outside of time, but the world outside of here is waiting for both of us. When we leave this cave, it will be together, hand in hand, made into something more if Helen was right about her cryptic message.

I pull back a heavy cloth curtain that parts the living area from this room I spotted while cooking breakfast the other day. Peeking behind it, I discover a half-lit room with canvases leaning against one another like patient bodies, bands of color frozen mid-argument.

Shelves run the length of the wall, packed with books, the spines blur together into a single, dusty horizon of knowledge accumulated over lifetimes. In the center of the room, a red velvet chair sits like a small throne, its padding sunken beneath the weight of sunlight that doesn't exist here. A side table holds a chipped mug and a stack of sketches: hands, a bar counter, an indecipherable map.

I move along the outer wall, fingers brushing spines the way some people finger rosaries. Each book has the same hush about it, as if they are waiting to be read aloud, their stories eager to be spoken into existence again. My footsteps are careful, not because the room would shatter but because it feels private in a way the rest of the cave isn't. Like reading someone's handwriting in the margins.

At the far end, a canvas on an easel catches my attention. I stop without intending to, drawn by something familiar. It's my bar...seen from the outside: the sign half-painted, the awning a cascade of unfinished brushstrokes. Behind the painted counter, a man is frozen mid-wipe, his hands a smear of light and shadow. I can almost feel the grain of the bar top under his sleeve.

I trace the painted man with a thumb that doesn't touch the canvas. There is something domestic in the image, ordinary enough to be heartbreaking.

"You weren't in bed."

The cloth falls back into place, and Sera steps into the room. She doesn't look surprised to find me here, as if she expected this eventually.

"I was restless." I say. "Did you do this?"

She moves closer, and the lamplight picks out a dust halo around her hair, making her look ethereal. "I did all of them." She says, and the pride in her voice softens the room around its cold edges. "A hobby from the road with Lucien. I taught myself to paint, and I read as much as I could."

My eyes sweep the shelves again, taking in the sheer volume. "You've read all of these books?"

"Every single one." She says with a smile. "Eternity is a long time, Killian."

I cross the room and take her hands in mine. Her skin is cold, but she lets me lift them without pulling away. I press small kisses to each of her fingers, savoring the intimacy of the gesture.

"Are you trying to make me change my mind about being with you?" I ask, half teasing.

She lets out a breath that trembles. "We just don't know what's outside of this cave, or what we will face when we leave." She lowers her head, vulnerability written in every line of her body.

She's frightened of the unknown, as am I of course. Her court has abandoned her. I left the hunters. Her generals are gone, sisters betraying her and ruining everything she has built over centuries. The man who raised me tried to kill me, and the woman who helped shape me into the weapon I am today, turned out to be the fucking witch who started all of this.

"You're afraid I'll leave." I say, the words as plain as the rock under our feet. Saying it aloud is like dropping a stone in clear water, the ripples immediately spreading.

Her head comes up, and for a second she looks small, brave, and desperate all at once. "I..." Her voice is clipped, struggling. "Everyone I have ever trusted has left me. I'm...I'm tired of the empty spaces."

I smile, the kind of smile that isn't trying to fix everything but exists to understand her. "Come on."

I lead her back into the living room before turning and walking towards the bathroom. The stone is cool under my feet, grounding, and her hand is a warm steady pressure as I turn the water on.

"We don't know what's waiting for us outside this cave..." My fingers trace the edge of her sweatpants before slipping them down. "But whatever it is...we will face it together."

I feel her lean into my touch as I pull off the tank top she was wearing before pulling her into the cascade of water with me. The warmth surrounds us and steam begins to fill the room, curling around us like embracing ghosts. The sound of water rushing over stone is soothing, but my fingers threading through Sera's hair has her melting into my chest and it brings a smile to my face.

"Together," she whispers, sinking further into me.

"Forever doesn't scare me, knowing you will be at my side." My lips ghost over her ear. "Let's finish this shower, have some breakfast, and then make me immortal."

She laughs softly, eyes flicking up to meet mine. "Pretty sure it's dinnertime, Killian."

My hand slides up her chest, fingers curling around her throat in a teasing grip. I press her back against the slick stone wall. I nip at her ear lobe.

"Pretty sure I wasn't talking about food."

I feel a shiver work down her spine, and it only deepens my smile against her skin. We emerge from the shower and dry off. Sera heads to the bedroom to find us clothes, while I begin cooking for the both of us. Something I have done for every meal since we got to the cave.

The smell of seared meat and garlic fills the cave, warm and oddly domestic for a place carved in stone. I smile, plating our food and picturing what life will be like once we are openly ruling together.

My bar comes to mind, and how much I miss being behind the counter. Even in Sera's painting, the joy seen in my painted self's eyes was evident. I miss the boring routine of taking care of people, listening to their stories, offering my advice, and cheering them up with alcohol.

I turn to place our plates on the table, catching Sera in a gorgeous red dress, a slit high along the leg to allow freedom of movement. The fabric clings perfectly to every beautiful curve of her body, and my eyes quickly find her neckline. I watch the pulse of her vein as my eyes wander to the ruby pendant resting against her throat.

My eyes drift lower, drinking her in until I see what she's holding in her hands. My smile vanishes instantly as I begin shaking my head.

"Absolutely not." I say.

"It's this or a dress." Sera shrugs.

"Then a dress." I say, not hesitating for even a second.

She laughs, tilting her head. "Come on, Killian. You'll look good. Your days of ripped jeans and leather jackets are done. You're about to wield power most men only whisper about. You should dress like it."

I groan, dragging my hand down my face. "I'm just your little mannequin, aren't I?"

"Finally. He gets it." She teases.

Still grumbling to myself, I cross to her and take the clothes from her hands. Dark gray slacks, a black belt holding sheaths for weapons, and a black button-up shirt that tucks neatly but stretches tight over my forearms. I roll the cuffs to just above my elbow before sliding into a red sleeveless vest with black linear embroidery.

I stretch out my arms and arch a brow, spinning slowly so she can get a full picture. "So?"

Sera bites her lip, her gaze raking over my body shamelessly. "You look...better than good. I love it."

I roll my eyes, but I feel the corner of my mouth twitch upward despite myself. We settle at the table, steam rising from our meals. Between bites we continue sharing stories of our lives and unwrapping more of each other's pasts. I keep my smile in place, listening to her, but behind it the nerves are still there, waiting to spill out.

Finally, I set my fork down and let out a sigh that causes Sera to pause. She smiles and meets my eyes.

"You really aren't afraid, are you?"

I smile. "Of becoming what you are? Becoming more? Definitely not." I lean forward, elbows resting on the table. "The only thing I'm afraid of is what happens if we don't do this. If we stay the way we are, divided and hunted."

Sera's face twists through multiple different emotions before landing on a smile that reaches her eyes. She tilts her head as she raises a curious eyebrow.

"You talk like a man who has already chosen his grave."

I give her a sly grin. "Maybe. But if I'm digging my grave, at least I get to share it with you."

She rolls her eyes, but the smile doesn't falter. "You're impossible."

"And you love it."

"Let's see if I still love it once you're immortal and unbearable."

I lift my glass of wine. "To unbearable immortality then."

I clink my glass with hers, and we laugh together at the absurdity of how casual all of this is. War is brewing outside these walls, but here, in our own little sanctuary from the world, none of it matters. It's just the two of us.

Finally, after a moment of silence between the both of us, I give a soft clap and lean forward on the table. "So. How does this work? Bite in the neck, drip a little venom, snap my neck after feeding me your blood? Sacrificial chant, a dramatic lightning bolt?"

Sera lets out a laugh that I can't help but match. Of course I'm trying to make light of this situation, as if we aren't about to shatter fate itself. She matches my posture on the table, crossing her fingers as she lets out a little huff. She's so fucking beautiful, I can't get enough of her.

"You watch too many movies and read way too many novels." Sera says. "It's actually much simpler than that."

"Do tell." I smile.

"When the witch made us, she warned us not to spread her secrets." She begins. "My sisters and I drifted apart. Loneliness is a dangerous thing and when we learned we could pass our blood to humans, we took advantage of that and began spreading like wildfire."

"Understandable." I say, hoping to ease her mind that what she's about to do isn't a mistake.

"They changed as we did, but there were subtle changes." Sera continues. "Sun kills them, their wounds don't close like ours do. They are...faded copies at best, but they were loyal to us."

"The witch wants us to do this." I say. "She said it would create something new, and you don't have any ideas what she could be referring to?"

Sera shakes her head.

"Have you ever turned a hunter before?" I ask.

Again, Sera shakes her head. "I've thought about it. But as the centuries went on, my hatred for them deepened and all I wanted to do was kill them. Over and over again."

I let out a laugh. "Lovely."

"Vampire blood is stronger than human blood," Sera says. "When we exchange blood, ours overpowers the human blood and turns it completely. It's painful, but bearable."

Sera stands and walks around the table until she's standing next to me. She places a gentle hand on my shoulder, and I lay my head against her cold hand.

"The hunter gene is powerful, and you come from the original hunter bloodline, which means you aren't a diluted copy of his blood. You come from the very magic that created him."

"Hence why combining our blood will create something new..." I say.

Sera holds out her hands to show me the soft pads of her fingertips. "We make cuts at our fingertips, place our hands together and let our blood mix. It'll flow from me into you, just as yours will flow from you into me."

I stand, walking over to the center of the living room and turn to face her. I give her a smile before laying my arms out before me, palms up. "Whenever you're ready."

I see a mixture of emotions in her beautiful red eyes, all of which I'm sure are positive in nature. She crosses the room in a blur until she's standing in front of me. She drops the glamour that she's had on since we got to the cave and lets her nails lengthen. My hunter gene come to life under my skin, reacting to the threat of a queen in my presence.

I meet her eyes and give a subtle nod, smiling to reassure her I'm here with her. "I choose this, Sera."

She jabs into the soft pads of my fingers, scoring the skin with tiny crescents. She does the same with her own fingers and together we raise our hands up and press our fingers together.

The moment our fingers touch, everything snaps into focus. The smell of blood fills my senses, hot and metallic. My chest answers with a rush of memories: The smell of her, the sound of her pulse beating, the precise rhythm of her heart. My blood mixes with hers and the cave leans closer, watching.

It feels like my skin is on fire as her blood enters me and fills every vein in my body. I feel it threading through me with a purpose, changing me down to the molecular level. I feel the hunter's strength become more. My heightened senses somehow sharpen further. Time slows around me until I realize it's actually me—thinking and processing so fast, looking around at such speed that the world is stopped.

I look at Sera as if for the first and last time. Her jaw is clenched, feeling her own change in a much subtler way than mine. I'm not sure what my hunter blood can provide for her that she doesn't already have, but the way her brows knit together, I can tell she's feeling something much deeper than a simple transition.

I open my mouth, making room for fangs that are sliding into place in my gums. I feel them with my tongue and a tickling sensation filters across my skin in a wave. I catch a glimpse of my reflection in the smooth stone and realize it's my own glamour masking the predator that is being born.

There is something raw and dangerous in my eyes and I watch as they shift from the forest green they've always been to a dark crimson hue. I can't help but smile when I look back at Sera, her mouth open in awe as she takes me in.

Pain rolls through both of us in waves, and we throw our heads back in unison. Something else begins twisting its way through us. Older and more primal than the hunter blood, or the vampire magic. This feeling weaves its way through every fiber of my soul and reshapes my being into something new. I can taste my fear, feel Sera's bravery on my skin. I hear Helen's laugh echo off the cave as it whirls around the space. A fury of wind begins blowing around us, coming from somewhere beyond the cave.

Paintings rattle against the walls, statues rock on their stands, and the heavy curtains hanging over doorways fold in on themselves. Sera's hair is a mess of tangles as the wind dies down before disappearing all together.

The apex of transformation passes. The world returns to focus not with the dullness of relief but with the crisp clarity of a struck bell. Our hands glow faintly where they've been bleeding. I watch as the wounds close, leaving behind only tiny little scars that I now realize mark us as vampires.

I stare into Sera's eyes, seeing her in a whole new light. I'm her equal. Not just a hunter beneath her, or a vampire serving her. I feel it just as I feel her running her fingers across my chest. We are more. We are new.

"Are you okay?" I ask, my voice deeper now.

Sera nods. "I feel better than okay."

I take a step back and take her in. The beauty I saw before has somehow been magnified into something words can't even describe. I watch as she smiles at me, her glamour gone completely.

"My king."

Hearing her say those words, acknowledging me as her equal makes my chest swell with something bigger than pride. I pull her against my chest and wrap my fingers behind her neck, pulling her into a kiss that is deeper than any we've shared before. Every nerve in my body is on fire. I can't get enough of her touching me.

I pull back, taking her in again.

"If eternity is a curse, then let it be one I suffer gladly. Because loving you is the only forever I want."

I take her hand and drop to one knee.

"I choose you. Not just for this life, but for every endless night that will follow. I was born and raised to hunt monsters, but I will burn the world to belong to you for all of time, Seraphine."

I kiss her hand, before bowing, submitting myself before her.

"I kneel to no crown but yours, and I will stand beside you through every immortal night. My Queen."

I stand, pulling Sera into my arms and leaning into her. Brushing my lips against her cheek, moving to the other cheek, finally finding her lips. When I step back, I see the smile on her face, and it fills me with hope for our future together.

"So, my King," Sera says, "are you ready to face my sisters and the hunters?"

Nodding, I take her hand and brush a gentle kiss across her knuckles. "Beside you, I'm ready for anything. Lead the way."

END OF BOOK ONE

Continue Killian and Seraphine's story in
To Rule with The Crimson King.

Before You Go...

Thank you for stepping into this world with me.

Stories only truly come alive when they're read, and the fact that you chose *The Hunt for the Crimson Queen* means more to me than I can put into words.

I hope this story stayed with you long after the final page. I hope you found pieces of yourself in these characters, in their struggles, their hope, and their fight to survive.

And thankfully this isn't the end.

Book Two is coming.

If you'd like updates on the next installment, future books, behind-the-scenes content, and everything still to come, follow me on social media and join me for the journey ahead.

TikTok: @justinpcshaughnessy

Instagram: @justin.pc.shaughnessy_author

Subscribe to my newsletter: justinpcshaughnessy.beehiiv.com

Until next time,

Justin